THE LONGEST JOURNEY

THE LONGEST JOURNEY

Betty McInnes

severn
House

This first world edition published 2010
in Great Britain and in the USA by
SEVERN HOUSE PUBLISHERS LTD of
9–15 High Street, Sutton, Surrey, England, SM1 1DF.
Trade paperback edition published
in Great Britain and the USA 2010 by
SEVERN HOUSE PUBLISHERS LTD

British Library Cataloguing in Publication Data

McInnes, Betty (Elizabeth Anne), 1928-
   The Longest Journey.
     1. Families–Scotland–Highlands–Fiction. 2. Highlands
     (Scotland)–Social conditions–19th century–Fiction.
     3. Judgments, Criminal–Fiction. 4. Family secrets–
     Fiction. 5. Domestic fiction.
     I. Title
     823.9'14–dc22

ISBN-13: 978-0-7278-6862-6   (cased)
ISBN-13: 978-1-84751-216-1   (trade paper)

Except where actual historical events and characters are being
described for the storyline of this novel, all situations in this
publication are fictitious and any resemblance to living persons
is purely coincidental.

All Severn House titles are printed on acid-free paper.

Severn House Publishers support The Forest Stewardship Council [FSC],
the leading international forest certification organisation. All our titles that
are printed on Greenpeace-approved FSC-certified paper carry the FSC logo.

Mixed Sources
Product group from well-managed
forests and other controlled sources
www.fsc.org Cert no. SA-COC-1565
© 1996 Forest Stewardship Council

Typeset by Palimpsest Book Production Ltd.,
Grangemouth, Stirlingshire, Scotland.
Printed and bound in Great Britain by
MPG Books Ltd., Bodmin, Cornwall

One

Wednesday 1st March 1848.

Mary-Ann Macgregor penned the date. It was satisfying to start the month at the head of a page in the ledger. Almost like turning over a new leaf . . .

In careful script, she wrote:

Brought Forward £3 12s 6d

Frowning, she paused a moment to contemplate the figures.

Not an auspicious start to 1848 for her husband's business, yet Forfar townsfolk swore that Ewan Macgregor was the best blacksmith in the whole valley of Strathmore.

Of course, the figures would look healthier if the laird of Graystones had paid for the repair of two carriage wheels, way back in January. She made a mental note to send that august gentleman a reminder. She had a good mind to add interest to compensate for the inconvenience, but she knew her husband would not hear of it. She could guess what he would say:

'The laird's the magistrate, my love. He sits on the bench and hands out justice. It's a wise man that keeps the right side of the law.'

Ewan was too lenient with debtors in Mary-Ann's opinion, although she knew injustice made the hot Macgregor blood boil. Her husband in a righteous rage was a frightening prospect, though it always fell to the blacksmith's wife to pursue bad debts. Mary-Ann's Irish charm and cheerful persistence usually resulted in payment. Either in cash or victuals for the blacksmith's table, equally acceptable.

The Macgregor family lived in troubled times. Famine and disease throughout the Scottish Highlands had worsened dramatically since rents were raised impossibly high, and impoverished tenants turned off crofts in favour of sheep. All through the winter landless folk had arrived at the door in pitiable state, begging scraps of food, many supporting elderly folk and half-starved bairns. Overcome with pity, Mary-Ann sent them on their way to mills or emigrant ships fortified with broth and bread, though sometimes hard pressed to feed her own five children.

However, the market town of Forfar had escaped the worst. The fertile valley of Strathmore lay around the town, cradled between rounded Sidlaw hills and glens and foothills of the Grampian Mountains. The town itself was a brisk walk down the road from the 'smiddy', which was the popular local name for Ewan Macgregor's blacksmith's business. The road led past bleach fields and down the brae to the marshy shores of a well-stocked loch, and beyond that to the township proper. Long ago this pleasant area had been the peaceful summer retreat of Scottish kings and queens; by March 1848 it was the busy hub of the local linen trade.

Although it was freezing outside, the substantial stone cottage, which housed the blacksmith's wife and family, known as the 'smiddy-seat,' was pleasantly warm, being attached directly to workshop and forge. Mary-Ann was working by the light of a window overlooking the yard, a coal fire blazing in the hearth. She leaned forward and cleared an area of frost-patterned glass. This morning everything sparkled with frosty rime. It was good to work cosily indoors, and she smiled.

Mary-Ann would be first to admit she fell short of the fashionable ideal of rounded prettiness, popularized by young Queen Victoria, who was not yet thirty. Mary-Ann's thirty-second birthday was past and she considered herself a skinny, mature matron. Soon, silver threads would appear among the raven black. However, since she spent little time in front of a looking glass, she was unaware that her glowing smile was memorable.

She considered herself fortunate. Married to Ewan for fifteen years, caring for five children and leading a busy, useful life keeping an eye on her husband's finances. Their home was simply but comfortably furnished, her husband was kind and hard-working and she'd spent many happy hours seated by the warm hearth with a bairn on her lap, singing the old Irish songs, while the children listened. Mary-Ann's beautiful voice was a delight, accompanied by Ewan on the violin. He had a silver touch with the instrument, as sympathetic with music as he was with frightened or injured animals encountered in the daily round.

Mary-Ann Macgregor's life was filled with quiet contentment these days. It seemed an age ago since heartbroken Mary-Ann O'Malley, aged seventeen, had married Ewan Macgregor, Scottish blacksmith, a man for whom she felt affection but not love. In sorrow, shame and desperation she had hastily married a good man who deserved better. Yet strangely enough, for fifteen years they had lived together quite happily.

But sometimes, wistfully, she would remember another house, another man – Mary-Ann quickly banished the thought. She would not allow memory to stray down that dangerous path.

She dipped the pen into the inkwell and resumed the sobering task of their monthly expenditure . . .

2 gross best quality six inch clout nails – 1s 3d

3 tons smiddy-gum – that was specially selected small coal for use in the furnace, and it seemed it became more costly with every trundle of the coal cart from the railway wagon.

Next came tallow candles, oil for lamps, and cartridges for Ewan's gun.

Though she grudged the price of ammunition, the gun was essential. Her husband shot rabbit, hare and pigeon on authorized common ground for the stew pot. In his careful way, Ewan kept the gun on a high ledge above the mantelpiece, out of the children's reach, although David, at fourteen the eldest of the family, had been allowed to try his hand at shooting under Ewan's strict supervision.

There was a tug at her sleeve. She glanced down at the anxious face of her youngest son, Daniel, aged four.

'What is it, Danny love?'

'Come quick, Mama. They're fighting in the smiddy.'

'What about?'

She was not unduly worried. Arguments were a normal part of daily life now that the two older boys were working there, with Ewan.

'Davey set fire to the wheel. There was flames!'

Daniel's eyes were round with alarm. He idolized his older brother, but David's mischief was a constant source of anguish.

Mary-Ann laughed.

'Danny dear, don't worry! Papa will put the flames out.'

'No, Mama! Papa put Davey out. He threw him in the horse trough.'

That sounded serious. She hurried to investigate.

The smiddy proper covered a large area, consisting mainly of a high-roofed workshop with double doors facing on to a yard. The arched opening was made high and wide enough for a massive Clydesdale horse to pass easily through.

The anvil and forge were at one end, and working accessories included jigs and tools required to make metal-bound wheels for carriages and carts. Both Ewan and Wullie Ogilvy, his journeyman, were highly skilled wheelwrights and craftsmen.

But today clouds of smoke, steam, and the stench of charred wood greeted Mary-Ann. The forge was roaring white-hot and furious, in keeping with her husband's temper.

Ewan was fishing David out of the trough by the scruff of his jacket. He deposited the dripping youngster on the floor beside a badly charred cartwheel screwed to the tyring platform. Ewan bellowed.

'Maybe that'll teach you!'

The shivering youngster scrambled to his feet.

'It was only a lark, Pa!'

'The place for larks is the sky! You've ruined two days work, and will you look at the state of your brother and Wullie?'

Mary-Ann whirled round to inspect the pair.

Matthew, their thirteen-year-old, was burly like his father, and already almost a head taller than David. Both boys had left school at the end of last session to begin an apprenticeship in the smiddy. Matthew had left school willingly, but David with reluctance.

'What happened, Matt?' she asked.

Matthew and Wullie were soaked too, standing in pools of water.

'Davey flung cold water on me and Wullie instead of the wheel, Mama. The iron rim was white hot. Icy water bonds it tightly to the wood.'

Davey was defiant.

'Pa told me to soak the fellows, so I did!'

Ewan scowled.

'Felloes are the wooden sections making up the round of the rim. You know that fine!'

'It was a joke, Pa! I didn't know the wheel would burn.'

'Any fool knows white-hot metal sets fire to wood unless it's doused, my lad. Where are the brains the schoolmaster praised to the skies? I've yet to see evidence of 'em!'

Davey Macgregor was wet and miserable. It had seemed funny at the time to pour icy water over the living fellows instead of the wooden felloes. The play on words had appealed to his sense of humour and he couldn't resist acting on the pun.

Now the joke had misfired, he could have wept. Davey loved his father and longed to earn his approval. His brothers and sisters made their father laugh. Why couldn't he? He'd been clever at school, top of his class, but Papa didn't seem to care. He'd made him leave school to learn to be a blacksmith, a job he hated. It was heartbreaking.

'You don't need brains working in this stinking hole, Papa, sweating in heat and dirt!' he said miserably.

Ewan took the remark personally. He reddened and lifted a fist.

'If it's teaching you need, my lad, I'll teach you a lesson you'll no' forget!'

'Stop it, Ewan!' Mary-Ann flung herself between them. She looked into her husband's face, contorted with rage, and said softly, 'Ewan dear, remember!'

He stared at her, anger slowly fading. His expression showed a mixture of shame and weary defeat. Then he sighed and wiped angry sweat from his forehead with the back of his hand.

'Yes, Mary-Ann, I know. I suppose it's not Davey's fault.'

He turned to the journeyman. 'Go home and change your breeks, Wullie. I apologize for my son's bad behaviour.'

'Och, laddies will be laddies, Ewan,' Wullie said charitably.

Mary-Ann put her arms round her two sons.

'These lads will catch their death of cold in these wet clothes. Will you need them to help clear up the mess, Ewan?'

He closed the damper on the forge with a clang, avoiding her eyes.

'No, I'll manage. Send them to meet Shona and Agnes from school. The wind's rising. It could snow.'

As Ewan had predicted, there was a flurry of snow, but the girls escaped the worst on the walk home. The boys had attended Forfar academy, but Mary-Ann had decided Mrs Carnegy's small private school was ideal for her girls' education, conveniently sited a short distance away at Zoar village. Mrs Carnegy was a minister's widow who had turned to teaching to keep a roof over her head. She taught reading, writing and arithmetic, and those who showed an aptitude were taught music, singing and embroidery. It was a struggle to pay a five-shilling fee, but Mary-Ann believed in education and considered the advantages well worth the scrimping and saving.

'Maybe there won't be school tomorrow,' said Agnes hopefully, nose pressed to the windowpane, watching the snowfall.

Agnes was the younger one, a domesticated little ten-year-old that would rather stay home and help her mother about the house. She'd little interest in lessons, apart from embroidery.

Her sister Shona joined her anxiously at the window.

'I must go! I have a singing lesson tomorrow.'

'You sing better than anyone in the school. You don't need lessons,' Agnes said.

'Yes, I do! Mrs Carnegy is teaching me to breathe.'

'Och, I've been breathing since I was a baby, nae bother,' Agnes scoffed.

Shona gave her a look, but it was beneath her dignity to argue. Shona was two years older and on the threshold of womanhood, already showing signs of a rare beauty which could turn men's heads.

Danny crossed from the fireside and leaned against Agnes, who was his favourite.

'Play jacks with me, Aggie?' he begged.

'I thought you'd lost the chuckie-stones, Dan?'

'Papa found new ones.'

The two children settled down on the rug to play, while Shona drifted across to her mother's chair and perched on the arm.

'Sing for us, Mama? Please!'

'Not tonight, dear.'

The spat in the workshop had upset Mary-Ann more than usual. She sympathized with her husband. Davey's contempt for work that kept a roof over their heads and food for the table must be hard for Ewan to take. The boy was growing more rebellious every day, since he left school. No wonder she had no heart for singing!

She caught Ewan's eye. He was sitting by the oil lamp, dressing fish hooks with feathers. He raised an eyebrow.

'My throat's a little sore,' she lied.

Agnes looked up. 'Wrap one of Papa's socks round your neck, Mama.'

Davey held his nose.

'Phew!'

With a sinking heart, Mary-Ann watched Ewan's fist clench till the knuckles showed white. It was only a boyish joke, but everything the boy did appeared to irritate him now.

Matthew stepped into the breach. He held out the boat he was making, and the dangerous moment passed.

'Pa, is the hull all right?'

Ewan smiled and examined the model.

'It's perfect, son. Well done. You're making a grand job.'

Only Mary-Ann saw the look Davey gave them. It nearly broke her heart.

Mary-Ann was sure Ewan would have something to say about David's conduct when they were alone that night. She sat in front of the bedroom mirror, slowly brushing her hair. Waiting.

He was a fastidious man, nightly washing away all trace of sweat and grime under the pump in the scullery. She had hot water ready in the ewer, and home-made soap to shift sooty grime from face and hands – a small luxury for the man who had given his heart to her unreservedly.

A small token of her gratitude.

He came into the room stripped to the waist and washed face and hands, before turning to face her.

'I'm sorry I lost my rag with Davey. Sometimes I think the lad goes out of his way to annoy me!'

She looked at him, tears in her eyes.

'It's all my fault!'

He put his hands on her shoulders.

'Mary-Ann! You know I would never blame you.'

'I know.' She wiped away a tear. 'If only Davey could be more like the others!'

'That's not possible, and you know it. It was easy to love your son when he was little. Now it's not so simple. I've only to look at him to see he's not mine.'

She sighed.

'Davey doesn't know that, of course, but he senses you favour the others. Maybe that's why he's so troublesome.' She met his eyes tentatively. 'Are you sorry you married me, Ewan? Maybe it was only out of pity.'

He laughed.

'No, I wanted you for my wife. I was lucky to win you!'

Ewan longed to take her in his arms and make love to her, but hesitated. She would submit, he knew. She never resisted his advances, but he wished she would turn to him of her own free will. Tonight, he felt dejected and defeated. Maybe the fight with Davey had upset him more than he'd suspected. He rubbed a hand wearily across his brow.

'I'm tired, Mary-Ann. It's been a long day.'

She was on her feet in an instant, handing him the clean night-shirt airing by the fire. He slipped the fresh garment over his head and felt comforted. Maybe she did not make a show of emotion, he thought, but her thoughtful care spoke volumes.

He climbed into bed. Mary-Ann snuffed out the candle and settled down beside him. She waited till he was warmed and relaxed before broaching the thought uppermost in her mind.

'We could send Davey to school in Dundee to finish his educa-tion, Ewan. He could board with your aunt and attend the grammar school,' she suggested. 'He's a clever lad. Who knows what he could do if he was given the chance?'

Ewan laughed.

'It's tempting to send the rascal back to school for a taste of discipline, but where would we find the money?'

She took a deep breath.

'There's the money his father sends for his upkeep. It's in the bank and never been touched.'

'And never will be, by me!' Ewan's good humour vanished.

'It'll stay there till the boy comes of age, then he can do with it what he wants. I vowed I'd bring him up as my own, so I'll see to his welfare. We'll say no more about grammar schools. Good night!'

He turned his back on her and tugged the quilt round his ears.

Davey had risen early, before anyone was up. In the kitchen, he carved a slice off the loaf, spread it with butter and washed it down with milk. Then he pulled on a bonnet, tied a sacking apron round his middle and went into the workshop. There, he raked ashes and clinker from the forge and put a brush up the flue. He was determined to be a credit to his pa today.

Even if it killed him.

The snow had come to nothing, only a light powdering blown by the wind. The girls set off for school, Agnes sulking, Shona skipping.

Ewan was pleased to find both lads hard at work when he and Wullie entered the workshop. The forge was stoked, floor brushed, tools neatly arranged by the anvil.

He smiled to himself as he studied the book in which his wife entered work in hand.

'Two Clydesdales from Heatherstacks to be shod by nine thirty, Blairyfeddon's chestnut mare at noon. Bogie Mitchell's harrow needs repairing and new hand tools to be delivered to Graystones. A full day's work ahead, my lads, not taking account of casual trade!' he announced.

'I'll deliver the tools now, Pa. That'll save time,' Davey offered.

Ewan nodded.

'That would be a help, son.'

They smiled at one another, yesterday's aggravation forgiven.

Davey set off whistling, carrying the new tools wrapped in sack-cloth. It was a beautiful frosty morning and his breath steamed in the clear air. He breathed deeply. Glad to be out of the smiddy's heat and stink. He had not walked far along the main road before he noticed all was not well. The wind had brought down a rotten old tree, which had fallen by the roadside, knocking down the dyke in the process and tumbling stones into the burn. The blockage had dammed the stream and water was rising, threatening to flood the main road to Brechin.

As he drew closer, he saw to his astonishment that a young girl was working up to her knees in water, tugging at the stones with bare hands, struggling to avert the catastrophe.

'Hey, that's no job for a lass!' he called.

She stopped and stared. She'd been crying. Her muddied face was streaked with tears.

'I know! But my father's the roadman for this stretch, and he's ill. He'll lose his job if the road floods.'

She went on working frantically without much success. Davey remembered the crowbar included with the new tools and quickly unwrapped the bundle.

'Wait. This'll do it!'

He eased the stones out of the stream with the crowbar's help. The water receded, gurgling through the culvert, and the danger was over.

Davey smiled at the girl. She looked a sight, blue with cold, wet and muddy.

'I haven't seen you around. What's your name?' he asked.

'Janet Golightly. We've only been here a week or two. My father was a soldier, but he left the army to care for me after Mama died. This job was the only one he could get. He's often ill, you see, and there's only me to help.'

He studied her. She was much too skinny, not in the least bonnie, but there was a tough, independent air about her, which was appealing.

'I could bring a rabbit or two for the pot till your father gets well,' he offered.

Two spots of colour rose in her wan cheeks. He could see she and her father were in dire straits, but reluctant to take charity. She looked down at her feet.

'Thanks.'

'Off you go home before you catch your death,' he said.

She obeyed with alacrity. The roadman's cottage was just along the road, a broken-down old bothy intended to house a single labourer, not an ex-soldier and motherless daughter. Frowning, Davey watched the girl hurry inside. He picked up the tools and went on his way thoughtfully.

Gunfire echoing from the direction of Graystones estate made him stop. No doubt the laird and his friends were out shooting deer, enjoying their sport behind high sandstone walls that kept common people out. There must be enough game running wild in the laird's estate to feed Forfarshire! he thought. Why should sporting gents have their pick of it? It's not fair!

As weeks went by and the laird made no attempt to settle the bill, Mary-Ann's patience was running out. Magistrate or not, her hard-working husband should not suffer loss.

She said nothing to Ewan, but one fine May morning she set off innocently with a basket over one arm as if heading for a shopping trip to town. Once out of sight, she turned sharp right in the direction of the laird's mansion. She did not take the longer route to the servants' doorway, but marched up the driveway to the front entrance and pealed the bell.

A housemaid she knew well answered the summons.

'I'll speak with the laird, if you please, Phyllis,' Mary-Ann said.

Phyllis stared, open-mouthed.

'I'm no' sure if the man'll see you, Mary-Ann.'

'Oh, he'll see me! Tell him the blacksmith will be out to remove the carriage wheels if the bill's not paid forthwith.'

'Tell him yoursel', hen. He'll have apoplexy!' Phyllis crowed with delight. Mary-Ann was ushered into the laird's study. It was a large intimidating room, but as a young woman she had been nursemaid in a much grander London mansion, and was not intimidated by a show of wealth. The laird sat glowering behind a huge mahogany desk while she delivered the ultimatum, quite pleasantly.

'This is most irregular and inconvenient, Mrs Macgregor! I am entertaining a guest at the moment.'

She smiled.

'Then you'll be anxious to keep the wheels on your carriage, sir.' She settled down on a convenient chair. 'I suggest you settle the account today. I can wait.'

'How much am I due ye?' he growled.

'One pound five shillings.'

'Daylight robbery!'

'There's extra charge for extended credit, sir.'

Muttering under his breath, the laird opened a drawer and took out a cash box. He counted out the required sum and pushed it towards Mary-Ann. She swept it into her purse.

'I'll need a receipt!' he grunted.

She produced one from the basket and laid it on the desk.

'There. You'll find that's all signed and correct.'

The elderly gentleman sat back and stared at her with grudging admiration.

'You were confident, weren't you, Mrs Macgregor?'

She stood up, laughing.

'Yes, sir. Very confident that a legal gentleman like you would see sense. And now I'll wish you good day.'

She walked out feeling pleased with herself, Ewan's hard won cash in her purse. In the hallway, she bumped into a young gentleman. This would be the laird's guest, no doubt.

He steadied her, and then smiled delightedly.

'It's Mary-Ann!'

She looked blank, and he laughed.

'I'm not surprised you don't recognize me, since I was only ten when you left to marry the blacksmith. Then Papa sold the Scottish estate, and there were no more Forfar holidays for me and my sisters.'

'Torquil St Clair, of course!' She hugged the grown man she'd cared for when he was a little boy and she was his nursemaid. 'How tall and handsome you are! No wonder I didn't recognize you. What brings you to Forfar?'

'I'm to marry a beautiful Edinburgh lass on the 15th of August, in St Giles cathedral, no less! The laird's son is to be best man, so this is a flying visit to settle a few details.'

'A Scottish lass? I'm happy for you!'

'She's a darling, and insists upon a Scottish wedding. All our English guests must arrange to come north.'

'Good for her!'

Torquil laughed.

'The guest list will include plenty of well-known names, as a result! Maybe you remember Alistair Ross, who was my older brother's best friend at university? He's quite a famous MP now with a reputation in the House for wit. He has agreed to speak at the reception. That should be memorable!'

'Yes.' she said. She laid a hand on the young man's sleeve. 'I hope you and your lass will be very happy, Torquil, but I must go.'

He kissed her cheek.

'It's been grand seeing you again, Mary-Ann. You left so suddenly we children didn't even have a chance to say goodbye! My sisters cried and so did I, because it seemed the end of our happy childhood. I went to Eton afterwards, and Mama and Papa never came back to Forfar again.'

Outside. Mary-Ann paused to take a deep breath. She understood why Mr and Mrs St Clair had never returned to the district. They would not care to meet the nursemaid who had been seduced under their own roof.

'Alistair!' Mary-Ann whispered. The first time for years the name had been on her lips.

Alistair Ross, quite a famous MP.

David's father.

Next morning started peaceably enough.

The boys were up early and busily at work, which pleased Ewan. Danny was still asleep, and Mary-Ann let him lie. The girls kissed their ma and pa and set off for school while Mary-Ann and Ewan lingered over breakfast. Ewan had been surprised and delighted that the laird had paid the outstanding bill at last. He had tactfully refrained from questioning his wife about a generous sum added for late payment.

There was no urgency to go to work that morning, since the boys and Wullie could easily cope with the work in hand, but Ewan had an uneasy feeling everything was not as it should be.

He glanced up at the empty ledge above the mantelpiece, and his blood ran cold.

'My gun! Who dared take my gun?'

Mary-Ann turned pale. She met her husband's eye. He looked grimly furious.

'Davey! The young fool's been hunting rabbits for the roadman's lass. So the catapult's not good enough for him now, is it? He must take my gun!'

He strode angrily to the workshop doorway. His suspicions were confirmed. Davey was nowhere to be seen and Matthew was a picture of guilt.

'Matthew, where's Davey?' Ewan bellowed.

The lad looked young and frightened beside the big, angry man.

'There are few rabbits left on common land, Papa. Davey's had no luck for days and the roadman's lass says her pa's growing weaker. Davey took the gun and went off very early this morning to try his luck on the laird's land.'

His father groaned aloud. This was even worse than he'd thought.

'Lord save us. The laird's land!'

Then Ewan was outside and running fast along the road towards the laird's estate. It was a fair way to go, but he settled down to a dogged pace. Under his breath he prayed he would not be too late to stop this foolishness . . .

For days, Davey had toyed with the idea of borrowing the gun as rabbits became scarcer on common ground. The plight of the roadman and his daughter hardened Davey's resolve to try his luck on the laird's hillside. He had brought Matthew into the plan to cover his absence should he be longer than expected, and had crept out of bed while it was still dark.

The roadman's lass was waiting outside her father's bothy, as arranged. Janet Golightly looked scared when she saw the gun. He had threatened to bring it instead of the catapult on this poaching trip, but she had not believed him.

'Davey! Do you think you should? They'll hear the shots!'

'No. The gamekeepers will be asleep. They won't be expecting poachers at this time of the morning. We'll bag a couple of rabbits and be back home before my pa misses the gun. You don't have to come with me, if you're scared.'

'Of course I'm not scared!' she cried.

'Come on then!' He shouldered the gun, gave her the empty game bag, and the two youngsters scaled the sandstone wall.

Once inside the grounds Davey had planned the route carefully, keeping high ground between them and the keeper's cottage. There was dense undergrowth and trees on both sides of the narrow track he had chosen, leading upwards to open hillside and the rabbit warren. His spirits were high, though the place was dark and gloomy before daybreak. The plan was working and he relished a hint of danger, holding the gun cocked, ready for action.

The stag appeared out of the gloom, thundering down the track towards them, its eyes wide and gleaming.

Davey froze in terror. He knew they were in deadly danger. Rutting stags crazed with rivalry and lust at mating time could inflict terrible injuries and death. He dropped to one knee and fired at the charging beast. The aim was true. The stag faltered in its stride then toppled over and lay still.

Shaking in every limb, he lowered the gun. Janet clutched his arm.

'Oh, Davey! What have you done?'

'I had to! It would have killed us!'

He was almost in tears, with no idea what to do. The dead animal couldn't be hidden, and the gamekeeper might have heard the shot.

'Somebody's coming!' the lass cried in panic.

It was too late to run. They were caught.

Ewan came pounding up the track. He halted abruptly, taking in the situation.

'God help us!' he groaned.

'Pa, I had to! It would have killed us!' Davey cried desperately.

Tears ran down his cheeks. He looked very young, the lass with him was white as death and near to fainting with fear. Ewan felt only pity for the terrified bairns. Retribution could come later, once he'd dealt with this disaster.

Ewan bent over the dead stag. At least it had been a clean kill.

'Take the lass to her father and go home, Davey. What's done can't be undone. I'll drag the deer into the undergrowth and hide it there. Maybe when it's found, a stray shot from the laird's shooting party will have the blame.'

'But, Pa—'

Ewan gave Davey a shove.

'Go on, run! There's no time to waste!'

The two youngsters took to their heels as the blacksmith heaved the dead stag through the bushes into the trees. Ewan Macgregor was stronger than most, but even so he was forced to rest. He was taking up the burden again when two men stepped out of the undergrowth and confronted him.

Ewan knew them well, of course. One was Spence, the laird's gamekeeper, rather a surly character, and the other Henderson, the brawny head stalker, a man not renowned for brainpower.

The gamekeeper looked surprised.

'Weel, blacksmith! I never thought you would turn poacher.'

Ewan spread his hands.

'I'm no poacher. I heard a stray shot on the laird's land and came to investigate. I found this dead beast. Do you see a gun in my hands?'

'Guns is easy hidden,' Spence said.

'I did not shoot the stag. Do you doubt my word?'

The man nodded.

'Aye. I do. It's well known your wife feeds vagrants. Folk wonder where she finds the meat. I say you are lying, blacksmith.'

Ewan stiffened.

'No man calls me liar. You will apologize, Mr Spence.'

'Apologize to a thief? Never!' He yelled to his companion. 'Grab him, Henderson. We'll take him to the laird.'

Ewan struggled. He realized resisting only made matters worse for him, but it would give the youngsters more time to escape. Besides, punching Spence gave him certain amount of satisfaction. The gamekeeper was not popular in the town. In the end there was quite a battle between the three of them.

Davey and the lass had almost reached the safety of the road when he heard Spence yelling, followed by the sound of fighting. He stopped running and looked back.

The girl tugged at his arm, frantically.

'Come on, Davey!'

He pushed her away.

'No, you go. Something's happened to my father. I must help him.' He turned and ran back, disappearing up the path.

Janet hesitated indecisively for several moments, and then followed him, stealthily.

Davey burst out of the undergrowth into the middle of the fight, just as Ewan had been overpowered and brought to the ground. The blacksmith cried out when he saw the boy.

'No, Davey, no!'

But it was too late. The young lad flung down the gun and pounded Henderson's back with both fists.

'Let my pa go! He's innocent. It was me that shot the stag.'

Ewan groaned despairingly. Spence nursed an aching jaw and stared at the lad venomously.

'Did you now? So we have the son's confession to add to the father's lies. The laird will be very interested indeed to hear what ye have to say, my lad!'

Janet Golightly lay trembling in her hiding place in the bushes. She pressed a hand to her mouth to stop a sob. This was a terrible disaster and she felt responsible for it, but there was little she could do to help Davey and his father now. She crept quietly from the scene till she reached the safety of the road, and then ran towards the smiddy, sobbing as she went.

Mary-Ann had been unable to settle to housework after her husband went dashing off after her son. As time passed she became worried and went into the yard to keep lookout. She was sweeping the cobbles when the roadman's daughter came rushing in.

'Terrible news, Mistress Macgregor!' the youngster gasped.

Mary-Ann's heart lurched, but she put an arm round the skinny girl and led her indoors. Danny was playing on the rug by the hearth with the little boat Matthew had made for him. He sat up wide-eyed as his mother seated Janet Golightly by the fire and began chafing her hands. The day was mild, but the child was icy-cold and shaking.

'Now then, my dear, tell me exactly what happened,' Mary-Ann said.

The whole story came pouring out amid tears and sobs. She listened to the girl's account with growing dismay.

'Oh, Mrs Macgregor, what'll happen to them? Poaching's a crime. They'll be sent to the ends of the earth!' Janet wailed.

Mary-Ann forced a smile.

'No, dear. Nowadays nobody is transported for poaching a rabbit or two. Shooting the deer was obviously not intentional and I'm sure the laird will let Davey off with a warning, when he knows the facts.'

'But the blacksmith punched Mr Spence and Davey thumped Mr Henderson. That makes it much worse!' the girl wept.

Mary-Ann could think of nothing to say. Assault did indeed make the crime a hundred times worse. Oh, the hot Macgregor blood! She thought despairingly.

Danny climbed on to her knee and she clutched the little boy close to her breast with a sudden feeling of utter desolation.

'Is this a bad day, Mama?' he asked.

She nodded.

'Yes, Danny, it is a very bad day. For all of us.'

Two

The laird was not pleased to be summoned from breakfast. He was even less pleased to find a bruised and battered gamekeeper with the blacksmith and his son in custody. He frowned.

'Well, Spence, what's this? I was told you had caught two poachers.'

'And so I have, sir. Macgregor was caught in the act with a new-killed stag, and his son claims to have shot the beast. Here's the gun in evidence. The pair o' them resisted arrest and the blacksmith closed Henderson's eye and near broke my jaw. The young lad's language and behaviour was wild an' threatening, sir.'

The laird might have an irritable reputation, but he was a fair-minded man. He had known Ewan Macgregor as a lad learning the trade in his father's smiddy. Aye, and learning it better than the father, with greater skill and more veterinary knowledge. If the laird's opinion had been asked, he would have sworn that honest Ewan Macgregor would never be found in this predicament.

'What do you have to say for yourself, Macgregor?' he asked with interest.

'I take full responsibility for my laddie's prank, sir.'

'Hardly a prank. There's a dead stag to be accounted for.'

'He had to shoot it. The beast was crazed and might have killed the boy. He had no right to trespass on your land, but food is scarce and there's hardly a rabbit left on common ground. My son took pity on starving folk and I found out his intention too late to stop him.'

The laird believed him. Normally, he would have given the boy a blistering warning he would not forget, left discipline to the father and sent them on their way. But there was the question of assault.

The crime of poaching aggravated by assault was a much more serious matter, and he could see that Spence was nursing a swollen jaw and nose which had received attention from the blacksmith's fist. Spence was a loud-mouthed braggart and the ferocity of the struggle and extent of his injuries would be greatly exaggerated by nightfall. This crime could not be hushed up, unfortunately.

He felt genuine sympathy for the two, yet the whole affair puzzled him. Why had the blacksmith resisted arrest, surely the man must have realized he could only make matters worse? The laird sighed.

'I have no option but to charge you and your son with this serious crime, Macgregor. You will be held in custody till your case can be dealt with.'

'Not my son, sir!' Ewan objected, dismayed. 'The lad's actions were foolish, not criminal.'

Davey was almost in tears.

'You mustn't punish my father, sir! It was my fault. Pa was only protecting us.'

The laird raised his eyebrows. 'Us?'

'Davey means – the pair of us, sir,' Ewan said hastily.

Davey met his father's warning glance and froze. He had nearly incriminated the roadman's daughter. He was scared to open his mouth now. Janet was his friend. If she and her father suffered because of his stupidity he would never forgive himself.

The laird waved them out of his sight. He was sure there was more to the incident than met the eye, and that worried him, but what could he do? The law was the law.

'Take them to the constable, Spence. Tell him I'll be in to see the fiscal this afternoon to press charges.'

Sam'l Birse, the Forfar constable, took it upon himself to inform Mary-Ann of the morning's events. He had left Ewan Macgregor and his son in the cells under the watchful eye of the turnkey, and found East and West High Street buzzing with the news. You couldn't hide a jelly nose like Spence's, though most Forfar folk were agreed that the injury was long overdue.

When he reached the smiddy-seat, Sam'l took off his helmet and held it respectfully under his arm as if attending a funeral. In hushed tones, he informed Mary-Ann of the outcome of the crime. She was pale but composed. Her bairns were grouped around her and a handsome picture they made, he thought. He couldn't help but notice that it was a tidy place. You could eat your meat off a spotless floor.

'So what happens now, constable?' she asked.

'They'll be taken to Perth to await sentence, ma'am.'

The room was warm, but Mary-Ann felt chilled.

'Why Perth? Surely it's a local matter?'

'There's more to it than poaching rabbits, ma'am. There's assault and grievous bodily harm to the keepers to be accounted for.'

Oh, that wild Macgregor temper! she thought despairingly.

'What might the sentence be, Mr Birse?' she asked with dread.

He felt heart sorry for the bonnie wee woman.

'It'll depend what view the judge takes. It might be weeks, but there's no denying it could be years.'

Mary-Ann sat down weakly in Ewan's favourite chair after the constable left, her children gathered round her. She lifted Danny on to her knee and cuddled him. Agnes crouched at her feet, her head against her mother's knee. Shona perched on the chair, an arm round her neck. Their young faces showed their deep distress. Ewan was a caring father, and now that he had been taken from them, they turned to their mother and expected her to take charge.

Mary-Ann felt weak and inadequate, but she must try not to fail them.

Matthew stood apart.

'Don't worry, Mama,' he said. 'We all know Papa's not a poacher. I expect Spence and Henderson pounced on him. Davey was wrong to do what he did, but he didn't mean any harm.'

Matthew's emotions were confused. He felt indignant and angry, which was right and proper, but a heady sense of jubilant freedom seemed inappropriate.

For thirteen years Matthew had lived in David's shadow, chasing after a bright star and hoping to catch a sprinkle of stardust. He could never match his brother's cleverness at school and teachers had grown impatient and accused him of laziness.

Yet he'd always tried so hard!

But once Matthew and Davey started work at the smiddy, the tables were turned with a vengeance. Ewan was impressed by Matthew's ability and enthusiasm, while Davey had made no attempt to hide his boredom. Matthew had discovered to his delight that he was every bit as clever as his brother, though in more practical ways. He could study a piece of machinery and see at once how it worked – and even how it could be improved. At school he had hated sums, yet his eye was true to the smallest fraction of an inch when forging a farm implement.

So Matthew's self-confidence had grown, and now he faced up to the greatest challenge of his life with determination. He had to take his father's place; his mother was looking to him for help.

'Matthew, they couldn't keep your father and Davey in prison for years, could they?' she asked tearfully.

He laughed.

'No, it makes the bobby's life easier if he frightens folk, Mama. Pa will be home in a week or two. Wullie and I will keep the smiddy going till then.'

Smiling, he headed for the smiddy and took in a long, satisfying breath of hot, smoky air. He found the lingering smell of horsehair and hoof inspiring. There were two chestnut Clydesdales waiting to be shod and Matthew couldn't wait to get started . . .

Mary-Ann rose next morning with renewed hope and energy. She knew her man was innocent, and her boy Davey just an impulsive, reckless lad. Laws were harsh, but she had faith in justice. Two weeks imprisonment could be endured. Ewan would suffer the sentence without loss of face and wild young Davey would benefit from the lesson.

She bustled around, preparing a bundle of clean clothing and a basket of food for the prisoners. The girls had gone to school as usual, but Danny's usual minder, Mrs Wullie, was working at the weaving sheds, and Mary-Ann was at a loss for someone to look after him for a few hours. The wee lad would never see the inside of prison, if she had her way, but leaving Danny in the workshop with Matthew and Wullie was too risky an option.

Then Mary-Ann remembered the roadman's lass. She hurried to the bothy, promising Janet Golightly sixpence and a piece of pie if she would come to the smiddy-seat and keep an eye on the child. Janet agreed with alacrity.

Mary-Ann drove the gig to the jail, a forbidding grey stone building set on the hill.

She tethered the horse, patted it, and fitted a nosebag on the patient beast. Then she squared her shoulders, picked up her burden and set off for the entrance.

Mary-Ann nearly wept when the turnkey brought her husband and son to her in a cold, bare room, where he kept an eye upon the meeting. The man had some sympathy for the blacksmith and his lad, and tactfully turned his back and contemplated the heavily barred window with a view of the yard beyond.

Ewan was unshaven, clothes torn and muddied. Mary-Ann was overcome when she saw him, knowing how his filthy state must distress him. She ran to him and kissed him. Ewan held her close. Her spontaneity delighted him.

'Ewan, I'm so worried! Birse says you could face a long prison sentence.'

'Hardly that.' He laughed. 'How would the town fare without a blacksmith? No, Mary-Ann, I don't anticipate that. Fourteen days at the most, I'd say, but Davey and I can face that.'

'Prison's not so bad, Mama.' Davey nodded reassuringly.

He hated to see his mother upset, so remained tight-lipped about dirty bedding, stale bread and murky water.

But Mary-Ann was not deceived. She could see for herself how her loved ones had suffered. The injustice angered her.

'Never fear. I'll find a way to have you both freed. Then we'll have a grand celebration,' she promised staunchly.

'Time's up, I'm afraid, ma'am,' the turnkey announced suddenly, turning away from the window. 'I see the brake's just arrived to take the prisoners to Perth.'

'Perth? It's forty miles away!' Mary-Ann cried. 'How can I visit my husband and son there?'

The warder shrugged.

'I'm sorry, but these two will be tried at the next assizes.'

Mary-Ann stared at the man in horror.

'But that's for rogues and murderers!' She clutched her husband's arm. 'Ewan love, you can't let them do this to you!'

'I can't fight the law, Mary-Ann. We'll plead not guilty and trust a jury to see sense. I worry about the smiddy meantime, though. Wullie's a good lad but he can't run the business, and I can't afford to lose customers.'

'At least you can stop worrying on that score, my dear. Matthew has taken over. He was shoeing a mare when I left, and Wullie was busy making cartwheels.'

'So long as he wasn't turning them, like last Hogmanay after a couple of drams,' Ewan remarked dryly.

'Still, something must be done about this, Ewan! I'll speak to the laird.'

'No, my dear! You must not!' Ewan was alarmed. He had visions of a battle royal if his feisty wife and the wily old lawyer should meet head-on.

'But what else can I do?' she demanded tearfully.

He kissed and hugged her tenderly.

'Go home, dear lass. Matthew has the skill, but he'll need your help. Go home and wait for me, my love.'

Davey looked away. They did not hug and kiss like this at home, and he was embarrassed and afraid. This unusual behaviour had brought home to him the gravity of their situation.

His mother turned and kissed him. Her perfume was light and flowery, so foreign to the quicklime and rotten cabbage smell of prison he nearly wept.

'Have courage, darling,' she said softly. 'Remember we love you.'

Does that include Papa? Davey wondered. He stole a glance at his father.

Ewan stood watching the farewell with folded arms. Davey was no stranger to that guarded stance.

Instinct told him that Matthew was the favoured one, and experience in the workshop had proved the suspicion. But why should that be when his father must surely soon realize it was just the old adage of the square peg in the round hole, and Davey would never make a blacksmith? He excelled in literature and mathematics, while his brother was a genius with machinery.

The two brothers were poles apart – and now he'd had time to think upon it, that seemed rather odd too . . .

Matthew had put in a power of work that morning, but by noon Wullie noticed the youngster was flagging.

'Lowsing time, Matt. Put your feet up for an hour,' he suggested kindly.

Matthew accepted gratefully. The gruelling work had tired him more than expected. His muscles ached.

But I'll get used to it! he thought as he pushed open the door and went into the living quarters. Danny's laughter greeted him, and the sound of a lassie singing.

'Ten green bottles, sat upon a wall . . .' she was singing. 'C'mon Danny, join in!'

She was laughing and dancing, but the laughter ceased when she and Matthew came face to face.

He smiled.

'Please carry on. Danny likes the exhibition.'

She looked hurt.

'You think I'm making a daft exhibition of myself!'

'No, no!' he said, red-faced.

She turned away.

'We were stopping anyway for dinner. Do you want any? There's broth, bread an' cheese an' apple pie.'

Her actions were quick and birdlike; she flew to the stove without waiting for his reply. Matthew was left with his mouth hanging open.

Janet Golightly had been in heaven that morning. The smiddy-seat had reawakened memories of the home presided over by her own dead mother. The room was clean, warm and comfortable. Fancy having a pump and sink in the scullery, so you did not lug heavy buckets from the burn! She hastily dismissed the sin of envy, because her father approved of the Macgregors.

'Hang in with smiddy folk, lass,' he had advised. 'There'll aye be horses to be shod and implements forged, even while poor folk starve. When there's war there are ploughshares to be beaten into swords. Smiddy folk will never want!'

Pa was right. Just see their larder!

Smoked hams, cheeses and pickles. Pots of jam, tubs of butter, dishes of milk – the smell itself was nourishment without a bite to eat!

Since Mrs Macgregor had not yet returned, Janet selected a few slices of ham, cheese and a baked fruit pie. Mutton broth simmered in the stockpot on the stove, and Janet took credit for that, since she'd kept the fire stoked, and salted the broth.

She admired the beautiful stove, handcrafted by the clever

blacksmith to fit the ingle. It had an oven, a spit for roasting meat, hooks and swees on which to hang kettles and pots to swing over the fire. Janet ladled steaming broth into three china bowls.

Matthew could think of nothing to say to her. He felt clumsy and awkward sitting beside the dainty girl. Fortunately, Danny was chattering nineteen to the dozen.

'You cook as good as my mammy, Janet,' he was saying. 'Stay with us while my papa's away. You can play with me all day an' sleep in Matthew's bed, now Davey's gone.'

Matthew choked. 'No, she couldn't!'

The girl looked at him seriously.

'I'm very sorry about Davey an' your da, Matthew. It was all my fault.'

He stared, shocked.

'Your fault? How can it be?'

Haltingly, she explained what had happened on the hill and the real reason behind the expedition.

'Do you think the laird would let them off, if I told him about me and my da?' she asked.

Matthew shook his head.

'No. It would make matters worse. He might send you and your father to prison as well.'

She looked terrified.

'He mustn't do that! My da's ill.'

She toyed unhappily with the broth, suddenly losing appetite.

'There's nothing else for it then. I'll need to be taken on at the sheds.'

'You mean the weaving sheds?'

'Aye.' She nodded. 'They say wee bairns can earn nine pence a week, cleaning lint from under the machines. I may start learning to be a weaver, and the wages would help Da get better.'

He was horrified at the suggestion. She looked such a frail wee lass.

'No, Janet, weaver's work is much too hard for bairns.'

She looked insulted.

'I'm not a bairn, I'm thirteen!'

He studied her. She was too skinny to be bonnie, but looking into her eyes he felt as dazzled as a fuddled hare caught in a lantern's beam. Strange new sensations were stirring.

At school the boys had whispered and laughed slyly about girls, but now that he was smitten himself Matthew did not feel like laughing. He wanted with all his heart to protect Janet Golightly from hardship and hunger.

But that might prove difficult. His own family were depending upon him now.

Janet took the apple pie from the oven and eyed the crisp sugary crust hungrily. She made a rapid decision.

If I cut four slices, two big and two small, I can give the boys a big slice each, and perhaps they won't notice if I eat one small slice and hide the other under my plaid, she thought. She calmed an uneasy conscience. A slice of pie was promised to her, and she was just sharing her portion with her da . . .

Sam'l Birse the bobby had a soft spot for Mary-Ann. He made a detour by the smiddy a few weeks later to inform her that a date for Ewan and Davey Macgregor's trial had been set. He also offered to arrange a return journey for her on the Perth stage-coach. She accepted gratefully.

The news set in motion a flurry of frantic activity in the smiddy-seat.

Mary-Ann's Sunday best clothes must be washed and ironed to keep Forfar's end up with the fashionable ladies of Perth. Her girls were on holiday from school that day, so when the time arrived she had no qualms about leaving Danny. Mrs Wullie had finished her stint in the weaving sheds and kindly volunteered to keep a watchful eye on the bairns.

Mary-Ann tiptoed out of the house at dawn on the appointed morning, and hurried down the brae to East High Street, where the stagecoach waited.

She sat in the corner seat reserved for her, too worried to pay more than scant attention to the friendly overtures of her travelling companions.

Afterwards, Mary-Ann could remember little of the journey through the sunny vale of Strathmore that peaceful morning. Time passed like a dream for her, too preoccupied with troubled thoughts to notice the beauty of her surroundings. She was restless during the leisurely stop in Coupar Angus to change driver and horses, but despite her impatience Mary-Ann found that fresh

horses brought the travellers at a spanking pace to complete the
journey across the Tay, to the outskirts of Perth.

She stepped down outside the courthouse with an hour to
spare before the trial, glad of the respite to collect her thoughts.

The courthouse overlooked the river, which was much narrower
at that point. To the east of the town, quite large ships could
navigate the river at high tide, sailing the twenty odd miles through
the Carse of Gowrie from the port of Dundee and the open sea
beyond. The sound of rippling water was usually soothing, but
today it set Mary-Ann on edge.

A crowd was gathering in front of the courthouse, for the
assizes attracted curious onlookers. Mary-Ann did not mingle
with the townsfolk. Cholera was more virulent than usual in the
towns that summer. She'd heard that the Queen was considering
a national day of prayer, for relief from the deadly scourge . . .

'Good day to you, Mistress Macgregor.'

With a start, she glanced up to find the laird doffing his hat.
She smiled, though she at once recalled their last meeting, when
she had demanded money with threats. How she wished now
that she had hung in with the law, as Ewan had advised!

'It grieves me to find your husband and son detained with
rogues and – ahem! – debtors, ma'am,' he remarked.

She inclined her head politely, but her heart sank. Debtors? So
he did remember!

He went on quite kindly.

'However, I believe there are mitigating circumstances, and I
have entered a plea with the court for clemency.'

Mary-Ann was grateful to the point of tears.

'Thank you, sir. You are very kind.'

'Aye – well, but don't raise your hopes too high, mind!' he
warned.

The laird knew the judge who would be trying the Macgregors'
case. A fair enough man, but unpredictable . . .

Presently the doors opened and Mary-Ann filed inside with the
others. The public benches were well filled, the selected jurors
took their places and gowned and bewigged counsel conferred
in low tones beside the judge's empty dais. She chose a seat next
to the passageway, near to the dock.

There was a scuffle of feet as the judge entered and everyone rose. Mary-Ann eyed the jury nervously as they were sworn, praying there were no landowners among them. Shopkeepers and townsfolk might take a more lenient view of poachers.

She almost cried out when her husband and son were brought up from the cells. Ewan scanned the crowded chamber eagerly and caught sight of her at once. He smiled broadly. It took courage to smile bravely in return. His healthy tan had faded and his eyes were darkly shadowed. Davey looked very young and defiant and Mary-Ann feared for him. Humility might serve him better.

She listened with increasing dismay as the charge was read out. The bare facts sounded damning, the truth hidden beneath layers of legal jargon.

The gamekeeper Spence took the stand. After a colourful account of the fight weighted to his advantage, he opened his mouth to point out missing and broken teeth. The defence counsel could make nothing of Spence, who stuck to his story grimly. The stalker Henderson corroborated every detail.

The laird was not called to the stand, but the defence counsel spoke eloquently on Ewan and Davey's behalf, and demanded clemency. When the jury rose to consider the verdict, Mary-Ann was feeling optimistic.

The jurors did not spend much time in deliberation. There was an excited stir within the courtroom as they filed back inside. The case had aroused much interested speculation, for the Colonial Secretary, Lord Grey, had changed the law on transportation of criminals to penal colonies. Nobody could guess what the sentence might be.

Everyone held a breath, for the verdict.

'Guilty, my lord!'

Mary-Ann made no sound, but felt as if her heart had turned to ice. Guilty! Oh, the injustice!

She watched the judge with terrified apprehension, for this man held Ewan and Davey's fate in his hands. He frowned. What was he thinking?

The judge pondered the facts of this unusual case, the laird's plea for clemency adding weight to the decision. He had been impressed by the dignified demeanour of the blacksmith and his son. The same could not be said for the gamekeepers!

Although the accused were guilty as charged, he was inclined
to take heed of the laird's testimonial and pass a light custodial
sentence for the poaching offence. But, there was the question
of the assault. He must not appear too lenient. Hardened criminals might take leniency as licence. The law must be upheld!

Thoughtfully, his fingers tapped a rhythm on the bench. In his
pocket lay a letter from his friend, Governor-General Fitzroy of
Her Majesty's penal colonies in Australia. It contained an urgent
appeal:

'Can you not send out skilled men, instead of thieves and cut-
throats? Our colonies need craftsmen, not criminals, if we are to
prosper!'

The judge knew, of course, that transportation to the penal
colonies had ceased for two years past, to pacify campaigners in
Britain and honest settlers in New South Wales who resented the
convict stain. British prisons were bursting at the seams as a result.

There was another option open to him, however. He could
sentence this highly skilled man and his son to a period of imprisonment in Britain, followed by shipment to Van Diemen's Land
on probation to complete the sentence. In this way, the wily
Colonial Secretary had pacified the objectors. No criminals would
be sent to the penal colony in future, only 'exiles' that were
repaying a debt to society. Very neat!

Wives and families were encouraged to follow, if of suitable
moral character. He eyed the handsome pair in the dock and
made up his mind.

'Ewan and David Macgregor, you have been found guilty as
charged. It is therefore ordered and adjured by this court that
you be detained in custody in such place as Her Majesty's officials shall think fit to direct and appoint, and thereafter, if in a
state of penitence, exiled from this land for a term of ten years.'

The silence was broken by a few loud gasps. The judge was
well pleased with this reaction.

It could be that I am doing these two a good turn, he thought
complacently. Skilled men could prosper and grow rich in Australia.
The blacksmith and his son might do very well for themselves
and decide never to return to Scotland.

Satisfied, he dismissed the court . . .

★   ★   ★

Mary-Ann walked out of the courtroom in a daze. Her husband and son had been ushered away so quickly there had been no chance to exchange more than a few words. There was a uniformed constable standing in the passageway. She approached him.

'Please let me speak to my husband and son, Ewan and David Macgregor.'

'Sorry, ma'am. Contact with convicted prisoners not permitted in court.'

'Then I can visit them in prison!'

He smiled grimly.

'I doubt it. Perth prison's so overcrowded they're to be shipped out with a batch of convicted prisoners leaving at high tide, in an hour or so.'

This was terrible news.

'Where are they taking them?'

'Pentonville, I believe.' He grinned. 'They're lucky. It's new-built.'

'Is it far?'

He laughed.

'Far enough. London, to be exact.'

Mary-Ann turned from him without a word and walked blindly out into mild sunlight. Despair had turned to anger. She would not give in so easily to this great injustice. She would fight to free her innocent husband and beloved, misguided son. Oh yes, she would fight! She would think of a way.

Danny was too young to grasp the full extent of the disaster, but the older children were grief-stricken. The effort to remain cheerful and appear optimistic for their sake left Mary-Ann drained by the week's end.

Matthew, a youngster doing man's work, was exhausted and aching in every muscle. He was given the luxury of a hot bath in the tub in front of the fire, modesty preserved by a blanket draped over the clothes horse.

They were all unnaturally quiet that Saturday evening. Nobody felt like a sing-song while Papa's violin lay silent in its case. Agnes refused Danny's request for a game, and he was huffed. What was wrong with everyone, now Papa and Davey had gone?

'Agnes was bad at the school, Mama,' he volunteered vengefully. 'Shona says Mrs Carnegy stood Agnes in the corner.'

Agnes turned red and glared daggers at the little boy.

'Danny, you clype! It – it was nothing, Mama.'

'Mrs Carnegy wouldn't stand you in the corner for nothing!' Mary-Ann said.

The girls exchanged a look. They knew their mother wouldn't rest till she had uncovered the truth. Agnes sighed.

'Beattie Murdoch refused to sit aside me, Mama. Her ma told her she wasn't to mix with jailbird's bairns, so I hit her.'

Mary-Ann was furious, but she could not blame the children. Spiteful folk had begun to cold-shoulder her innocent bairns already. She hugged Agnes.

'Mistress Murdoch had no right to say such a cruel thing. Your papa is innocent. I will take you both away from Mrs Carnegy's school. We must economize anyway, till – till your father comes home—'

Her voice broke and she couldn't go on. Fortunately, the girls were too stunned by this change in their fortunes to notice.

'Are we to go to the Spoutie school?' Shona asked anxiously. Castle Street narrowed to an outlet known locally as the 'spout'. The school situated at that location catered for a more robust breed of pupil. Shona feared this would be the end of music lessons.

However, Agnes welcomed the adventure. She quoted a well-known saying aimed at dawdlers and lasses showing off finery.

'East the town, west the town, up the Spout, and home.'

That made everyone smile, and somehow the future appeared less bleak.

Mary-Ann could not sleep that night, tired though she was. A pale half-moon sent cool moonlight filtering into the room. The night was beautiful, but beauty must be shared, and she was all alone. Even with eyes tightly closed she imagined she heard echoes of Ewan's voice, saw him smile, remembered the play of muscles on his back.

'Ewan!' she whispered in sorrow and tears, 'I did not value your faithful love highly enough, forgive me, dear husband!'

And she had Alistair Ross's treachery to thank for it! she thought bitterly, turning restlessly in the lonely bed.

On a night such as this Alistair had told her he loved her and

wanted to marry her. And she had believed he meant it, innocent little fool – as if a wealthy, ambitious young man would
marry a nursemaid whose father was an Irish navvy, working on
the railroad!

She had tried to put the past behind her when she'd married
Ewan, but how could that first disastrous love affair ever be
forgotten? Davey was born as a constant reminder. Alistair Ross
remained unforgettable, all their married life.

She sat up in bed as a sudden thought struck her. Torquil had
told her Alistair was a member of parliament now, and MPs could
intervene in court cases if an injustice had been done, could they
not? Perhaps he would agree to help Davey, his son. He had
shown some interest in the boy, sending the gifts of money which
her husband scorned to touch – but would he use his influence
to help Ewan too?

Mary-Ann rose restlessly and crossed to the open window,
breathing gulps of cool night air to calm her agitation.

If she went ahead with this plan, she must meet her former
lover. The matter was much too delicate to be entrusted to pen
and paper.

Fortunately, there was a way. She knew Alistair Ross would be
in Edinburgh very soon to attend Torquil St Clair's wedding. She
could be there to speak to him, to plead Ewan and Davey's case
in person.

Mary-Ann shivered, but not because the night had turned
chilly. Would he offer to help, or turn his back on her and walk
away?

He'd done it before. He might do it again . . .

Three

Mary-Ann outlined her plan to the children at breakfast next morning. It was greeted with suspicion.

'Who is this man?' Matthew asked.

'He's an English gentleman. I remember him when I was nurse-maid to the St Clairs, in London. He's a member of Parliament now.' She ladled porridge into Danny's bowl. He howled.

'Don't want it!'

'Stop your nonsense and sup it. It'll put hair on your chest,' his mother snapped.

Matthew frowned. She wasn't usually so ill-tempered.

'Wullie says politicians are useless,' he said. 'Wullie wrote to one about bad Forfar water, but nothing's ever been done. Don't trust the water in the well down by the Muckle Drain, he says!'

'Mr Ross has an influential job in government and he's an eloquent speaker by all accounts. If anyone can persuade the Home Secretary to grant a pardon, he can. So that's an end to the argument, if you please, Matthew!' Mary-Ann declared.

She retreated to the scullery and pumped water vigorously into an empty kettle.

Matthew could not let the matter rest. As man of the house he felt responsible for his mother's safety, and her plan to visit Edinburgh to ask a stranger for help bothered him. Besides, it wasn't like Mama to fly off the handle like that.

He outlined his concerns to Wullie, in the workshop.

'The man's name's Alistair Ross, and Mama remembers he was a friend of the St Clairs when she was a young lass working in London. He's an MP now, but have you ever heard tell of him?'

'Alistair Ross? Aye, so happen I have.'

Wullie put a taper to the forge and lit a pipe.

'Well?' Matthew prompted.

'I mind that was the name whispered round the dinner table, last time the St Clairs came to Forfar on holiday. That must be about fifteen year ago. Mrs Wullie used to wait at table in the big house, and she telt me.'

This information made Matthew uneasy.

'Why would they whisper?'

'So's the servants wouldna latch on to scandal, of course. My Florrie's ears are sharp though, and she took note o' the name.' Wullie eyed the forge, which Matt in an abstracted use of the bellows was making white-hot. 'I wouldna raise that fire ony higher if I was you, laddie,' he warned, and strolled off to put another spoke in the wheel.

Ewan, Davey, and a batch of convicted men and boys were herded into the hold of a small coastal steamer that had offloaded iron ore for Perth foundry and would make the return journey south with human cargo.

Despite overcrowding, heat from the boilers and coal dross seeping into every corner from the stokehold, Ewan found the ship's hold preferable to the confines of a cell. He and Davey were reunited and free to talk. The guards were Scottish soldiers on detachment from Perth barracks who sunned themselves on deck, leaving the prisoners pretty much to their own devices, confident there was little chance of escape.

Dusty sunbeams filtering into the hold revealed a sad sight. Ewan sat resting wearily against a bulkhead. Davey's face was streaked with dirt, his fair hair matted, a shapeless prison smock and trousers accentuating a skinny body. But still he looked undaunted, while most of the other convicted youngsters snivelled miserably.

Ewan felt proud of him. He could see no trace of tears on this young man's cheeks.

Man? The thought startled Ewan. He looked more closely at the lad. This was not the mischievous boy he'd flung in the horse trough not so very long ago. Recent events had forced David Macgregor to grow up quickly. Maturity was evident in the strong set of the features, and made his foster-father ponder the future.

'What did the judge mean by exile?' Davey asked presently.

'What he said. We'll be exiled to Australia to finish the sentence, after a spell of imprisonment in England.'

'That's not fair, Pa. We haven't done anything bad!'

'It's the law that's bad, not us. Never forget it, Davey.'

The youngster sighed.

'I keep remembering my mother's perfume. To me it's like a lifeline, to drag us out of this stinking hole.'

Davey's flights of fancy often left Ewan floundering, but this one flew straight to the heart. For one brief moment after the trial Mary-Ann had grasped Ewan's hand. Her perfume had drifted to him; her despairing cry had followed them as they were led away.

'Remember – I love you!'

He would always remember her sweet perfume and loving words. Every detail of the parting would stay fresh in his mind, tormenting him for ten long years.

They had been told that the boys were destined for a reformatory for 'correction', when the ship docked in the south. The men would be sent to various prisons or – God forbid! – a rotting hulk swinging at anchor in some lonely harbour. It was possible that he and Davey might not see each other again for many years.

Aye, Ewan thought, the time has come to wipe the slate clean for the lad's sake. Whatever the outcome, Davey should be told that Alistair Ross is his father.

Fortunately, many wearisome hours lay ahead of them aboard ship. Ewan could take his time in the telling, and do it kindly . . .

A journey to Edinburgh was not to be undertaken lightly, and Mary-Ann found that there were many irksome details to attend to. The date of Torquil St Clair's wedding was easily ascertained. All Forfar knew that the laird's son was to be best man at grand Edinburgh nuptials, and draper and shoemaker confirmed the date of an event for which fine linen, the tartans made fashionable by Prince Albert, and black brogues had been ordered.

Danny tailed his mother like her shadow, in case she suddenly disappeared. He howled if Mary-Ann was out of his sight for more than a minute and sorely tried her patience. She made allowances though. The little boy had lost father and brother, and was in terror of losing his mother as well.

She sat Danny on her knee.

'If I ask the roadman's lass to stay till I come home, will you let me go to Edinburgh without a fuss? You like Janet, don't you?'

'Aye. But Agnes doesn't.'

Agnes glanced up.

'I never said so!'

'You're jealous 'cause I like Janet best. She plays better games than you.'

'You think I care, you wee scunner?' Agnes yelled.

Shona had been on edge since music lessons stopped, and the argument tipped her over the brink. She put her hands over her ears and screamed.

'Stop it! Why must we always fight since Papa left? Any more of this, and I swear I'll leave home!'

Mary-Ann was in despair. Once there had been harmony in this house, now tears and squabbles were the norm and the family was falling apart.

Matthew came to the rescue. He'd been at the desk, keeping tally of income and bills. Calculations were easy now that none stood over him with the strap.

'Janet can't come, Mama. She's working in the weaving sheds. The linen trade is picking up, and she works long hours. She can hardly keep her eyes open by the day's end.'

Mary-Ann was surprised to find her son so interested in a lass. Yet why not? Matthew was fourteen past, a man already, carefree boyhood lost forever, and shouldering heavy responsibility much too young.

The thought made her more determined to approach Alistair Ross and beg him to bring an end to this terrible situation.

'It's no matter, Matthew,' she said lightly. 'Mrs Wullie is to stay in the house and see to you all, and Maggie the mangling woman will do washing for an extra three pence we can ill afford.' She looked at her children with a steely glint in the eye. 'That's the way it's to be while I'm away, my dears, so you might as well put a bold face on it.'

They eyed her with surprise. Their father had always had the final say, but Mary-Ann's expression heralded a new approach . . .

Mary-Ann set off for Edinburgh one fine morning. The Forfar–Arbroath railway line had been opened in January 1839 but Forfar station remained a huddle of sheds. There was no direct rail link from Forfar to principal cities, and she would travel first to the coastal fishing town, and thence to Dundee. Wisely, she had allowed two clear days before the wedding, to cover a long, tedious route by rail, road, and ferry.

Mary-Ann was no stranger to long journeys. As nursemaid to the St Clair household from the age of fourteen, Mary-Ann had often travelled with the family from London mansion to Scottish estate. But that had involved a leisurely progress in considerable luxury and with frequent stops along the way.

This journey promised to be very different. She was troubled and alone. Worst of all, while she sat in the carriage worrying about her husband and son, memories of Alistair Ross stirred. She relived the hurt and heartbreak of that disastrous incident in her life.

What will happen when I meet him? She wondered. It would be difficult to control bitterness and anger, but she must try. She would make an appeal to his sense of responsibility as Davey's father, but above all, she dare not offend the man who had treated her so abominably.

Matthew watched his mother leave the smiddy. She turned to wave when she reached the top of the brae and he raised a hand in reply. He was uneasy about the journey and her reasons for it. He didn't like what he'd heard about this man.

'Breakfast's on the table, Matthew,' Mrs Wullie called from within.

She had arrived early that morning with a rattle at the door-knocker, bringing a bundle of clothing and a basket of medications. In Mrs Wullie's experience, bairns were always the better of a dose of something. It didn't much matter what.

Matthew went inside.

The others had not come down yet. No doubt they were awake, but cowering in bed. He sat down and got on with the porridge, while Mrs Wullie rattled and poked at the fire.

'Fancy your ma going off to Edinburgh, alone,' she remarked.

'It's a fine day for it.' Matthew took a spoonful of porridge.

'I don't hold wi' travel, Matt. It unsettles folk. I went on a weavers' jaunt to Glamis once and that was enough for me.'

'My mother's used to travel. She came from Ireland with my grandparents, and when she was working as a nursemaid she often travelled from London to Forfar and back again.'

'You dinna have to tell me. I was in table-service with the St Clairs at the time.'

Matthew was interested.

'Did you meet this famous MP Mama's gone to see?'

She sat down and poured herself a cup of tea, ready for blether.

'No, I never met him. I only heard whispers about his goings-on.'

He leaned forward anxiously.

'What were they whispering, Mrs Wullie?'

She sipped the tea, studying him thoughtfully over the rim.

'It's strange, Matthew. If anyone ever asked, I expected it would be Davey, not you.'

He stared, puzzled.

'Why Davey?'

'Because—' She hesitated, then came to a decision. 'You might as well know, Matt, seeing as how you're man o' this house, now your pa's gone. Davey was born barely seven months after your ma and pa were married, and I was midwife at the birth. Ewan Macgregor insisted Davey was born afore his time, and the rest o' Forfar took him at his word, but Davey didna look like a seven-month baby to me. I didna ken what to think. I'd heard whispering around the table about another man, and I knew Ewan Macgregor would never bring trouble on Mary-Ann. He'd watched her grow up in service to the St Clairs and anybody could see he worshipped the ground she trod. Besides, your ma married the blacksmith scarcely a fortnight after she arrived from London on holiday wi' the St Clairs.'

Matthew pushed the bowl away. He could not touch another mouthful.

'Are you saying this man was Davey's father, not Pa? Is that what they whispered?'

Mrs Wullie stood up.

'I'm no' saying another word, Matthew. I'm surprised at ye, keeping me away from my work, blethering!'

And she scuttled off hastily to the scullery to prepare the washtub for Mangling Maggie.

Matthew did not want to believe her. To believe destroyed precious illusions. Yet he knew in his heart Mrs Wullie had spoken the truth.

It explained everything that had puzzled him for years. He loved and admired Davey, but they had never seemed like real brothers.

The reason sickened him. His mother had always seemed a shining example of womanhood, her virtue beyond reproach.

Now it seemed she had made cynical use of his father's devotion to get herself out of trouble and save her reputation. If Matthew had not been aware of his status as head of the household, he would have wept.

He scrambled to his feet as a thought struck him. There had been scandal whispered round the table about the man his mother had gone to meet. Was he Davey's father, the man who had led her astray? Of course he must be!

Matthew had watched his mother leave the smiddy that morning with a glow in her eyes and a spring in her step. She'd insisted she must ask this influential man's help, but was she telling the truth? Would it suit her better if Davey was set free and Papa never came back?

The thought of his mother's treachery was so appalling; Matthew could not contemplate work that morning.

He left the smiddy and walked fast, striding at a great pace down the brae towards the windmill whose canvas sails creaked round in the favourable wind. He came at last to the extreme point of St Margaret's Inch and could go no farther, staring out across the loch. There he cried the last of his boyish tears, with uncaring ducks going quietly about their business, dabbling in the shallows.

When it was over Matthew sluiced his face in the loch and returned to the smiddy.

Wullie looked up. 'Whaur have you been?'

'Out.'

'I was thinkin' that's whaur you were.' Wullie nodded, sympathetically. The young lad looked older, someway, and a good deal more manly . . .

Mary-Ann broke her journey at a Dunfermline lodging house, then set off with other travellers next morning in a rattling brake, along the riverside to board the ferry. The crossing over the river Forth was calm that morning, and the large coach and team of horses awaiting them on the southern side rolled briskly along the nine miles remaining, to the centre of the city.

Alighting from the coach, the excitement of being once more in a great city gripped her. She felt almost carefree, relieved of responsibility for household and children. Valise in hand, she dawdled along, gazing in shop windows. The air seemed to buzz with life, crowds of fashionably dressed folk thronged the pavements and the thoroughfare was choked with carts, coaches, brewery drays and omnibuses drawn by hefty horses. What trade Ewan could enjoy here, she thought.

Thinking about her husband reminded her of the purpose of her journey. She had taken note of an address in London Road which Ewan frequented when delivering wrought ironwork to Edinburgh customers, and was delighted to find clean lodgings in a reasonably priced room with a view towards the distant river. A good, plain meal was served later. Her fellow guests seemed to find nothing unusual in a young matron travelling alone, to visit the sights of the city. They eagerly offered directions to St Giles, and the proprietor volunteered information about a big wedding in the cathedral the following day at one o'clock. She must be sure not to miss the show! he said.

Next morning dawned hazy, promising a mild, sunny day later on. Mary-Ann had slept restlessly and wakened with a wildly beating heart. Dressed in her best walking-out costume, she studied the reflection anxiously. With her trim figure and glossy black hair, she decided she did not look old enough to be the mother of five children. And for a treacherous moment, she was glad . . .

Meanwhile, Mrs Wullie was enjoying herself as mistress of the smiddy seat. She'd kept Mangling Maggie hard at work all morning, and Maggie had departed with three pence clutched in her fist and a promise to attend to the ironing first thing.

Agnes was outside, busy pegging washing on the line. She was a couthie wee lass Mrs Wullie could get along with – unlike the older one, a flighty piece!

Shona was nowhere to be seen. Mrs Wullie tightened her lips. Out after the lads, no doubt.

She turned her attention to the evening meal. Wullie would be dining with the bairns, and she fancied showing off culinary skills. She studied the contents of Mary-Ann's larder.

There was a plateful of liver under a muslin cover and Mrs Wullie had already noted tender onions in the vegetable garden. Wullie would walk ten miles if there were liver and onions at the end of the journey.

She frowned, though, studying the shelves.

'Och. There's no fat!'

You couldn't have tasty liver and onions without roast fat in the frying pan.

Her eye alighted upon Danny, who was lying on the floor playing coach and horses with sticks and string. He was a sturdy, biddable wee bairn.

'Danny, go to the butcher's in East High Street and ask for a pennyworth o' fat to fry liver. There's a good laddie! And here's a halfpenny to yoursel'.' She doled out the money generously from Mary-Ann's tin.

Danny scrambled to his feet with alacrity. Mama would never let him venture into town on his own, even though he was a big boy, nearly five. Agnes always accompanied him. Danny grabbed the money and ran, intent upon being far down the road before Agnes discovered he'd gone.

It was safe to dawdle once Danny was through the Spout and into Castle Street.

He pressed his nose to the window of Peter Reid's sweetie shop, the halfpence hot in his hand. Peter Reid rock was famous, and a particular favourite of his.

He went inside. Peter Reid himself stood behind the counter.

Shyly, Danny laid the coin down.

'Ha'pennyworth o' Peter Reid, please, sir.'

The genial man laughed.

'Which piece o' him would you want, laddie? Brains might be worth a ha'penny.'

He weighed a portion of broken pieces into a paper bag.

Danny went grinning on his way.

The butcher's shop was crammed. There were trays of freshly baked meat and onion bridies on the counter, a pastry delicacy that is a powerful draw for all Forfarians. Danny wormed a path through the crowd to the front and slipped Mrs Wullie's penny on to the counter. The red-cheeked butcher leaned over.

'Whit can we do for you, son?'

'A pennyworth of fat to fry Mrs Wullie's liver, please sir.'

Everyone laughed.

The adult world is strange, Danny thought, once outside. All the same, he'd learned that if you made people laugh you put them in a good mood, and they were more generous. Witness a paper bag containing a large lump of congealed beef dripping the butcher had given him, and a pocket bulging with a generous ha'pennyworth of Peter Reid's broken rock.

In future when he wanted to have his own way, Danny decided to abandon gurning and howling in favour of riddles and jokes. He had quite a few up his sleeve, and Wullie knew some good ones.

He was trailing slowly homewards past cattle pens set up in High Street for the farmers' market, when a familiar sound stopped him in his tracks. He could swear that was Shona singing!

He tracked the voice to a pub door. Danny was intrigued. Mama always hurried him past these dens of iniquity when he was inclined to loiter. He put his eye to the door and peeped through a crack.

Shona was standing ankle deep in sawdust in front of the bar, singing quite beautifully.

Two men and a lady with bright red hair were listening. Danny recognized them as strolling players who visited the town from time to time. He'd been taken to a very rude pantomime once, and Mama had vowed never again.

There was a hush after Shona finished. Then one of the men sighed.

'A lovely voice, my darlin', but you'd best go home to your ma now. If you're still of a mind to leave home in two, three years, maybe come and see us.'

Danny hopped backwards as Shona came out. Her cheeks were tear-stained and she yelled with fright when she saw him.

'Danny! What are you doing here?' She glanced around in terror. 'Wh—where's Agnes?'

'Dinna fash yourself. I'm on my own.'

She was so relieved she hugged him.

'Promise you won't tell a soul where I've been, Dan?'

He drew a finger across his throat.

'I promise. Cut my throat an' hope to die!'

Danny's chest swelled importantly as he and Shona walked home hand in hand. He was a big boy, entrusted with a secret. Just wait till he told Agnes that!

Mary-Ann had not fully anticipated the interest a large society wedding would arouse in Edinburgh. When she reached the cathedral she found hardly a space to stand on the pavement and the street packed with coaches, carriages, gigs and carts, all brought to a standstill.

Her heart sank as she surveyed the scene. Even if she reached the front, it would be almost impossible to catch Alistair Ross's attention in this melee, far less speak with him. Her plan had been hopelessly optimistic. The only slim chance might be after the wedding service, when crowds began dispersing.

She took up a position across the street, sharing a flight of steps with some others. She was eager to inspect the young lady Torquil would marry.

The St Clair family arrived together, and it brought tears to Mary-Ann's eyes to see her charges again, the little girls grown into young ladies. The parents had been kind employers and had treated her well. Mrs St Clair was a motherly soul who had been very distressed at her young nursemaid's betrayal and had gone out of her way to find a happy solution, namely marriage to the blacksmith.

A great cheer went up as the bride's carriage arrived. Yes, she is lovely, thought Mary-Ann, but every bride looks lovely on her wedding day. However, the young lady had a warm smile and was laughing, as if she found the great fuss amusing but quite unnecessary for their future happiness. Torquil had been a nice, kind little boy, and Mary-Ann had no reason to believe he had changed. She was pleased with his choice.

There was still no sign of Alistair Ross, and she grew anxious. Had there been a change of plan, and he would not be attending the wedding after all? Her view was restricted, so she left the vantage point and joined the crowd on the opposite side, outside the cathedral. She tried to struggle to the front. Several times her bonnet was knocked sideways and she could hardly breathe as constables forced the crowd back.

No matter how she struggled, she was forced farther back. Another wild surge from the crowd as the wedding party appeared after the service sent Mary-Ann staggering into the gutter on the outskirts, as carriages filled with guests rolled by, heading for the reception. She had no idea where that was to be held, either.

Mary-Ann was sunk in despair when suddenly, she saw him.

He was seated in a coach, which was just drawing level, but his attention was focused upon the lady at his side. His companion made some arch remark, and he laughed. The coachman had checked the horses momentarily, but now urged them on. The coach picked up speed and rumbled past her.

'Alistair!' she screamed despairingly.

How could he possibly hear?

But it is strange how hearing one's name, however faintly, always grabs one's attention. He started, glanced round at the crowd, and for one vital instant their eyes met and she glimpsed his amazement and disbelief as he recognized her.

Then the carriage picked up speed, and he had gone.

Mary-Ann stared after it and wept frustrated tears. Her last chance of freedom for Ewan and Davey had gone. How could she struggle on alone, with no hope of seeing her loved ones for ten long years?

Aimlessly, she followed the crowds dispersing down the Royal Mile and over the bridges. She did not know what to do or where to go now.

Go home, common sense told her. There was no hope of finding Alistair Ross now.

'Mary-Ann!'

A hand held her arm and there he was, looking down at her. Older, a few silver hairs at the temple, more distinguished-looking, but still Alistair.

'You!' she said weakly.

'Yes. I never thought to see you again.'

'I never wanted to see you again!' She had forgotten the resolution to remain calm.

'Yet you called my name. Why?' He still held her arm, and she drew back.

'You have a speech to deliver at the reception. Shouldn't you be making haste?'

'It's in the Assembly Rooms, within walking distance. I'll walk with you, if I may.' He fell into step beside her. He glanced at her sideways.

'You seem remarkably well acquainted with my duties.'

They walked along North Bridge in silence. It was strange, but she sensed a hostility and anger in him, which did not bode well.

'I came to ask a favour,' she said.

'I suspected as much.'

His tone infuriated her. She rounded on him angrily.

'You have no right to take that high-handed attitude with me, Alistair. I am the wronged one!'

'Are you?' His eyes were cold. She had hoped for a calm and unemotional discussion, but her feelings were running high.

'What is this favour?' he said.

She told him everything as they walked, and he heard her out in silence.

'Can you help them, or don't you care a docken what happens to your son?' she said at last.

'Of course I care!'

Cautiously, she began to hope.

'Then can you persuade the Home Secretary to review the case and correct this injustice? Davey's just a boy – and my husband is completely innocent.'

'Hardly! He punched a gamekeeper. Thousands have been transported for less.'

'Do you think I don't know?' She clutched his arm in desperation. 'Alistair, please, you must help! You are their only hope.'

He glanced down at the hand on his sleeve.

'I'll do what I can to have them set free, but I can't promise, Mary-Ann.'

'Thank you. I know you will try. You were always—' She hesitated.

'A man of my word?'

'So I believed, until you deserted me.'

'I deserted you?' He stared at her, astounded. 'On the contrary, I was ordered to sail for India as secretary to the Governor-General. I told you in my letter.'

'Letter?' Mary-Ann stared at him. 'What letter?'

'I arranged our wedding in great haste and planned a honeymoon on board ship. I wrote you a letter explaining the arrangements I'd made.' His expression darkened.

'But I was left standing waiting at the church like a fool, as you well know, and next day I sailed without you.'

'I had no letter from you, Alistair!' she whispered in bewilderment. 'I waited for you to send for me, but there was no word. Then I heard that you had left for India. I realized you had deserted me. I was left alone, and in serious trouble!'

He stopped and swung her round to face him.

'Listen, Mary-Ann, I wrote that letter, I give you my word. It went astray somehow.' His expression changed suddenly. 'My father! He was against the match from the beginning, but I thought I had won him over. He gave us his blessing, and like a fool I trusted him with your letter. I had so much to see to – and he promised faithfully that your letter would reach its rightful destination . . .' His voice trailed away as Alistair realized what his father had done.

Those were the very words his father had used! No doubt the letter had ended up in the fire. 'He lied to me!' he said brokenly, and again, 'he lied to me!'

They stood holding hands on the bridge, the ancient Castle behind them, years of misunderstanding between them finally ended.

'Alistair, if the letter had arrived, I would have been waiting at the church. Nothing would have stopped me,' Mary-Ann said. The truth must be told, even if to admit it seemed disloyal to her faithful husband.

'I know.' He pressed her hand. 'If I had known about the baby I never would have left England, believe me. I didn't learn about David until I returned on leave after three years. Mrs St Clair called me all the scoundrels of the day for leaving you alone and in trouble. She told me you had married Macgregor the Forfar blacksmith and were settled and happy. You can imagine my feelings!'

Mary-Ann looked away. 'Are – are you married?'

'No. I couldn't marry anyone else. All these years I've believed it was because you had destroyed my faith in women. But now we've met again—' He paused for a long moment. 'I think perhaps I lost my heart forever, fifteen years ago.'

'Alistair, I'm sorry,' she said.

And yet she had no right to regret a life they might have shared. She would never again know the wild love of her youth, but she was happily married nevertheless, with five fine bairns she adored.

She should be content, but the east wind blew icy cold upon tears and his hand touched her cheek, wiping them away.

'Please don't cry, Mary-Ann. I know the truth now, and the anger has gone. So there's comfort for me, at least.'

They walked on towards Princes Street at the end of the bridge. Then he took her hand.

'I must go, I have a speech to make. Can I see you again?'

She hesitated. The temptation was strong, but Mary-Ann knew that he would do his best for Davey and Ewan now. She dared not see him again when there was no need.

'Better not,' she said 'Write to me at the Forfar smiddy when you have news.'

'Very well.' He released her and stepped back. 'Don't say goodbye, Mary-Ann. I hate the word!'

So she nodded, smiled through a haze of tears and walked away. Alistair stood motionless, watching her slender little figure disappear at last in the crowded street.

Four

Mary-Ann left the city next morning. She departed as planned, despite the landlord's entreaties to spend more time sampling the delights of Edinburgh. It was a wise decision not to meet Alistair Ross once more, but even so, she remained in a nervous state of indecision until the coach was on Queensferry Road, heading out of town.

The meeting had upset her and their parting did nothing to ease the pain of the discovery she had made. For fifteen years she had nursed a grudge against an innocent man, and yet she couldn't help wondering if his father's intervention had proved more beneficial for Alistair's career. Would he have been quite so successful as a politician, with the distractions of a wife and family?

Besides, though she had never felt the reckless passion of young love for Ewan, he was a kind and considerate husband and together they had made a success of their marriage. They were not wealthy, but they valued their five healthy bairns more highly than riches.

On quiet reflection as she journeyed homewards, Mary-Ann decided that reviving painful memories was a small price to pay if it would secure Ewan and Davey's release. But that was before she arrived back home, to discover the destructive power of past events . . .

The young ones welcomed Mary-Ann with boisterous joy, and her critical eye could find no fault with Mrs Wullie's housekeeping. A reassuring reek of smoke drifting from the smiddy told her that Matthew was busily occupied.

Mary-Ann saw Mrs Wullie to the door with two shillings to herself and the gift of a crystal bottle of perfume.

'Just wait till Wullie gets a whiff o' this!' She beamed.

Alone with the children, Mary-Ann sat down to watch them open the gifts she had bought with such care – a sewing-box for

Agnes, a journal with a songbird on the cover for Shona, and a spinning top for Danny.

For Matthew, she had bought the most expensive gift, a penknife with small tools hidden in the hilt. Anticipation of her children's delight had helped to soothe a troubled mind.

Danny climbed on to her knee. She hugged him.

'Have you been a good boy'?

'Of course!' He held up a finger. 'Mrs Wullie tied horsehair round the wart on my finger an' she says it'll drop off. Agnes and Shona got rhubarb an' liquorice mixture twice, 'cause once didn't do the trick.'

Mary-Ann laughed.

'Mrs Wullie's a grand nurse. She's better at dosing bairns than the doctor.'

'I know a joke, Mama,' Danny said. 'Why did the farmer cross the yard?'

'I've no idea, lovie.'

''Cause he only has two feet!' he cried gleefully. 'There's three feet in a yard, Wullie telt me! Are you laughing, Mama?'

Agnes sighed.

'He only has one stupid joke, Mama. We've heard it dozens of times.'

Agnes and Danny were not on the best of terms. Danny and Shona were close as bugs in a rug these days, and she felt excluded.

Danny was furious with his playmate.

'You're green 'cause I know Shona's secret and you don't!'

Shona gave a horrified wail.

'Danny, you promised!'

'I never said what it was!' he protested.

Agnes snorted. 'I know what it is anyway! Shona told Lizzie Murray, and Lizzie told me. Shona's planning to run away with the strolling players.'

Mary-Ann was shocked.

'Shona dear, you must not!'

Shona burst into tears.

'Everything's horrible now that Papa and Davey have gone, Mama! I don't want to bide here any more!'

Clutching the precious journal, she rushed upstairs to her room. When she calmed down she decided to start writing in it.

She would tell her love and hate to its sympathetic pages, confess all the emotions and strange feelings that frightened her with their intensity.

This talk of running away had alarmed Mary-Ann. Like many gifted people, Shona was sensitive and volatile, quite liable to up and run if upset, and that could spell disaster for an innocent girl. Already Shona's beauty turned men's heads as she walked by, and Mary-Ann knew that she could not keep a watchful eye on her lovely daughter, every minute of the day and night.

Leaving Agnes and Danny to settle their differences outside on the doorstep with the entrancing spinning top, Mary-Ann rose and set about preparing a meal. She ached with weariness after the long journey, but welcomed the activity. Mrs Wullie, bless her, had left the larder well filled, and the first early potatoes had been gathered from the vegetable plot. Prime Minister Robert Peel had fought to abolish Corn Laws that kept the price of bread artificially high. Cheaper bread would help everyone, especially the poor—

'So you're back!'

Matthew had come in from the smiddy. She turned and smiled.

'Yes, my dear. The train arrived at four.'

She'd expected him to meet her with the gig, and been disappointed when there was nobody there. The baggage had seemed heavy on the lonely tramp up the brae.

'Did you meet the man Ross?' Matthew demanded.

'Yes, I did.'

She stared at her son, realizing something was wrong. He seemed hostile, unsmiling. She went on bravely. 'Mr Ross would make no promises, Matthew, but after some persuasion he agreed to do whatever he could for Papa and Davey.'

'You mean you persuaded him? I wonder how!'

Mary-Ann stiffened. The tone was deliberately insulting.

'How dare you, Matthew! What ails you?'

'Nothing but a dose o' the truth from Mrs Wullie. She was present when Davey was born, and hints she dropped confirmed my suspicions. Davey and I never seemed like brothers, and that was because we had different fathers. It was Davey's father you went to see, wasn't it?'

'Yes, it was.'

No point telling lies, she thought, though at fourteen he could not be expected to understand the overwhelming power of love, nor forgive its consequences. All the same, Matthew's contempt was hard to bear.

'So!' he said bitterly. 'My mother is not the saint I thought she was.'

'My dear lad! I never professed to be a saint!'

'But – but I thought at least you were virtuous. What a fool I was!' His voice sounded choked. He turned and fled.

She sank down in Ewan's chair, hoping to find some strength. But it was only an empty chair. Her strong man had gone.

Wee Danny came in. He clambered on her knee, touched her face and found it tear-stained.

'I have a funny riddle to cheer you, Mama. It's a wee round man in a red, red coat, a stick in its hand an' a stone in its throat. What is it?'

She moved her head listlessly; she had no heart for guessing.

'It's a cherry, Mama!'

She covered her face with her hands, her shoulders shaking.

'You – you're laughing, aren't you?' the wee boy asked anxiously.

'Yes, Danny, I'm laughing,' Mary-Ann sobbed.

Time had ceased to exist for Ewan Macgregor. He knew summer had passed, because he no longer sweated under a hot sun while coaling naval steamers at Woolwich docks. Leaves had fallen on the coal dust, rustling dryly round his feet, stirring memories of Forfar and the forest of Platane. He knew it must be winter. He and the other prisoners shivered in thin canvas. He was a big, strong, muscular man, and could labour harder to keep warm. Other poor devils, fresh from towns or malnourished in unhealthy city alleys, did not fare so well.

Hard labour did not bother Ewan overmuch, but coal dust did. His nails were black rimmed, hands, arms, face and body ingrained with oily black dust. His hair was dull and stiff with it; it grated between his teeth and tasted foul and acid on his tongue. No matter how vigorously he scrubbed with icy water and coarse yellow soap, he could not make himself clean.

That was a cruel punishment, for a fastidious man.

When the turn of the year came and spring 1849 lay just ahead, Ewan and several others were taken from an antiquated hulk moored on the river, that had been their winter quarters. They were offloaded at a new prison in North London, recently built since transportation to penal colonies had become controversial and expensive. It was named Pentonville, and the inmates of the 450 cells became known as 'Pentonvillains'.

'You 'ave friends in 'igh places, Macgregor!' remarked the warder as he unlocked the door of Ewan's cell several weeks later. 'There's a city gent come to see ye.'

Any diversion from the monotony of prison life was welcome. Ewan was marched into an interview room furnished with table and two chairs. A high barred window in one blank wall let in a meagre light. The warder took up a position with back to the door, arms folded.

A handsome man about Ewan's own age was seated at the table. He indicated a chair.

'Please sit down, Mr Macgregor.'

Ewan eyed the stranger curiously.

'What do you want with me?'

'Mrs Macgregor contacted me in the hope of gaining a pardon for yourself and David. I'm afraid that's out of the question, but it does appear the sentence was much too severe.'

'Isn't that comforting!' Ewan said caustically.

'Unfortunately, it cannot be overturned, and you will be transported to Australia at the beginning of May, but I have persuaded the Colonial Secretary to make sure you get a ticket of leave when you reach Sydney. That means you will be your own master while you serve the remainder of the sentence. You're a fine tradesman with skills much in demand in the colony, Mr Macgregor. You could do so well, you may not even choose to return to Scotland.'

'But what about David, my son?'

The visitor met his eyes.

'Ah, but David is not your son, is he?'

Ewan was startled. He stared at the man.

'Who are you?'

'My name is Ross, Alistair Ross.'

'You!' Ewan cried bitterly. A year ago he might have hit the rogue who had deceived Mary-Ann, but prison life had taught control of the impulsive Macgregor rage. 'If I'd known Mary-Ann intended to approach you, Mr Ross, I would've forbidden it. I'd rather bide in jail than be indebted to a scoundrel.'

'I swear on my honour I would have married Mary-Ann if it had been possible – but that is over and done with now.' He leaned across the table. 'Where is the boy?'

That surprised Ewan.

'Don't you know?'

'I was hoping you would tell me.'

Ewan shook his head.

'Davey and I parted company months ago, when the ship docked in London, I've no idea where they took him.' An alarming thought suddenly struck him. 'Have they sent the laddie to Australia already?'

Alistair frowned.

'It's possible. I have checked every reformatory in England without success.'

Ewan stood up. 'The sooner I leave the better. When I reach Sydney I'll move heaven and earth to find him.'

'Yes, he must be found! There are reforms on the statute book soon to be made law, that could free David.'

Alistair Ross had never met his son, yet the boy was incredibly important to him. Believing himself rejected by the only woman he had ever loved, he remained unmarried, dedicated to a political career. Once he had dreamed of having children of his own but now it seemed that Mary-Ann's son was the only child he would ever father.

Studying this man, Ewan was confused. He considered himself a good judge of character and he would have sworn he was an honest fellow. But Ewan had always believed Mary-Ann would be a faithful wife, yet the moment her husband was out of the way she had run to her former lover. What had transpired between them? Did she still love Alistair Ross?

Ewan's imagination was running riot, and he did not know what to believe any more. Captivity bred cruel fantasies in the loneliness of a prison cell. He turned abruptly to the warder.

'Take me back.'

'Wait!' Alistair said. 'Is there anything you need?'

'Only pen and paper, to write to my wife.'

'It shall be done.'

Ewan bowed, and Alistair found himself alone in the cold, bare room.

Ewan's letter arrived while Mary-Ann was pegging sheets on the line and keeping an eye on changeable weather. Her hands shook as she recognized Ewan's writing.

She was alone in the house these days. Danny aged five and bright as a button, had been accepted at North Burgh School, better known as the Spoutie. Mrs Carnegy had kindly offered to take Agnes back as pupil-teacher, paying her a few pennies to teach the younger girls knitting and sewing. Shona, newly turned thirteen, had begged to start work and Mary-Ann had given in. Her daughter seemed happy, working in a bookshop in West High Street, and the few shillings Shona contributed were welcome.

Mary-Ann would have welcomed Matthew's support as she opened Ewan's letter, for her heart was beating fit to burst with dread of what it might contain.

But Matthew was lost to her now. He rarely spoke to his mother. He was working hard, gaining a reputation for skill beyond the ordinary. His expertise had caught the eye of factory owners, and Baxter's Glamis spinning mill boasted a faster hackling process for raw flax, because of an adjustment to hackling pins, suggested by Matthew Macgregor.

Mary-Ann wiped away a tear and began to read . . .

> *My dearest wife, it is great joy to write to you at last. Hard labour does not include the use of pen and paper, since the system brands all prisoners uneducated. Mr Ross secured these sheets for me. I need not describe my emotion when he visited me in Pentonville, but at least we talked civilly and he prepared me for my fate. I am to go to Australia with a selected group of Lord Grey's Exiles, all skilled men of good behaviour. I do not know which ship, nor the precise date of sailing, but it is rumoured we leave these shores within the first week of May. Dear Mary-Ann, my heart is heavy at leaving you, the dear children and my beloved land, but it seems certain that David has already been sent off to the penal colony*

*and I will spare no effort to find him there. Bear with me if you
hear no word for many months, for the journey is long and tedious,
though I am assured it is not so rigorous for us exiles, as once it
was for other poor souls. The distance between us will be immense,
dear one, but I promise I will keep faith with you, Mary-Ann. I
pray you will keep faith with me . . .*

She was in tears by the end. She glanced at the wall almanac.
Today was the 20th of May. Ewan would be on the high seas.
In winter she had clung to hope, now there was none. Her dear
ones had gone far away. Perhaps forever.

A week after his father's letter arrived, Danny was dawdling home
from school all by himself. The wee ones were let out early and
Agnes was not released from Mrs Carnegy's till four. Mary-Ann
was so busy, and she trusted Danny to dander down the Spout
and up the brae himself. He enjoyed independence. There was
time to stop and stare. He picked up a tiny dark-green frog by
the roadside and examined it with wonder. He put it back out
of danger into the mire.

He could smell the Arbroath fishwife a mile off. She had a
creel of herring and haddock on her back and carried a basket
filled with seaweed, buckies and mussels. She called out to
him. 'Tell your ma I have braw fresh herrin' the day, wee
laddie!'

She patted Danny and left her smell on his jacket.

He walked on; puckering his lips and trying to whistle, but
could not. Papa could teach him how, but Papa was far away.
The older boys laughed and pushed Danny over, and then they
whistled and called Papa a jailbird. It hurt. Thinking about the
humiliating treatment, Danny began to cry.

'What's wrong?' A man had stopped and was bending over
him. He was a stranger, dressed very fine.

'Nothin'.'

Mama had warned him not to talk to strangers, especially
Dundee strangers, where cholera was rife once more.

'You look so sad,' the gentleman said sympathetically.

'I want my papa,' Danny gulped.

'Are you lost? Is your papa at home, maybe?'

'No, sir, he's in the jail. My papa's a jailbird an' that's why I canna whistle!'

The man straightened. He was very tall, as tall as Papa.

'Will you tell me your name?'

Danny told him. The man produced a handkerchief.

'Here, Danny Macgregor, blow your nose. You'll feel better.'

He watched Danny's ministrations thoughtfully.

'Is your papa Mr Macgregor the blacksmith?'

'Aye!' Danny beamed and handed back the handkerchief. 'Do you know him?'

'I met him in London,' Alistair Ross replied. 'In fact, Danny, by coincidence I was on my way to see your mother. May I accompany you?'

Danny eyed him suspiciously. 'Have you come frae Dundee?'

'No, by coach from Perth.'

'That's all right then,' Danny decided, and accepted the gentleman's comforting hand . . .

Mary-Ann could not believe it when her small son walked in with Alistair Ross. She looked so stunned Danny reassured her.

'He's not got the cholera, Mama. I made certain.'

Alistair smiled.

'Danny's right. I have a clean bill of health, Mrs Macgregor.'

She put a hand to her throat.

'What are you doing here?'

'Your husband said he would write, but I had to be sure you knew what had happened.'

She sighed.

'Yes, I had Ewan's letter. I know Ewan and Davey have been sent to a penal colony.'

'I'm sorry, Mary-Ann. There was nothing I could do.'

She turned to the little boy, forcing a smile.

'Go upstairs and change your school clothes, Danny, there's a good laddie.'

Alistair watched him go.

'He's a fine boy, but he misses his father sorely.'

'Of course he misses him!' Mary-Ann cried. 'We all miss him. I've cried till I've scarce a tear left, missing my strong man and beloved son!' She had begun in anger and finished in tears.

He crossed the room, and rested a hand on her shoulder.

'You forget David's my son, too, Mary-Ann.'

She struck his hand away.

'Don't touch me!'

He backed away.

'I'm sorry. I'll leave now, if you wish. I had to see for myself if all was well with you and your family.'

He glanced round the comfortable room. The blacksmith had prospered, but how would his wife and children fare without him? He broached the subject with trepidation.

'Forgive me, Mary-Ann, but I wonder how you can manage on your own? With your permission, I could arrange a monthly sum for your upkeep. It would be my pleasure. I have more money than I need.'

'I thank you, but of course I refuse. You mean well, but I can guess what scandalous rumours would fly around town, if that arrangement became public knowledge!'

He hesitated. 'There is another option. The Colonial Secretary has an agreement with the Legislative Council of New South Wales to encourage wives and families to join their menfolk in the colony. They hope in that way to dilute the criminal stain. I could arrange a passage to Australia for you.'

She lifted her head and gave him a level look.

'So. It would ease your conscience to be rid of me.'

He met her eyes.

'No, Mary-Ann. I only wish to be rid of temptation.'

She looked away. Love light shone in his eyes, and she must be strong.

'I would rather sell the smiddy than be indebted to you!'

'This is no time for pride. Be practical!'

'Pride does not enter into it. I have another son to consider before I can even think of leaving Forfar, or selling the smiddy,' she told him. 'Ewan's son Matthew is only fourteen, already as skilled as his father, and the lad has worked hard to support this family. Matthew is steady and reliable. Ewan's son won't let us down.'

He winced.

'I find the comparison unkind.'

'I'm sorry, I meant no criticism of your son.' She sank down on a nearby chair. 'I love David. He's clever, with a keen intellect much more suited to study than practical work. He is your son in every way, Alistair. Ewan saw that likeness in the boy, and resented it.'

He nodded.

'I can understand the friction it would cause.'

He picked up hat and gloves, preparing to leave. She put out a hand and stopped him.

'Don't go yet! You've come a long way, and I'd be neglecting a duty to my guest if I sent you away unfed.'

Mary-Ann felt safe to issue the invitation, since Matthew was out of the way. He had left for Glamis that morning and was not expected home till late. She was pleased when the offer was accepted. It would be a relief to talk to another adult who understood the situation she faced. The need to stay strong for the children's sake was wearing her down . . .

Matthew had mounted the mare that morning and trotted the few miles to Glamis village. He found the mill manager outside, champing at the bit. The mill was at a standstill because of the breakdown.

'How long will you be, Macgregor?'

'As long as it takes, sir.'

The man cursed.

Matthew hid a grin as he fetched tools from the saddlebags. He had heard Dundee mills had secured a government contract with the Deptford Naval depot for canvas. They had cut the price to the bone to get it, and the Navy had rejected the consignment of power-loom canvas. Every hand-loom weaver in Forfarshire had cheered; such was the rivalry between old and new.

They had closed the sluice and the water wheel lay idle. Matthew soon saw where the trouble lay in the power drive to the spinning frames. It was a clumsy piece of machinery anyway. He could see how it could be much improved, and set to work.

It took some time to make the adjustment, but even so Matthew finished earlier than expected, much to his delight. He had a more pleasant plan in mind for the evening.

He whistled and sang as he rode back to town at a smart clip, just in time to catch the butcher before he closed. Matthew came out clutching two piping hot bridies. Leading the mare, he headed for the weaving sheds, and there was Janet just hurrying out, work over for the day.

Matthew paused just for the pleasure of watching her.

Janet Golightly. She was well named, small and quick and dainty. A lump came to his throat and a sentimental mist to his eyes.

He was frowning when he stepped in front of her.

'What time o' night is this for wee lassies to be working? Nine hours a day is the law!'

'I'm thirteen. I can work longer.'

'But you should not!'

She was so slender a puff of wind might blow her away. Her eyes lit on the paper bag.

'Is that bridies?'

'Aye, it is. I'd no dinner, so I bought two. One for me and one for you.'

He laughed and lifted her in his arms, setting her on the horse's back. She felt no lighter than a feather. Her cheeks were scarlet.

'Matthew, where are you taking me?'

He led her down beside the loch. He let the mare graze, and they sat upon the rocks and ate the bridies. The water was like rippling silver under the night sky.

Janet hugged her knees.

'I'm worried about my father. He's so weak and tired he can hardly work; yet I feed him well. I think there is something seriously wrong, Matthew.' She turned to him, in tears. 'I don't know what I'll do if anything happens to my da!'

'You'd come to live in the smiddy with us,' he said. The thought filled him with joy.

'Your ma has enough on her plate.'

His expression hardened.

'Forget about my mother. I'm the man of the house. The decision rests with me.'

Janet looked at him sideways. This was an aspect of the gentle lad she'd never seen, and she wasn't sure she liked it. She pulled her plaid closer round her shoulders. It was colder now.

'I want to go home, please,' she said.

'It's early yet.'

'I don't care. I want to go home.'

Once more he picked her up in his arms. He could hardly breathe for the pounding of his heart and the strength of his love as he put her in the saddle. He led the mare in silence along the Brechin road to her father's bothy. He helped her dismount, and might have kissed her, but quite purposely she turned her head away and bade him cool goodnight.

Matthew was in confused and frustrated mood as he fed and watered the mare in the stable. It had been a strange day, ending strangely, with Janet acting as if she did not like him much.

But there was worse, much worse, to come.

A sudden burst of laughter from the smiddy-seat startled Matthew. Laughter? There had been very little laughter since Papa and Davey were taken! He pushed open the door and stood in the doorway.

His mother sat facing him. She half-rose from her chair. 'Matthew!'

There was a strange man sitting in his father's chair, Danny on his knee. Agnes sat on the rug, at his feet. Shona sat opposite, obviously smitten, where the lamplight was most flattering. But Matthew could not take his eyes off the stranger. There was something vaguely familiar about him. And then he knew. The resemblance to Davey was striking.

His mother was on her feet making a nervous introduction.

'This is Mr Ross, Matthew. He has come from London to make sure all is well with us—'

Matthew ignored her.

'Danny, get to bed! You others, go upstairs!' he ordered.

The little boy whimpered, and ran to his sisters. The three young ones stared at Matthew in fear. They had never seen him like this. Something terrible was happening to destroy the happy time they had spent with Mr Ross. Shona gave Matthew a scared glance, and hustled the two young ones out of the door.

Alistair had risen to face Matthew. The youngster was tall, a younger version of his father. It was as if Ewan Macgregor himself had burst in to shatter a dream of what might have been.

'So, Mr Ross!' Matthew said. 'Now my father's safely out of the way, you thought to draw in your chair. Well, sir, you reckoned without me. I'm master o' this house in my father's absence, and I would be obliged if you never return to insult my father with your presence.'

'Matthew!' Mary-Ann cried in horror.

Alistair reached for his hat. The last thing he wanted was to distress Mary-Ann. He smiled at her reassuringly.

'I can see I leave you in capable hands, Mary-Ann.' He paused for a moment, a hand on her arm. 'Remember what I said. Leaving here might be best – for all of you.' He gave the young lad a glance, and was gone.

Mary-Ann was heartbroken, beyond tears.

'Matthew how could you?'

He shrugged. 'He's lucky he escaped so lightly.'

'I'm ashamed of you. He came as a friend, to offer help!'

'What help did he offer? To take my father's place?'

'No, he did not!' she cried, scandalized. 'Mr Ross wanted to arrange a passage to Australia for us all, a chance to be reunited with your father and brother. I told him I would take time to consider it, but after this outburst, I can see the wisest course is to sell the smiddy and make a fresh start for this family.'

Matthew was horrified.

'You couldn't do that without my permission!'

'I don't need it, Matthew. You are a minor.'

He knew her well enough to realize he had pushed her too far. She meant every word.

Janet! he thought in panic. He couldn't leave Janet when she was in such a desperate plight. He loved her, dreamed about her, tossed and turned, wanting her. Leaving was out of the question.

'If you go, you go without me,' he said.

Mary-Ann was startled.

'You don't mean that!'

'Aye, Mother, I do.' He crossed to the doorway and stood looking at her. 'You can take the others and go, but I'm staying here.'

Five

Mary-Ann was left alone with her thoughts, which were not cheerful. Until Matthew burst in to ruin the evening, it had been the happiest she could remember since her husband and son were taken. She had watched the children blossom under Alistair's kindly influence. The quiet, courteous man knew how to amuse, listen and sympathize. For the first time in weeks Mary-Ann had relaxed.

Until Matthew came.

Her son's rudeness angered Mary-Ann, but she was relieved that the unwelcome task of telling Alistair to go had been taken out of her hands. Matthew saw life in simple terms; he could not imagine the dilemma facing his mother.

Alistair had mentioned temptation if she remained in Scotland, and she could see the danger. There had been temptation in her pleasure in his company. Life was difficult for a lone woman trying to run a home and business on her own. How long before the struggle wore down her resistance?

Her mind was made up. They would follow Ewan and Davey to Australia. Scotland had nothing to offer the Macgregor family now but shame. The smiddy would be sold despite Matthew's objections. They would need proceeds from the sale to pay for the passage and necessities for the voyage.

Matthew spent a restless night, but was up at five next morning as usual. His mother had left oatmeal steeping in the porridge pot overnight and soon he had the pot bubbling over a blazing fire. He wondered how he would fare without a roof over his head. It was a gloomy prospect, but nothing would change his mind.

He had the furnace raised to full power and was riveting new tines on an old harrow when Wullie strolled in. It suddenly struck Matthew that when the smiddy went, Wullie would lose his job. He lost concentration, misplaced the rivet and the tine twisted out of line. He swore.

Wullie raised his eyebrows.

'Bad language afore seven gets worse by eleven.'

Matthew shoved in the damper to check the fire.

'Did you see the man that visited my mother yesterday?'

'The tall stranger that came wi' Danny, in a London coat, grey waistcoat, gold watch an' chain, grey breeks, white shirt, blue stock, grey lum hat? Naw, I only caught a wee glimpse.'

'Tell me when the man leaves town, Wullie. He's bad luck.'

'Och, he left on the early coach this morning. He'll be well down the Perth road by now.' Wullie hung his jacket on a convenient nail.

'Your ma's a bonnie wumman,' he observed.

'I know.' Matthew roused the forge to an angry roar. 'What the hell do I do with this harrow, dammit?'

Wullie sighed.

'I telt ye! Bad language is gettin' worse . . .'

Ewan Macgregor would never take to life at sea, but had learned to thole it since the transport bound for Australia left Portsmouth in May. The ship bore a fine Scottish name – 'Mount Stewart Elphinstone' – although the vessel itself left much to be desired. Its human cargo consisted of 'specials' including forgers, swindlers and educated felons. More privileged were the 'assisted exiles' like Ewan himself, skilled men who had done hard labour and served time in Pentonville, and were now deemed reformed characters who had earned a conditional pardon to be paid within the confines of the penal colony. There were also a few hard cases, kept under close captivity below decks by a muster of Dragoon guards. Known to the unwilling passengers as 'goons'.

The exiles performed daily tasks around the ship and had a privileged amount of freedom. Of course they grumbled about cramped quarters, food and violent storms encountered while taking advantage of trade winds on the route to southern Australia, via Rio de Janeiro and Cape Town. They were reminded that conditions aboard were much improved since the bad old days, and they should thank their lucky southern stars.

Ewan felt like a human being again and less like a Pentonvillain. He had been issued with underclothes and shirts, decent jacket and breeches, hose and shoes. He suspected Alistair Ross had seen to that, and was deeply grateful. He could hold up his head once more, having discarded prison canvas.

As the journey progressed Ewan made a friend – all because he could play chess. His father had taught him as a lad, and Ewan had shown a natural aptitude for the game.

Thomas Bryant was a naval surgeon, his presence aboard a fairly recent innovation by the authorities. His official duties were to supervise the captives' health and ensure they were fit for work when they reached the other side. It was not too taxing a job this trip, and the doctor was delighted to find a worthy opponent among the exiles for a game of chess. He spent many evenings with Ewan, absorbed in a chessboard battle.

'Sir, what can we expect when we reach Sydney?' Ewan ventured during a lull in the game

His friend frowned.

'That depends.'

'Upon what?'

'The graziers.'

Ewan was encouraged.

'There are sheep, cattle and plenty of horses out there?'

The doctor frowned at the chessboard.

'Aye, grazing on vast leases of land in the outback. Graziers hold much of the wealth and power in the state, and Lord Grey will do anything to keep them content. If that means a supply of cheap labour by some clever loophole, now transportation is out of favour, so be it.'

'Am I fated to become cheap labour for a cattle baron?' Ewan demanded angrily.

'Not necessarily. It depends what happens in the Legislative Council. New South Wales has rebelled at last, demanding honest settlers, not vagabonds and thieves.'

'Some of the other exiles intend sending for wives and families to join them. It's a tempting plan. Would you say it was wise, sir?'

'On the contrary! Do not ask your loved ones to attempt the journey, Ewan. It would be wise to wait and see what transpires.'

It was a bitter disappointment. Ewan sighed.

'I'll think on your advice, though I'll not promise to heed it.'

Thomas Bryant shrugged.

'That's up to you.'

He captured a chess piece and sat back to await the next move. If what the captain had told him in confidence were true, it would be a brave wife who would venture out to join Ewan Macgregor, where he was going . . .

The three younger Macgregors had closed ranks since their brother had driven the kind visitor out of the house.

'I don't know what demon's entered into Matthew recently,' Agnes sighed. She and Danny were headed for school; Shona was bound for the bookshop.

Shona nodded. 'He's grown too big for his breeks since Papa left. He's maybe big, but he'll never be a gentleman like Mr Ross.' Her heart fluttered. She had confided to her journal that she had fallen in love with a man old enough to be her father. Mature men were much more interesting than boys.

'Matthew's in love,' Danny volunteered.

He was wearing highly polished boots this fine day, and wished he could go barefoot, like some other Spoutie pupils. Some hope. Mama would faint if he suggested such a lowering of standards. His sisters stopped and stared.

'What do you know about love?'

'Matthew's in it. A boy at school telt me.'

'Who's the lass?' Agnes demanded.

'Janet Golightly.'

'Och, her! The roadman's daughter!'

'I was thinking of marrying her myself,' he protested. 'She's bonny!'

Plump Agnes, dark pigtails sticking out at rebellious angles, was touchy on the subject of beauty. She snorted.

'Marry that skinny-ma-linky-longlegs? You want your eyes looked at, Dan.'

'Matthew thinks she's bonny too, so there! He bought her a whole bridie to herself. Geordie Jamieson saw them down by the loch.'

His sisters exchanged a significant glance. This meant serious courting!

Danny's information was too sensational to keep. That evening Agnes bided her time until she and her mother were alone.

'Mama, Matthew's in love,' she said, confidentially.

'Who said so?'

'Geordie Jamieson saw Matthew and Janet Golightly down by the loch.'

'I see,' said Mary-Ann thoughtfully. That explained his reluctance to leave. First love was a deep and painful emotion. However, sometimes it was fleeting. Matthew was but fourteen and the lass not much more than a child. She saw no reason why calf-love should be allowed to break family ties. Somehow Matthew must be persuaded to change his mind.

This was a sensitive matter, to be handled with care.

'Agnes dear, I thank you for telling me, but promise you won't say a word of this to Matthew, nor will you tease him. That would be unkind, and might have disastrous results. Will you promise?'

Agnes loved secrets, and to share one with Mama was something special.

'Sure's death, Mama, I promise!'

Mary-Ann sought out Matthew in the smiddy on Sunday afternoon. There was a rainstorm in progress and nobody had ventured out. Matthew had planned to ask Janet Golightly to walk out with him, but the deluge had put paid to that. He was pottering around the workplace preparing Monday's job when his mother appeared.

'Have you decided what to do?' he challenged her.

'Yes. Have you?'

'I told you. I'll not leave.'

It struck Matthew suddenly how out of place she looked among the tools of his father's trade. Dressed in her Sunday gown, she would not disgrace a gentleman's mansion. It was an uncomfortable thought. She laid a hand on his arm.

'Matthew my dear, we must talk.'

'I'm not stopping you,' he said coldly. He did not want to remember how much he had loved and admired her once.

'I'm sorry, son, I've decided the smiddy must be sold.'

'You'd put Wullie out of a job?'

'Good craftsmen are hard to find. I'll persuade whoever buys the business to take Wullie on.'

'What about me?'

'You must come with us, dear. There's a new life awaiting us, when we join your father and Davey. A fresh start, Matthew! We can put the past behind us.'

'Maybe you can sell my father's business and leave the country without a backward glance, but I can't.'

The scornful response angered her.

'There's more to this than you'll admit, my lad! You fancy the roadman's lass, don't you?'

He turned red.

'Janet needs help.'

'No, she does not. She has a steady job in the weaving shed and is doing well.' She moved closer. 'That girl is bad luck, Matthew. She brought trouble to Davey and she'll bring trouble to you.'

'It wasn't Janet's fault!' For a moment he looked as if he might cry. 'Her father's sick and could die. She needs me!'

She pitied the boy, caught in the throes of first love.

'Matthew dear, I need you too, when we make this hazardous journey. I don't want to leave my home, but it's no home for me without your father.'

'Why can't you wait till he's free?'

'Wait for nearly ten years? That's a long weary time to be on my own, Matthew!'

'Aye it is,' he agreed reluctantly. 'Especially when the man Ross is hoping to step into my father's shoes!'

He was beginning to understand the quandary she faced. Matthew turned away unhappily.

'I don't know what to do!'

She clutched his arm.

'We're a family, Matthew. We should stick together. We need each another.'

But I love Janet, he thought. I love her!

Mary-Ann waited for a response, but there was none. She sighed. She could do no more. The final decision was Matthew's. Hers had been made, and would not change . . .

Monday morning turned out fine, but Mary-Ann abandoned thoughts of washday. She dressed in businesslike fashion and set off for the laird's mansion.

Phyllis the housemaid answered the doorbell. 'Heaven save us, it's Mary-Ann!'

'Has the laird finished breakfast?'

'Aye, and he's not for speaking to. But you can try your luck.'

Still grumbling, she led Mary-Ann along the corridor, knocked on a door and disappeared inside. She reappeared hastily.

'He says you're to go in.'

As before, the laird was at his desk. He studied her cautiously over the top of his spectacles. 'What is it this time, Mrs Macgregor?'

He waved a hand at a nearby chair and she sat down gracefully.

'I have come to offer a business opportunity you may find hard to resist.'

'Just try me!' he grunted.

'I am selling the smiddy and giving you first chance to buy it, sir, before offering the entire lot for public sale.'

He was a lawyer, his features well schooled, but he could not hide his surprise.

'What would I want wi' a smiddy?'

'I believe you have a keen nose for business. The smiddy lies close to your boundaries. You can either keep a close eye on your investment, or be faced with a neighbour you may not care for. At present the smiddy has steady farm trade and contracts with the mills for spare parts. You're welcome to study the books. A healthy profit has been made in the first six months of this year.'

'Why would you dispose of a gold mine, I wonder?'

'We are emigrating. We are to follow my husband and David, to start anew in Australia.'

He sighed.

'I begin to see your drift, Mrs Macgregor. You believe I was responsible for sending them there. You came here to prod my conscience.'

'I did not know your conscience troubled you, sir,' she said innocently.

He gave a dry bark of laughter.

'It's a pity women are barred from the bench. You'd have advocates trussed in knots.'

He drummed his fingertips on the desktop, frowning.

'I must admit the blacksmith's severe sentence still worries me.

I doubt if I reached the bottom o' the meal poke in his case. I'm sure there were extenuating circumstances that never came to light.'

Mary-Ann sighed.

'What's done is done, sir. My man and my son are far overseas, and we will join them.'

He studied her with sincere regret.

'If I were a seafaring man I would say you are burning your boats. Once burned, there's no sailing back, Mrs Macgregor. What price had you in mind for the smiddy?'

'One hundred and twenty five pounds.'

'Och away! Ninety!'

'One hundred guineas.'

'Make that pounds and I'll consider it.'

'Done! On one condition.'

'I micht have known there'd be a catch!'

'You employ Wullie Ogilvy in the smiddy, or the bargain's void.'

'Very well.' The laird nodded agreement. 'I'll have the smiddy and Wullie Ogilvy, for one hundred pounds. Wullie can live in the smiddy-seat; I've no need for another cottage. I daresay Mrs Wullie will be into that good house, quick as a mouse in the wainscot.'

The elderly man stood up and shook hands solemnly, sealing the bargain. He stared at Mary-Ann sadly.

'I'll miss the Macgregors. You've been grand neighbours. Is your passage booked? If not, I could see to it. The shipping agent for the Dundee London line will make sure you have good accommodation. Don't scrimp and go steerage, Mrs Macgregor! That's asking for trouble, with filth and pestilence in overcrowded conditions. Thirty guineas should secure a comfortable passage for you and your family.'

The expense made her gasp, but she accepted his advice for the sake of the children. She smiled.

'Thank you, sir. I would be grateful for your help.'

It was a memorable smile. The laird beamed.

'Sensible lass! Will you trust my clerk to prepare documents for transfer of ownership?'

'Certainly! But I will have a translation of any Latin phrase used, please, before I sign.'

He laughed and raised her hand to his lips.

'My dear Mistress Macgregor, Forfar will be the poorer without you.'

There were loose ends to be tied before departure, and Mary-Ann set about tying them. Next morning she set off to town carrying a shopping basket. Matthew stood at the smiddy door awaiting the arrival of Turwhappie's horses, and she gave him a cheery goodbye.

She could feel his speculative gaze follow her along the sunlit road until she was out of sight. After that she relaxed. The lad had no way of knowing that his mother's destination was the weaving sheds.

Mr Don's hand-loom weavers were granted an hour's respite at noon. They crowded out into the sunlight as Mary-Ann sauntered by. Trade had picked up recently. A recent consignment of flax from Riga was of good quality, and the sun had shone upon the bleach fields after a rainy spell. Forfar thrummed to the clack of thousands of hand looms from cottage and shed. Mary-Ann was forced to step aside as handcarts loaded with finished webs came rattling along the plainstones towards the stampmaster's office.

When Janet Golightly appeared amid the crowd of men, women and children, Mary-Ann fell into step beside the girl. The distinctive smell of Harefield potato starch clung to the weavers. Janet's hands were white with it.

'Going for your dinner, Janet?' she asked pleasantly.

'I'm heading to the well for a drink. It's thirsty work.'

'I've a spare bridie in my basket if you'd care for a bite, dear. We could sit and have a blether by the well while you eat. We seldom have a chance to talk.'

Janet gave her a quick glance. She was no fool, this child! thought Mary-Ann.

'Thank you kindly, Mrs Macgregor, but I'll not trouble you for a bridie. I have bread and cheese in my pouch.'

Mary-Ann tried a different approach.

'Janet, I must talk to you. About Matthew.'

'Oh, I see,' she said flatly.

A group of weavers had gathered round the well. Janet wormed her way through and sloshed water over hands and face, then cupped her hands in the bucket and drank. She returned to Mary-Ann.

'We can sit at the edge o' the green, Mrs Macgregor, but I'll need to watch my time.'

They sat under a shady tree. Janet produced bread and cheese wrapped in butter muslin.

'What about Matthew?' she demanded.

'Has he told you we're emigrating to Australia?'

'No, he has not.'

'Ah! I thought so. He's a kind, caring lad. Though he knows he should come with us to join his father, he insists he'll stay in Forfar. He thinks you need help. He pities you, Janet.'

She frowned.

'I don't want pity!'

'Of course you don't! But he refuses to leave, and it would be a great shame if he missed such a wonderful opportunity, just because he formed a false impression.'

'Aye, it would,' Janet agreed. She had lost her appetite. She broke the crust off the bread and tossed it to the sparrows. 'What do you want me to do?'

'Convince him you're in no need of his pity, my dear. I'm sure you can convince him to change his mind.'

Mary-Ann stood up and brushed grass off her skirt.

'Oh, and Janet – don't tell Matthew we had this talk. He'd be affronted if he knew I'd spoken so frankly.'

'I'll not breathe a word, Mrs Macgregor,' Janet promised tearfully . . .

Matthew had been looking forward to St James' market, for days. The fair happened once a year in July, and attracted hawkers, booths and cheap-johns of every description, along with sideshows offering fascinating sights such as a Californian Giantess and a Tattooed Lady.

Janet had completed sixty-nine weekly hours in the weaving sheds, the limit for a lass of her age, and had agreed to accompany him to the fair that Saturday. He whistled merrily as he stepped out along the turnpike to meet her at the appointed tryst.

She was waiting, but so changed in appearance it took his breath away.

She wore a blue gown and straw bonnet. When she walked beside him, he caught a glimpse of petticoat and slender ankles. Matthew swallowed.

'You're dressed so ladylike I hardly know you,' he remarked pettishly.

She tossed her head.

'I've taken a step up the ladder. I'm to be a weaver, and weavers are a cut above the rest. Maggie Soutar's hands are twisted wi' rheumatics and she can't work, so she's training me. I'll soon be well off, so I'm getting used to good fortune and bonny dressing.'

Some of the joy fled from Matthew's day as they walked along Castle Street.

'My mother's emigrating to Australia,' he said.

'Good for her. You'll be going too, of course?'

'Not if you don't want me to.'

She shrugged.

'Why should I care one way or the other?'

'I – I hoped you might care a little.'

'Well, I don't!'

He could not understand why she was so changed, so cruel.

'What about your father, Janet? You care about him!'

'Oh, he's much better, thanks,' she said.

The noise of crowds mobbing down the packed street ended the conversation. Matthew walked in an unhappy daze. The mingled smell of frying onions, fruit, candies and flowers sickened him. Janet did not appear to notice. She was radiant and smiling. Matthew trailed along behind her from stall to stall.

It was a relief when she tired of tawdry jewellery and cheap novelties and decided to go home. Conversation was awkward till they reached the door of her father's bothy. She faced him resolutely and held out a hand.

'Goodbye Matthew. I will be busy learning to be a weaver and working longer hours. I maybe won't see you before you leave, but I wish you good luck.'

'Thanks,' he said bitterly.

The brim of the bonnet shaded her face as they shook hands, then the bothy door closed.

Matthew stared at the blank woodwork for several seconds, and then strode furiously down the road to the smiddy-seat. His mother was on her knees putting a gloss on the grate with black-lead. She rose hurriedly when she saw his expression, hands clasping the sackcloth apron.

'What is it, Matthew? What's happened?'

'I've decided I'll go with you.'

'Oh, son, I'm glad!'

'Are you?'

He went out and walked blindly down to the lochside. Her adored father was better and she would do well as a weaver. They were a cut above the rest. Weavers could earn enough to marry young, stop work when they chose, go cut peats, help at harvest, lift tatties, make money. She had no need of him any more, and he should be happy for her.

But oh, how his heart ached! He covered his face with his hands and sobbed.

The laird was as good as his word and by mid-August the smiddy was his, and the Macgregors' passage booked to Sydney. Even after handing over thirty guineas for the tickets, Mary-Ann was wealthier than she'd ever been, and was in the nerves about keeping the remainder safe. She had no doubt they would need every penny, once they reached the other side. Prudently, she sewed sovereigns into the hems of her skirts, and made sure Agnes and Shona did the same. If by some desperate chance they became separated, they would all have money at their disposal.

She had closed the savings account kept on Davey's behalf with the New Bank. Ewan had refused to touch it and with interest it now amounted to the tidy sum of one hundred and fifty pounds. She mistrusted paper money, but the banker said notes were as good as gold, lighter and more convenient to carry on a long journey.

Mary-Ann persuaded Matthew to carry Davey's paper money, sewn into a concealed pocket inside his jacket. Because the fortune had originated with Alistair Ross, he had objected strongly.

'I won't carry that man's conscience money, Mother!'

'It's Davey's birthright, son. God knows he's suffered enough!'

And Matthew had said no more.

It was a sad little group that gathered in the yard one August morning. Mrs Wullie hugged each one in turn.

'I'll take good care o' your bonny house, Mary-Ann,' she promised.

Danny tugged at her skirts.

'Will you make treacle toffee when I come back, Mrs Wullie?'

'If I'm spared, lovie.'

'If you're not spared, maybe we could have a dumpling,' he said quite seriously.

They left for the station in laughter and tears, with Wullie driving the trap.

There was cholera in Dundee once again, and Mary-Ann would have preferred to give the city a wide berth, but they were already booked on the steamship *Iona*, leaving from Dundee's King William Dock, heading for Newcastle to offload passengers and cargo aboard the *Lady Kennaway*, bound for New South Wales . . .

'Put your handkerchiefs to your noses, and don't breathe!' Mary-Ann instructed the family when they arrived at Dundee's east station. Handkerchiefs charged with camphorated oil clamped to their noses, sure defence against infection, they followed a porter wheeling the handcart piled high with baggage.

The dock was conveniently sited. Smart new steamers, high-masted sailing vessels and old mouldering hulks lay berthed by the busy street. They dodged carts loaded with raw flax and others with finished bales of linen cloth. It was a rumbling, shouting melee.

Matthew scarcely noticed. In his miserable state, he would even have welcomed cholera. Janet Golightly had not come to wish him well. All he asked was a word, a smile, and a touch of the hand to show him she cared, just a little.

But – nothing!

He was too dejected to be impressed by the steamer and the family cabin reserved for their comfort. He saw the younger ones settled, then went up on deck and leaned on the rail. Presently his mother joined him. He looked so unhappy, Mary-Ann was filled with pity.

'Don't be sad, Matthew dear,' she said. 'Janet will prosper. She told me she was in training to be a weaver, a cut above the rest.'

Matthew stared at her. Janet's very words!

'She never told me you'd spoken with her.'

'I – I had a word with Janet, outside the weaving shed.'

He straightened. He could see it all now, clear as day! He did not know whether to laugh or cry.

'And I can guess what you said! You persuaded Janet she was standing in my light, keeping me from a grand new enterprise, didn't you?' He stared at Mary-Ann, and she could not hide her guilt. 'Of course you did! And Janet put on such a show of prosperity and indifference, I believed her.' Angrily, he leaned close to his mother. 'But it was only a show, not the truth. The truth is, Janet needs me. She needs me much more than you do, Mother, weighed down wi' my father's hard-won wealth!'

He gave Mary-Ann one last withering stare, then ran for the gangway and down on to the dockside.

'Matthew, come back!' Mary-Ann screamed frantically.

He paid no attention. Leaving the busy quay, he dodged down one of the dark alleyways bordering the harbour, and was lost to sight.

Six

The *Iona* was on the point of departure, and Mary-Ann panicked. She ran to the companionway leading to the bridge, only to find the way barred by a burly seaman.

'Can't go up there, Ma'am!'

'I must speak to the captain. My son is lost ashore. We cannot sail till the boy is found.'

The man was sympathetic.

'Wandered off, has he? How old is the mite?'

'Fourteen.'

'Fourteen?' He smiled. 'Lady, I'd been at sea two years when I was fourteen. If your laddie chooses to stay ashore, good luck to 'im!'

She was nearly in tears.

'You don't understand. We are emigrating. He'll be left behind, on his own.'

An angry, whiskery face appeared at the top of the companionway.

'What's the hold-up, bo's'n?'

'It's this wumman, cap'n. Her big son's gone ashore and she wants the ship held back for him.'

'Out o' the question! The pilot's aboard.'

A sudden thought occurred to Mary-Ann, and she turned cold.

'But my son is carrying money we'll need when we reach Australia!'

The captain frowned.

'The tide's not on the turn yet. I could wait five and forty minutes. After that we must leave, or risk going aground.'

Mary-Ann thanked him and ran to the ship's rail, staring towards a jumble of old buildings threaded by dark wynds and closes. She prayed Matthew would have a change of heart, but could see no sign of him.

★   ★   ★

Matthew had fled through a network of ancient buildings and stinking pends. The thought of cholera frightened him. This unhealthy area seemed a likely breeding ground. Matthew headed in what he judged was a northerly direction, towards the Glamis road and Forfar. Janet would be there. He had been deceived by her clever and generous act of self-denial, and loved her all the more, because of it.

Tall buildings obscured the view, crowded pavements and streets crowded with carts, drays and horse-drawn trams all served to confuse his sense of direction. He could not see the conical hill to the north of the city, which would give him a bearing. Massive factory walls rose sheer above his head on either side, and the plainstones trembled beneath his feet to the thunder of legions of looms. Matthew listened in awe. It seemed that the path to the future was opening right here. Machines were already doing the work of thousands of hand-loom weavers. He tried to imagine daily life driven only by machines. It was beyond Matthew's comprehension, but the idea excited him enormously.

He'd been too sick at heart to eat breakfast, but an aroma of cooking from a nearby pie shop made him suddenly realize he was ravenously hungry. Dundee pies were famously succulent.

Matthew thrust a hand into his pocket to search for loose pennies and his fingers encountered the wad of notes sewn into the lining. He stopped short in utter horror. He'd forgotten all about his mother's money. Money, which rightfully belonged to Davey, his half-brother.

Matthew turned and ran back the way he had come.

He wished he had paid more attention to the route. Several times he took a wrong turning in an attempt to find a short cut to the docks, but at last he heard the forlorn call of sea-gulls and found himself in a pend opposite the docks. Frantically, he leaped over dressed stones destined for the completion of an arch to commemorate Queen Victoria's visit and paused, looking around wildly. The docks were extensive, and he could not remember where the ship was berthed. Distraught, he ran along the quayside past sailing ships, small sprat boats, cargo and passenger steamers. At last he caught sight of the *Iona*, and groaned.

The ship was on the move, navigating a narrow exit from

the dock. Matthew felt renewed hope. Maybe he could attract his mother's attention and have the money sent aboard somehow.

A large crowd had gathered to watch the ship depart, and he tried desperately to find a way through. To make matters worse, Matthew glimpsed his mother and Danny standing by the rail.

'Let me through!' he yelled.

A hefty fellow held him back with a hand on his chest.

'Mind your manners, my lad!'

He struggled, but by then it was too late. The ship was out in the river, heading for the wider estuary and picking up speed. The crowd was dispersing and Matthew at last reached the forefront. He cupped his hands and shouted, but though he imagined that Danny turned and looked in his direction, the vessel was too far off to be sure.

Matthew felt sick. Whether he liked it or not, he was now custodian of his half-brother's patrimony.

Matthew arrived in Forfar in the gloaming, after a fifteen-mile tramp from the city. He had been sustained by a pie and pint in a Lochee pub, all he could afford with limited means. He had paid with his last shilling and was left with a few coppers. Ironically he was a pauper, with a fortune in the lining of his jacket.

He limped into the smiddy yard and tapped on the door. Mrs Wullie answered.

'Lord save us, it's Matthew!'

She ushered him in to where Wullie sat by the fire. Wullie nodded.

'Aye, Matthew, it's yoursel'.'

Absurdly, tears threatened Matthew.

'I couldn't go to Australia, Wullie. I ran away and they left without me. I've no money, no clothes, nowhere to go but here.'

Mrs Wullie took command.

'It's fortunate you an' Wullie are near the same size. Take off your boots and let's have a squint at your feet. You came hirplin' in like an auld man.'

He obeyed, and she doctored blisters with peppermint tincture. It did Florry Ogilvy's heart good to have a youngster to care for. She and Wullie had never been blessed with bairns, and it was a sad lack.

Matthew revived after a meal. He went across and sat hesitantly beside Wullie. Till now, Matthew had been stand-in for his father. Now he had no authority and just two pence ha'penny in his pocket. It was humbling.

'Would you take me on at the smiddy, Wullie?'

'It's not up to me, son. The laird's master now. He hires and fires.'

'So I have to go and beg for my own job back?'

Wullie nodded.

'Wi' bonnet in hand, if you're wise. The laird's a good man, but with a tongue sharp as a sickle if you get on his wrong side.'

Mrs Wullie bustled in. 'That's enough, Wullie. The poor lad's deadbeat. I have a night-sark airing for him, and fresh sheets on his own bed.'

'Thank you,' Matthew gulped.

To his shame, tears of gratitude slid down his cheek, which Wullie's keen eyes did not miss.

Mary-Ann was on the verge of collapse when the ship departed. Matthew had not come back, but her frantic appeals were ignored and the captain could not hold the ship a moment longer. She had seriously considered abandoning the voyage, but had decided too much was at stake. At least Matthew was resourceful and could look after himself, but she and the young ones had no prospects and no home in Scotland now. Her wise friend the laird had warned her she was burning her boats. There was no turning back.

Her daughters and Danny had found their way from the cabins, back on deck. Danny gripped the rail, watching the dock recede. Dundonians took keen interest in comings and goings at the docks and there was a fair crowd of sightseers gathered on the quay, waving and shouting. Mary-Ann turned away, too saddened to watch.

Shona stood with Agnes. She looked around.

'Mama, where's Matthew?'

Mary-Ann remained calm with an effort.

'He won't be coming with us, dear. He's decided to stay in Scotland.'

'But he didn't even say goodbye!' Shona cried forlornly.

Agnes scowled.

'It's that skinny-ma-link Janet Golightly! He's in love, the daft donkey.'

The wind blew more strongly as the ship headed for the open sea. Mary-Ann shivered. She remembered another sea voyage when she was just a child. Her parents had been leaving their beloved Ireland forever then. She remembered looking up at her mother's face, wondering why tears wet her cheeks. Now she understood.

'Let's go below and start unpacking,' she suggested, turning her back upon Dundee.

Danny trailed behind. He tugged at Agnes's sleeve.

'Matthew did say goodbye, Agnes. I saw him waving.'

She sighed.

'Danny, stop blethering. Can't you see Mama's sad?'

'Should I tell her a joke?'

She relented and hugged him. 'Aye, you do that, lovie.'

Danny ran ahead.

'When is a ship not a ship, Mama?'

'I've no idea, darling.'

'When it's a hardship,' Danny beamed. That was a good one. Wullie told it to him.

Mary-Ann laughed, but the word seemed charged with fore-boding. Who knows what hardships and dangers they'd face on the journey? She hugged this last remaining son, doubly precious now. Oh, Ewan! She thought. I am really truly on my own now . . .

Matthew set off for the laird's mansion next morning. Wullie had stressed the wisdom of humility, but Matthew marched boldly up the laird's driveway to the front entrance.

Phyllis answered his summons.

'I'll have a word with the laird, if you please,' he demanded.

She groaned.

'Michty me, here's another Macgregor on its high horse!'

Grumbling, she ushered him along a corridor, knocked on a door and shoved Matthew inside. Just in time, he remembered to remove his cap.

The laird was seated at his desk. He studied Matthew with raised brows.

'I understood you were off to Australia?'

'I changed my mind, sir. My future's here.'

'Oh aye? What sort of future were ye planning?'

'Working with machinery, sir.'

'You'll be on the lookout for work then?' the laird said mildly.

Matthew took a deep breath.

'No, sir. I've come to make you an offer to buy the smiddy.'

The laird eyed him thoughtfully.

'That's a fair sum o' money we're considering, my lad.'

'I have plenty in my – er – keeping.'

The hesitation was not lost upon the lawyer.

'In your keeping, is a good bit different from in your own pouch. Whose money is it?'

'It's money I hold in trust for my half-brother Davey. He's a convict serving time in Australia, as you know, sir, and I'm sure he would approve.'

'Your half-brother, eh? Well, well!' the laird mused.

He studied the youngster in silence for a moment. No mistaking this was Ewan Macgregor's son, but he had harboured suspicions about the other lad's parentage!

'A brave try, young Macgregor, but it'll no' hold water,' he said at last. 'If I made a deal wi' you, the transaction would be null and void.'

'Why so?' Matthew demanded.

'Because, if I'm not mistaken, Matthew Macgregor, you're not a day over fourteen. In the eyes o' the law you're a child.'

Matthew's lip trembled.

'What will I do? I hoped to save the smiddy for my pa.'

The laird smiled. A surprisingly kind and gentle smile.

'I suggest we enter into an agreement, Matthew. If you agree to an apprenticeship in the mill and train as a millwright, you can lodge in the smiddy-seat. I'll attend to board and lodgings. Till you can pay your way. How does that suit ye?'

'But sir – I wanted to be my own man!'

The laird rose and stood beside him. They made an incongruous pair, the old man spare and wiry, the youngster well muscled and tall. The laird patted Matthew's shoulder.

'You will be your own man one day, Matthew, I promise. In the meantime, when instruction's offered, it's wise to learn, is it not?'

Matthew sighed.

'Aye, sir,' he agreed . . .

Mary-Ann never forgot her first sight of the clipper *Lady Kennaway*, when the Royal Mail steamer *Iona* had brought them safely from Dundee to the Tyne and passengers began embarking in South Shields.

The clipper ship was a graceful lady, with three towering masts and a raking bow that hinted at speed. The Macgregors stood gazing in awe at the large, handsome vessel moored by the quayside, which would be their refuge and home for months to come.

The dockside was crowded as more passengers arrived. A large crowd of poor emigrants clutched pathetic bags and bundles and were herded into a nearby warehouse. They would not be allowed into the bowels of the ship till cabin passengers were all aboard.

As Mary-Ann watched the pitiful scene, a hansom cab drew up and a well-dressed gentleman climbed down and helped a lady of about Mary-Ann's own age to climb down. The lady glanced around; looking so nervous and anxious Mary-Ann gave her an encouraging smile as their eyes met. Mary-Ann's spirits rose. It would be pleasant to make friends on the voyage.

But to her astonishment the gentleman hurriedly picked up a small portmanteau then took the lady's arm and guided her into the crowded warehouse, where the couple were soon lost to view among emigrants destined for the poorest steerage accommodation. It was so totally unexpected, Mary-Ann was left feeling puzzled and curious about the well-dressed pair. She wondered if their paths would cross aboard ship.

Agnes tugged at her arm.

'Mama, there's Mr Ross!'

'Nonsense, Agnes! It can't be!' Mary-Ann said sharply.

But it was true. Alistair was threading his way through the crowd on the dockside.

He stopped in front of Mary-Ann, warmth in his eyes that made her catch her breath.

'Alistair!'

'Good day to you, Mrs Macgregor.' He raised his hat.

She was caught off guard. She was so pleased to see a friendly face she could have hugged him − if the children hadn't been watching every move. She gave a guarded smile and held out a hand.

'How thoughtful of you to come all this way to bid us goodbye, Mr Ross.'

Perhaps her eyes revealed her true state of mind, because his answering smile was tender. He took her hand and held it.

'Fortunately, you mentioned your travel arrangements in your last letter to my office, my dear. I travelled to Newcastle by train yesterday and have had a word with the ship's master to make sure all is well. It's useful being an MP sometimes.'

So she was not alone, after all! His thoughtfulness made her feel like crying.

'You are too kind,' she said formally.

He laughed.

'Nonsense! I must make sure my friends travel in comfort and safety. The skipper assures me he'll have you safe in Sydney harbour within sixty days. And he assures me the sails were made in Dundee!'

'Only sixty days?' Mary-Ann smiled again. 'That's good news. Do you hear that, children?'

Alistair smiled at the girls, winked at Danny and looked round warily for Matthew.

'Where's the man of the house who threw me out? He should surely be here to defend you?'

Mary-Ann looked uncomfortable.

'Matthew refused to go with us,' she admitted.

Agnes frowned. She suddenly remembered something that had been lurking at the back of her mind.

'Where's the money I sewed into the lining of Matthew's jacket, Mama?'

'He − he took it with him,' her mother said.

This was a shock to Shona. She had been overcome with shyness at the sight of Mr Ross, whom she greatly admired, but this news was a disaster.

'That's terrible, Mama!' she cried. 'You said we'd need every penny we had!'

'The young rogue!' Alistair exclaimed. 'So that's how Ewan Macgregor's son serves you!' He couldn't hide a small glow of triumph at the fall of the paragon. At least David, his son, hadn't stolen from his mother!

'It was accidental,' Mary-Ann said quietly. 'Matthew left in a hurry, Alistair, and there was no time. Besides, he will need money himself, and we have plenty.'

He looked at her keenly.

'I wish I could be sure of that, Mary-Ann, I know how devilish proud you are!'

She withdrew her hand.

'We should go aboard now, Mr Ross. It was most civil of you to attend to our safety,' she said formally, to cover the wave of feeling which threatened to make this a difficult and harrowing parting.

Once, long ago, she had loved him and borne his child. They would have married if fate – and Alistair's father – had not intervened.

She met his eyes helplessly. So much she wanted to say, so much must be left unsaid!

He understood, and found the right tone to help her out. His voice was matter of fact.

'Yes, you should settle in before the ship sails. She leaves in about five hours, on the tide.'

He picked up the heaviest bags and escorted her to the gangway, the girls and Danny followed, giving the two adults a few moments alone for hurried conversation.

'Alistair, have you any word of Davey? Do you know where they sent him when he reached Australia?'

'I've checked lists of boys transported in the last year and found nothing, but that's not surprising. The records are badly kept.' They had reached the foot of the gangway, and he clasped her hand. It trembled in his, though she looked calm. 'I'll keep looking, my dear. Send me your address and I'll tell you all I know.'

She shook her head slightly.

'Goodbye, Mr Ross.'

'Mary-Ann, write to me! Please!' he begged softly.

She pulled her hand away.

'Perhaps, when I find Ewan and Davey.'

Alistair had never felt such longing, never felt such bitter anguish since that last terrible time he had sailed away from Britain believing himself rejected, with no idea where Mary-Ann had gone, or what had happened to her.

Their eyes met and he glimpsed uncertainty there and hoped for a breathtaking instant that she might change her mind. Then the children pushed eagerly forward between them and she turned away from him and began to climb the gangway.

'Goodbye, Mr Ross!' Agnes and Danny chorused cheerfully, while Shona choked back tears and glanced sorrowfully over her shoulder as she climbed the gangway.

It isn't fair! She thought rebelliously. Mama commandeered Mr Ross, and I had no chance to speak with him. He was so distinguished and handsome, she was sure she was falling in love with him, and she would never see him again. No wonder she cried!

He was waving as they all stood by the ship's rail, looking down. Shona's heart eased a little and she shyly fluttered a handkerchief, till she suddenly noticed, outraged, that he had eyes only for their mother.

Mama has a husband already, yet she flirts with poor Mr Ross, Shona thought resentfully. It's disgusting!

They had been allocated quite a spacious family cabin on an upper deck. Shona was in a bad-tempered sulk, and the inevitable squabbles over bunks and unpacking helped Mary-Ann return to something approaching normality.

The poor emigrants were scrambling aboard, herded like sheep down into the dark bowels of the ship near the steering mechanism. Mary-Ann remembered the lady and gentleman she had noticed earlier, and pitied them.

The girls decided to stay in the cabin, but she took Danny on deck to watch the rowers who would pull the *Lady Kennaway* downriver to hoist sail. The ship began to move as the oarsmen in the cutter put their backs into the work. She mustn't cry, Mary-Ann thought, her heart still painfully divided. At the end of this long journey the grief she felt would have time to heal, when they would be reunited with Ewan and Davey.

She put an arm round Danny's shoulders.

'When one door closes, Dan, another opens,' she said softly.

That reminded him of a riddle he'd been saving for just such an occasion.

'When is a door not a door, Mama?'

'I can't guess.'

'When it's ajar.' He looked up at her searchingly. 'Are you laughing, Mama?'

She didn't answer. She was staring wistfully towards the shore as the ship moved steadily away from land. There were tears on her lashes, but Danny couldn't tell if they were laughter tears, or not . . .

Seven

David Macgregor was a lucky boy – or so the authorities told him.

He had been sentenced to transportation, but fortunately for him, the law had just been changed. David Macgregor at fifteen was now too young to be transported overseas.

They had sent him instead to the Isle of Wight off the south coast of England, to the notorious Parkhurst prison. Behind its walls, David Macgregor ceased to exist. He became prisoner No. 93, the number on the door of his cell.

The obligatory three months of virtual isolation had given him ample time to mull over the startling news Ewan Macgregor had told him on the voyage to London.

Knowing that the blacksmith was not his father had merely greatly increased Davey's respect and admiration for Ewan. At the same time, it had bred a deep hatred and resentment of Alistair Ross, his natural father.

He didn't know what to think of his mother's part in the shameful affair. She had shown herself to be weak, when he'd believed she was strong. She had used Ewan Macgregor's faithful love to save herself from shame. There was no getting around that, and Davey loathed the mere thought.

He had been given leave to write to his mother on his arrival, but had refused the offer. He'd no idea what to write.

Still, in the following weeks he had learned how to knit, which would have amused his sister Agnes. In the workroom they had given him wool and needles, and explained how it was done. In those three months he had knitted a blanket made of squares, sewn together. He had been pleased with the blanket, because the cell was chilly, but they had taken it away. Davey suspected the guard had sold it in Cowes.

After isolation, the Governor set young offenders to work. Davey spent summer days breaking stones for roadways within sight of Queen Victoria's recently built Osborne House.

In September, the weather broke and the youngsters were put

to work picking oakum, a caulking fibre made from unravelling old rope, used for waterproofing ships' decks.

When the guard wasn't watching, Davey used to stare out to sea. He could see ships sailing past the island, and the sight made him dream of freedom, of family and home.

His sad heart softened, and he found he could forgive his mother. All he wanted was to see her again . . .

After they had left Newcastle and sailed south with favourable winds, Mary-Ann had watched the pilot leave the ship at Start Point, the headland from which their long journey really began. The pilot cutter carried with it letters from passengers aboard the *Lady Kennaway* to those left behind. She looked on as the pilot cutter headed for the shore, carrying her letter to Matthew.

It was a loving, forgiving letter, giving him permission to use his half-brother's money, provided that one day he repaid Davey what was owed.

As the crew piled full sail on the clipper, the shores of England grew distant.

England – not her homeland. Yet it was as near to home as she'd see for years – perhaps for the rest of her life. Mary-Ann's eyes clouded with tears . . .

Storms in the Bay of Biscay tested all but the stoutest of hearts. Luckily, the Macgregors soon found their sea legs and though her daughters preferred to stay in the saloon with books and embroidery, she and Danny ventured out on the deck reserved for first-class passengers.

The helm was overhead, and they had a good view of the officer of the watch taking sextant observations at noon every day. The little boy was impressed when Mary-Ann explained this reading would help pinpoint the clipper's position when at sea. She was pleased. What an education this was for her son!

'I'm going to be a sailor when I grow up,' Danny declared confidently.

Sea air certainly agreed with him, his mother thought. Danny's cheeks were rosy with health and his blue eyes sparkled. He had been attempting to spin a top on the canted deck, and his laughter rang out, mingled with the sound of wind in the rigging.

Mary-Ann laughed with him, revelling in the elements as the wind tugged at her skirt and shawl. She felt free, almost carefree, released from the crinoline cage while aboard ship.

The fashion had been greeted with some amusement anyway, when it first appeared back home in Forfar.

'A braw playpen for crawling bairns,' Wullie had remarked.

And no use at all for climbing narrow companionways.

Thinking of Wullie made her realize she hadn't heard a single riddle from Danny lately, nor had she heard Wullie's name mentioned. Children soon forget! Maybe that was a blessing in Danny's case, she thought sadly.

He'd had very little success with the top and abandoned it, to take her hand and chat.

'I have a friend, Mama. He's called Abraham Stewart.'

She smiled.

'Danny, Abraham's a steward, who looks after us. That's his occupation. His name's not Stewart, dear.'

'He knows good riddles, though. Almost as good as Wullie's, though Abraham's are about the sea.'

So he hadn't forgotten Wullie after all, bless him!

'Why is a fishing boat crowded, Mama?'

'I can't think!'

''Cause the fish fillet. Fill it! Do you see the joke, Mama? Isn't it good?'

Laughing, Mary-Ann agreed, and shooed him off to try the latest joke on his sisters.

She remained on deck, the solitary passenger to brave the brisk wind today. Solitude was to be prized within the confines of the ship, and she savoured it.

After several minutes, Mary-Ann was surprised to hear a sound very like a stifled sob. It was so soft, and the wind in the rigging so noisy, she wondered at first if she'd imagined it, till it came again, unmistakable this time.

The sound seemed to come from beyond the first-class section of deck, from an area Abraham had pointed out to her, where steerage passengers took an airing at certain times of day. It was outside the hours they were permitted to do so, Mary-Ann knew, but someone was out there now, and in obvious distress.

Reaching the rope barrier, she at once recognized the woman

in bedraggled dress and bonnet. It was the well-dressed lady she had noticed on the quay at Newcastle.

On impulse, Mary-Ann removed the rope barrier and walked towards her. Hearing her footsteps, the woman whirled round. Her expression hardened when she saw Mary-Ann.

'What are you doing here?' she demanded. 'Have you come to gloat at discomfort?'

That shocked Mary-Ann.

'Oh, no, ma'am. Indeed not! I'm Mary-Ann Macgregor, and I've come to try to be of help to you.'

The woman stared at her hopelessly.

'I'm sorry. No one can help. I shouldn't even be here, breathing God's good air – I should be down in the stinking hold with my husband.'

'Then let us go down together, and I can see for myself what has to be done,' said Mary-Ann calmly.

'Do you mean it?' The woman stared, and then shook her head. 'Very well. But you won't like it. You may not be able to bear it.'

They went down one companionway, then another, steeper, scarcely more than a ladder, and through a doorway into noise and darkness.

As her eyes grew more accustomed to the gloom, Mary-Ann saw a dark host of humanity. In every corner of this large open dormitory there were people. They were cooking, eating; lying huddled on narrow bunks or crouched in cell-like family compartments with pathetic sackcloth walls.

Babies crawled with cockroaches on the floor, toddlers tumbled and wailed, and children ran to and fro . . .

Mary-Ann recoiled at the stuffiness and stench that caught at the back of her throat. The woman had been watching her reaction grimly.

'Not pretty, is it?'

Mary-Ann turned to her, almost in tears.

'Oh, ma'am, what has brought you to this?'

'Debt. My husband is a fine man, honest and kind, but too gullible, I fear! He trusted his so-called friends and business partners. Oh, I never liked them, and warned him to be wary, but by then it was too late. He had invested every penny in their fraudulent scheme. We were left destitute, with massive debts we could never hope to repay. We were forced to run, or else face prison, or worse. We shall never return to England again. We dare not!' She looked away, struggling with tears.

Mary-Ann was deeply moved. This was obviously an aristocratic lady of quality. It showed in every move she made.

'I'm so sorry, my lady!'

The lady gave a wan smile.

'Not my lady any more, my dear. Louisa will do.'

At that point, Abraham the steward came clattering down the companionway in a great state of alarm. The helmsman had noticed Mary-Ann had crossed forbidden boundaries, and alerted him.

He grabbed her arm.

'Mrs Macgregor, come away. This is no place for you!'

'Go away, Abraham! I'm talking to a friend!'

Mary-Ann struggled, but the steward had her firmly by the arm, guiding her to the stairs. She was forced to give in, but looked over her shoulder.

'I'll be back, Louisa!'

The other woman shook her head sadly.

'Not if you're wise, my dear!'

Back on deck, Mary-Ann faced the steward.

'That was unnecessary and unkind, Abraham. I want to help those poor people!'

'And it does you credit, ma'am. But sure as death there'll be illness down there afore the voyage is over. Do you aim to carry some vile infection to your young folk?'

Mary-Ann was silent. She shook her head slowly. She had not understood the dangerous risk she had taken . . .

David Macgregor was working quietly in the prison carpentry shed when the warder's shadow fell across him. He did not look up, though every nerve in his body tensed. What rule had he broken now?

'You're for the Guv'nor, 93. Look slippy.'

Davey nearly spilled the glue he was heating into the flame. The Guv'nor? That was serious. He couldn't imagine what he had done.

He was marched at the double to the governor's office and brought to attention in front of the desk.

The governor studied the lad before him thoughtfully, and glanced at the guard.

'Thank you, Mr Wilkins. Wait outside, if you please. I'll deal with this.'

It would be transportation after all, Davey thought in despair. He almost broke down and pleaded with the man, but pride came to his aid. He stared straight ahead at a point just to the left of the governor's ear.

The man looked up from the report he'd been studying.

'You are David Macgregor?'

Davey hesitated. He'd been a number so long; it was strange to hear his name.

'Aye, sir.'

'On the whole, you have been well-behaved and diligent while in our care, Macgregor.'

'Thank you, sir.'

'I consider you are no longer a threat to society, and have made my opinion known to the proper authority. Today I received the warrant authorizing your release. You are free to leave, Macgregor.'

It was so unexpected, the governor's features swam before Davey's eyes.

'You're setting me free?'

'Yes. You will be issued with suitable clothing, given free passage to Portsmouth, and the sum of seven shillings and sixpence to enable you to go home to your mother.'

He consulted the report, frowning.

'I see your father was transported some time ago. I trust you have a home to go to?'

Davey's head cleared.

'Yes, thank you, sir. My mother bides in Forfar with my brothers and sisters.'

'Scotland? That's a fair distance. Perhaps I should arrange lodgings for you in London for a night or two—'

But once out of the prison's clutches Davey wanted no more to do with it.

'Thank you kindly, sir, but that won't be necessary,' he said hastily. 'My mother has a relative in the city who'll give me a bed.'

That was a shot in the dark. Davey remembered his mother

had mentioned a cousin, Kathleen O'Malley, who worked in Covent Garden.

The governor looked relieved. He nodded.

'Good. I like to be sure that my boys are quickly reunited with their own flesh and blood, if possible.'

His own flesh and blood. How ironic that sounded! Davey thought. Alistair Ross, his father, was a rich, influential man living in London. Davey had never known him, and had no wish to make his acquaintance. Ewan Macgregor is father to me, he thought, but heaven knows if I will ever see him again.

The governor stood up, ending the interview.

'Good luck, Macgregor. I need hardly say I hope never to set eyes on you again.'

'You won't, sir,' Davey promised in heartfelt tones.

He left the office in a daze.

Freedom! He could scarcely remember what it felt like.

Davey was not the only youngster to be released that day. His companion in a prison cart, driven by Mr Wilkins, was a small, chubby-cheeked fourteen-year-old named Spooner.

'Am I glad to get out o' that place!' Spooner said.

'Me too.'

Davey took a deep breath of fresh air to clear his lungs. Ahead was an incredible vista of trees and green fields bathed in golden September sunlight, with cliffs and sea beyond.

A foreign landscape, but every inch of it available. He could go anywhere he liked. It was a heady feeling.

Down at the quay, the ferry was preparing to sail. Wilkins unlocked the cart and doled out two tickets.

'Hop it, you two. I never want to see hide nor hair of ye again.'

'Likewise, Mr Wilkins.' Spooner grinned and tipped his cap to the back of his head. He strolled hands in pockets, whistling merrily, towards the ship.

Davey followed more soberly.

Standing on deck once they were under way, Davey watched the white wake stream out behind them, and his heart leapt. He felt like a human being again. With three half crowns jingling in his pocket, breathing bracing sea air, he was his own master. And he was going home.

'Where's your home, Spooner?' he asked.

'I dodge about, here an' there.'

'No father or mother?'

'Naw. I've an auntie in Portsmouth.'

Davey's heart went out to the other boy. Home was far away, but at least he knew that for him, it was there, waiting. He could hardly wait to reach the warm and welcoming bosom of his family, in the smiddy-seat in Forfar . . .

The boys parted on the quayside.

'Are you sure you'll be all right?' Davey asked Spooner anxiously.

He grinned.

'Oh yer! Ta-ta, mate.'

He gave Davey a quick hug, and was off at the run, disappearing into the crowd.

Now to find transport to London, Davey thought happily. Train or coach? Train, he decided. He'd plenty of money for the fare. He patted his pocket confidently and suddenly realized that it no longer jingled.

He pulled out the single half crown he'd been left with and cursed himself for a fool.

He'd forgotten Spooner had been in the nick for picking pockets.

Davey stared at the single coin and wondered how far it would take him. He'd had no intention of searching for Kathleen O'Malley, but perhaps he would be forced to find her after all.

To his surprise, he found the disaster had left him still optimistic about the future. Nothing daunted, he was a free man who could deal with any adversity now. He set off with a spring in his step. He could hardly wait to see his mother again. How overjoyed she would be when he walked into the smiddy-seat. What a family celebration there would be!

Except . . .

Davey's stride slowed, and he sighed heavily. Pa wouldn't be there . . .

Ewan Macgregor stood on deck and surveyed the land ahead of the ship. So this was Australia. After months at sea they had reached their destination at last. But what did this strange land hold for him?

In a way, the ship had become home. Ewan knew every board

and splinter on the deck beneath his bare feet. He ought to! He'd scrubbed it many times. Every sea-scarred inch of the old ship was familiar. The smell of it was in his nostrils and the taste of salt on his lips.

The land ahead was a different matter though.

Strange, Ewan thought. The land ahead was a dark, brooding green, with a high misty wall of mountains rising beyond a huddle of modest buildings. It was not at all what he had imagined the town of Sydney to be.

'Journey's end, Ewan,' his friend the surgeon said, coming up behind him.

Thomas Bryant would be sorry to lose such a fine opponent at chess. The voyage home would be dull indeed!

Ewan had a moment's disquiet. He frowned.

'Where exactly are we, sir?'

The surgeon hesitated fractionally.

'Van Diemen's Land, Ewan.'

'Wha–at?'

Ewan wheeled angrily to face him.

'I was told we were going to Sydney! I was told I was to be given a conditional pardon if I agreed to complete the rest of my sentence working in the colony.'

The surgeon met his gaze. He had expected trouble.

'This is part of the colony, Ewan.'

He stared at the brooding landscape in despair.

'This evil place? How can I ask my wife and bairns to join me here? Even in Forfar, folk shudder at the very mention of Van Diemen's Land.'

Bryant remained silent. It was true the island had earned a brutal reputation.

'And I understood I would work at my trade till my debt to society was paid,' Ewan protested.

'So you will, man!' Bryant insisted, clapping him on the back reassuringly. 'This shipload of craftsmen has been brought here specially, at the request of Van Diemen's Land graziers. Craftsmen are scarce here on the island, so what matters it to you if you land in Hobart instead of Sydney?'

'Of course it matters, Mr Bryant!' he cried angrily, shrugging off the hand on his shoulder. 'Have you forgotten you told me there's hope I'll find my boy David in New South Wales? Besides, I've paid for my crime ten times over, for the minor fault it was! I'm willing to work hard and work well as a free man, not a sheep-herder's bond servant!'

Ewan felt he had been misled and shabbily betrayed, by a man he'd considered his friend.

He thrust his hot face close to Bryant's.

'It's true what they say, Mr Bryant. Never trust new friends or old enemies!' That said, Ewan turned on his heel and strode off along the salt-bleached deck.

The surgeon watched him go with narrowed eyes.

'And pride will be your downfall, I fear, you stiff-necked Scot!' he muttered.

But Thomas Bryant spoke sadly, for he had genuinely liked the man.

As Matthew Macgregor made his way through Forfar to the spinning mill to start work, he could hear the sound of the hand loom from nearly every cottage. It was gentle music to his accustomed ear – very different from the power looms he'd heard thundering in Lochee, a relentless sound, strangely exciting.

He made haste to visit the weaving sheds soon after his return. Janet Golightly looked startled, then smiled sweetly.

'So! I thought you might have died of shame at sight of me, after your play-acting, you sly wee besom!' he scolded.

She laughed delightedly.

'Och, somehow I felt sure in my bones you'd be back.'

'Are you glad?'

She wouldn't say, just shooed him outside to wait for the end of her shift, before the overseer saw him. But she did allow him to walk her home, down the Spout.

When relating his adventures, he couldn't resist telling her of the excitement engendered by the walk past the Lochee spinning mill.

'The very street trembled beneath my feet, Janet, just imagine the power! You'd be better paid working in the Forfar spinning mill, you know. There's improvements being made every day to safety and efficiency, and I could keep an eye on you. I work there now.'

She stopped in her tracks and glared.

'I'd never sink so low as work in the mill. Weavers are a cut above mill workers.'

'Oh aye? From what I hear, weavers stop work at the drop of a bonnet to go off to work in the fields,' he mocked.

'Why shouldn't they earn an extra penny or two at harvest, instead of slaving at a loom all hours to make fat profits for someone else?' she argued.

'You do!'

'That's different. I can't leave my da.'

She walked on quickly. He ran to catch up.

'Janet, how's your da faring?'

'Better. But he complained of pain this morning. Here.' She touched her chest.

'Can't the doctor do something?'

She glanced at him.

'Doctors cost money, Matthew.'

It was dusk as they walked along the road towards the bothy. Janet frowned.

'Da hasn't lit the cruisie at the window to light me home. Where can he be?'

'It's not dark yet. Maybe he's saving oil,' Matthew suggested.

But when they reached the bothy it was in darkness and eerily silent. Janet stood uncertainly in the doorway.

'Da, are you home?'

No answer.

She disappeared inside and presently the room was bathed in yellow light as she lit the lamp. She turned round – and screamed. Matthew ran to her side and held her.

The roadman lay on the floor by the cold hearth, kindling scattered around him. Janet crouched weeping beside her father. Matthew knelt, searching for signs of life.

'Fetch the doctor, Matthew. Quickly!' Janet begged.

'Will you be all right, left alone?'

'Yes, yes. Please, Matthew, run!'

He ran off through the darkness, but no matter how fast he ran, he knew nothing could save Janet's father.

When at last the doctor drove the trap to the door with Matthew by his side, they found Janet still crouched beside her father.

After a brief examination, the doctor took Matthew aside.

'Get the lass out o' here, Matthew. The man's been dead for hours.'

He nodded, and put an arm around her.

'Come away, Janet. There's nothing you can do for your da. There will be no more illness and pain for him now. He's at rest.'

To his surprise, she obeyed meekly. She seemed numb. Matthew could hardly imagine what she must be feeling, now that the moment she had dreaded for so long had arrived.

Janet roused from her dazed state when they reached the smiddy door.

'Where are you taking me?'

'Home, Janet,' Matthew answered. 'Mrs Wullie will look after you.'

Mrs Wullie Ogilvy, kindly soul, rose to the occasion when Matthew explained the sad situation. She took charge of the shivering lass.

'Come and sit yoursel' down by the fireside, lovie. The kettle's on the boil.'

Matthew left them together and went into the scullery. He washed away the grime of his working day in the slate sink under the pump, as fastidiously as his father had. He had been struck by the change in Janet, dispirited and prostrate with grief, clinging to him. It was sad, of course, but now that they were under the same roof he would see her every day. It was unseemly, given the circumstances, but his heart sang for joy.

Now that the reason for driving herself hard had gone, Janet fell ill.

The lass was so ill that Mrs Wullie had difficulty finding a remedy for the illness, even among her assortment of pills and potions.

Matthew was beside himself with fear, and voiced his concern to Wullie while working on a new wheel for Pluckerston's cart. Pluckerston was pernickety, and the wheel must be perfect, but Matthew couldn't concentrate.

'She won't die, will she, Wullie?'

'Not her! She's plenty spunk, that wee one.'

He eased his back and filled a pipe and settled down for friendly word.

'The lass can't bide here once she's on her feet, Matthew.'

This was a body blow. Matthew frowned.

'Why not?'

'You know as well as I do, my lad!'

Matthew went red.

'I'd never harm Janet. Never!'

'You'll not get the chance,' Wullie said calmly. 'I've told the laird. Who bides in the smiddy is up to him, no' me.'

Matthew was furious.

'If she's sent back to the bothy in her state, she'll die, Wullie. I'll not allow it! The laird will discover I'm not a dog that answers to any man's whistle!'

Wullie sighed.

'Dinna get your dander up, my lad. The lass has landed on her feet. She's to go into service in the big house. When she's trained, she'll make a grand wee wife for somebody.'

Matthew was silenced. He thought about it.

Under the laird's protection Janet would be expected to work hard, but she'd be warm, well fed and cared for. Nobody had ever ended up crippled and coughing in the laird's employ – unlike some poor old folk from the weaving sheds that Matthew knew.

And she'll be living close at hand! he thought. They could walk out together on days off.

The future suddenly looked bright.

But Janet didn't seem to care what happened to her, although she did agree listlessly that working for the laird was at least some place to go. Matthew longed to shake her out of her apathy, but Mrs Wullie warned him to hold his horses.

'It's cod liver oil, sulphur and treacle that set her on the road to recovery, Matthew. Skin an' bones, she was when you brought her in, poor lass. She'd been starving herself to feed her father and I've seen more fat on a whippet. A month o' good feeding in the laird's kitchen and you'll no' ken that lass,' Mrs Wullie predicted.

So Janet went off to live in the laird's mansion.

The housekeeper examined the graceful girl's clean, white hands and good teeth and decided to train her as a housemaid, presentable enough to serve at table. Janet was handed over to Phyllis, the head housemaid.

She was allocated a tiny box room in the topmost turret. It held bed, cupboard and chest and had a breathtaking view over Strathmore. Janet loved it on sight. It was the only room she had ever occupied that was hers alone.

Her best uniform and working overalls were laid out on the bed, along with two sets of underwear, black wool stockings and garters – the finest set of clothing she'd had for years. For the first time since her dear father died, Janet felt warmth creep back into her heart.

The working day began at five thirty, with Phyllis in charge.

Janet was ordered to clean out the grates and lift ashes noiselessly, before laying kindling for Phyllis to light the fires. This task was second nature to her, and Phyllis was pleased.

'After your porridge, I'll let you loose on the stairs to polish the banisters,' Phyllis decided, and offered some further cheerful advice. 'You'll soon get the hang o' housework in the laird's hoose, lassie. Just remember, if it's moving, curtsey to it. If it stays still, polish it.'

After a good breakfast in the servant's hall, Janet set to work on the beautiful, carved staircase with beeswax and dusters.

Engrossed in making the intricate woodwork gleam, she didn't hear the laird approach till he stood beside her. Janet jumped, tried to curtsey and nearly lost her balance.

He steadied her, smiling.

'You're Janet Golightly, the new lass.'

'Aye, sir.'

Her teeth were chattering with fear. This man had sent Davey and his father to Botany Bay and could do the same to her, if he only knew it. She could hardly bear to look at him.

'You're a friend of the blacksmith's lad,' the laird said.

She flushed guiltily. Was the man suspicious?

'You – you mean Davey Macgregor?'

His expression changed.

'It was Matthew Macgregor I had in mind. I did not know you were acquainted with his brother David.'

His eyes were piercing; they seemed to drill through her head. Janet was terrified.

'Davey is – I mean was – my friend. He was kind, he hunted rabbits for me and my da—'

She faltered, and then stopped.

Maybe she'd said too much already. The wise old man's shrewd gaze was fastened upon her thoughtfully, and Janet went to pieces.

'Oh, sir – the poaching wasna Davey's fault, nor his father's neither!' she wailed. 'Davey did it for me because my da was so sick. We only meant to shoot rabbits, but the deer would have killed us both. Then the blacksmith came too late, and the game-keepers were hurt, which made it worse, and it was all my fault!'

Tears were streaming down her cheeks. Janet was quite sure she'd go to prison now.

The laird was startled. The sobbing child was almost inco-herent, but he suspected that the answer to the puzzle of Ewan Macgregor's strange behaviour was right here before him.

He laid a hand gently on her shoulder.

'Come away into the study with me, lassie, and let's hear the whole story.'

Eight

The clipper *Lady Kennaway* was thirty-five days out from England. Mary-Ann and her family had never experienced such heat, even in the hottest summer back home. Trade winds had carried them to the Cape Verde Islands, and southwards into an area dreaded by sailors, the doldrums.

Sails swung limp on the yards and the ship wallowed sluggishly in a millpond sea. Usually the clipper romped through this troublesome patch, but this time luck had deserted her. Skies cleared, the wind dropped and a tropical sun blazed on scorching decks. Tarpaulins were erected for the cabin passengers' comfort and they lounged languidly on deck, praying for a cool breeze. The captain ordered the hatch covers opened to send a breath of fresh air to the poor souls sweltering below, and permitted steerage passengers limited access to the upper deck in the humid night.

The fate of those cloistered below was a constant worry to Mary-Ann. She knew that had it not been for the sale of the blacksmith's business, she and her children would be down there with them.

She had struck up a friendship beneath the tarpaulins with another lady travelling on her own, Mrs Evan-Jones, middle-aged wife of a Sydney government official, who was determined to educate Mary-Ann in colonial etiquette – penal style.

'Pull your chair farther under the tarpaulin, Mrs Macgregor, one would not wish to be brown and freckled,' she advised.

'I don't mind that, ma'am. I admire the healthy glow of women working in the fields.'

Mrs Evan-Jones raised her hands in horror.

'Heaven forbid, my dear! Sydney is trying to forget that some grandfathers, fathers and mothers were convicts labouring outdoors. You won't be welcome in the best houses, with skin tanned like leather.'

Mary-Ann did not inform the kind lady that she herself was

a convict's wife. She had no intention of allowing her small son and pretty daughters to be ostracized, the moment they set foot on land.

Fortunately, Shona and Agnes stayed voluntarily under cover, guarding fine complexions inherited from their Irish mother. Not so Danny, who was brown as a berry, a favourite with the crew, and ranged freely throughout the ship,

Agnes, who was twelve years old recently, had lost her endearing puppy fat. She was not blessed with Shona's delicate beauty, but promised to be slim and wiry, with plenty of spunk and a wonderful smile that transformed snub-nosed features into something quite memorable.

Unfortunately, Agnes was jealous of her sister's looks and touchy on the subject of her own, a complex that was destined to give all concerned much heartache in the future.

Danny dodged under the tarpaulin.

'Mama! Abraham Stewart says I have an a-come-splash-ment.'

'You mean an accomplishment, Danny?' She smiled.

'Come an' see!' He pulled her to her feet.

The sun's glare hit her like a blast from a furnace as she stepped out of the shade. She was glad of a wide-brimmed bonnet and loosened corset beneath a muslin gown. Danny, barefooted and lightly clad, seemed unaffected. He led his mother into a spot of shade beside the ship's cutter.

'Listen to this, Mama!'

He puckered up and whistled several clear, musical notes. Scarlet with success, he looked at her breathlessly.

'I can whistle! Abraham Stewart showed me. He says I must whistle for the wind.'

Mary-Ann applauded. She knew how important the achievement was for Danny, who'd suffered cruel teasing on the subject at school.

She hugged him.

'Darling, that was wonderful. We'll be out of the doldrums in no time now.'

Danny had paused, listening.

'Mama, they're singing hymns, and it isn't Sunday yet.'

Mary-Ann glanced along the deck towards the doleful sound. A small group of steerage passengers had gathered by the ship's rail. A canvas-wrapped bundle lay on a plank nearby the ship's rail.

To her surprise, Mary-Ann recognized her friend Louisa, who appeared to be chief mourner at the sad little ceremony. Louisa was beautifully dressed today, a fine lady to the tips of white lace gloves. She stood apart, unflinching.

Mary-Ann and the cabin passengers had heard rumours of an epidemic down below, but the crew kept quiet when questioned. Now she was seeing the evidence with her own eyes, and feared the worst.

She turned to Danny.

'Run and show your sisters how well you can whistle, dearie.' To her relief, he went off obediently. Mary-Ann made her way for'ard.

Abraham the steward barred her way.

'I was watching out for ye, ma'am. I had a notion you'd come, since it was your friend's husband that died.'

The news upset Mary-Ann.

'Oh, Abraham! What happened to him?'

'There's scurvy and typhoid down below. He succumbed, poor gent. Turn back, Mrs Macgregor. You don't want to go there.'

'Let me talk to the widow first.'

He sighed. 'I can't deny the poor woman your comfort, I suppose. I'll look t'other way, but only for five minutes!'

Meanwhile, the calm sea had closed with barely a splash over Louisa Polpatrick's husband. The small group of mourners had dispersed, but the widow stood alone, staring at the ocean. Mary-Ann touched her arm hesitantly.

'Louisa my dear, I'm so sorry.'

Tears would have been natural, but her friend was dry-eyed and angry.

'Mary-Ann, my darling husband would be alive today, if evil men had not deliberately ruined him. He could not fight the fever. He did not even try!'

Mary-Ann put an arm round her shoulders; there was nothing she could say.

Louisa sighed.

'I don't know what the future holds for me. Once I was rich, now I have nothing. But I will work hard, Mary-Ann, and one day, God willing, I could be rich again. I swear no ruthless men will ruin *me*!'

Brave words, but Mary-Ann had personal experience of the hard toil required to achieve even modest success, and doubted if a lady accustomed to be waited upon hand and foot, would ever have the necessary skills. She was too kind-hearted to say so.

'If you need help, Louisa. I promise I'll do all I can,' she said.

Louisa Polpatrick had known very little kindness in the last few weeks. She broke down in tears.

'God bless you, my dear, you are a true friend!'

Sobbing, she turned away and hurried towards the companionway, descending quickly down into the heat and stink.

Left alone, Mary-Ann counted her blessings. She had her children with her and was confident she would soon be joining her husband and son. She would never be alone, like this other poor soul.

Lost in thought, she had not noticed the limp sails stirring. But suddenly the topgallants flapped, an officer yelled an order, crewmen spilled out of the fo'c's'le and shinned up the masts on to the yards, piling on sail as the faint breeze strengthened to a wind. The turgid sea swelled lazily and waves chuckled beneath the bows.

Mary-Ann looked up and laughed. Danny Macgregor had whistled for the wind.

The clipper was under way at last . . .

Ewan's ship had reached Van Diemen's Land and berthed in Hobart harbour, a red and white pennant fluttering at the masthead proclaiming its human cargo.

News of the arrival of a convict ship had spread. Eager bidders had gathered in a dockside warehouse to view the latest intake.

The graziers grinned and winked. Not criminals now, remember. Exiles! A fancy name for a familiar breed.

Ewan Macgregor's anger at the betrayal was stamped darkly upon his handsome features as he entered the warehouse, the firm ground still rocking beneath his feet, after months at sea. Many buyers took one look at the big, glowering fellow with arms folded across a brawny chest and passed on. As his companions were chosen and numbers dwindled, Ewan began to hope he would not find favour with the graziers. If not, he might be free to find work for himself. Then a harbour official stopped in front of him.

'How about this one? He's big and ugly enough.'

To Ewan's surprise, a woman stepped forward and studied him. She shook her head.

'No. I want muscle, not flab.'

'There's no' an ounce of flab on me, you impudent hussy!' He declared angrily.

The official raised a fist to strike him.

'Mind your manners!'

The woman stopped him. She stared at Ewan.

'What's your name?'

He told her. The harbour official frowned.

'Don't touch this 'un, Miss Rose. He's a Scot. They're a load o' trouble.'

Miss Rose? Anyone less like a rose Ewan could hardly imagine. The woman couldn't be much older than Mary-Ann, but there the similarity ended. Her hair was scraped back from a long, thin face into a severe knot at the nape of a scrawny neck. On top rested a straw bonnet, tied beneath the chin. She was sallow, freckled and sun-bleached, with pale, veiled eyes. She wore blouse, dusty dark skirt, shabby coat and cotton gloves splotched with dried mud. He glimpsed dusty black hobnailed boots beneath the skirt hem.

Rose? Ewan very nearly laughed.

She looked at him with a grim little twist of the lip, as if she'd read the opinion accurately.

'We were promised craftsmen this time. What's your trade?'

'I'm a blacksmith.'

Miss Rose eyed him thoughtfully for a minute, and then turned to the official.

'I'll take Ewan Macgregor. The usual conditions to apply.'

'Very good, Miss Bates.' He jotted down a few sentences in a notebook and held it out while she scribbled a signature. Ewan intervened indignantly.

'Do I have any say in this arrangement?'

She looked at him with cool amusement. 'None whatsoever. Come along, Macgregor.'

She nodded to the official and walked away. She did not bother to check if Ewan followed her. He stood swithering, seething with rage.

'Go with Mistress Bates, Scotchman. You'll find it less trouble in the long run,' the official advised.

Ewan heaved the bedroll containing his few possessions on to a shoulder and followed.

He found a dust-covered buggy waiting in the shade. Miss Rose unhitched the horse from the hitching rail and climbed aboard. She glanced at Ewan.

'Stow your swag in the back and get in.'

He took his seat beside her as she shook up the reins. The horse set off on a route that the beast knew well, for it needed little guidance. Passers-by were few, but those who had braved the midday sun paused to watch. Ewan heard stifled laughter. If Miss Rose heard, she gave no sign.

He had no idea where the strange woman was taking him, or what she had in mind. He gave way to despair.

Oh, Mary-Ann, my dearest, he thought, if only I could kiss your sweet lips once more!

But he knew that was impossible. He had written to his wife warning her not to follow him to this notorious place. The ship's doctor's last act of friendship had been to take charge of the letter. He had promised it would be delivered to Mary-Ann in Forfar without fail, not more than six months from this day . . .

Back home in Forfar, the laird had let Janet Golightly off lightly. He'd coaxed the whole story of Davey Macgregor's poaching expedition from her, and assured the tearful lass he'd no intention of clapping her in jail. To be sure, there was no case to answer. The laird had contented himself with a stern warning about the dangers to lasses led astray by persuasive young lads, then sent her off to finish polishing the banisters.

In the weeks that followed the confrontation, regular meals brought about a remarkable transformation. Janet filled out and grew tall. Her cheeks were rosy, eyes sparkled with health.

Matthew noticed the difference at once when they met a month later, on Janet's first Saturday afternoon off. She was so bonny it nearly bowled him over.

'You've grown!' he cried accusingly.

His head was in a spin. Now she was so bonny, lads more handsome than himself were bound to come courting. She could take a fancy to someone else, and Matthew wanted her all to himself. He tucked her hand possessively into the crook of his elbow.

'What d'you want to do?'

'Let's go to the market.' Her eyes shone. 'I've a whole sixpence to spend.'

Matthew had hoped for a more secluded destination, by the lochside. Still, it was October, the wind cold enough to dampen even Matthew's ardour. They set off for the booths and cheap-john stalls set up in the High Street.

'The laird says he can have your pa and Davey pardoned, on the strength of what I told him about that awful day, Matthew. Davey could be home soon. Isn't it wonderful?' Janet said.

Matthew felt chilled to the fingertips.

'Australia's a long way off. They could take years to come.'

'Steamers are fast and don't wait for wind. Your pa and Davey could be home by Hogmanay. What a New Year that'll be!'

'Aye. What a disaster!' he predicted darkly. 'The smiddy sold and my mother off to the ends o' the earth, searching for them.'

But nothing could dampen Janet's spirits. She was still smiling as they rounded the corner into High Street, and came face to face with trouble.

A knot of unemployed men stood around idly outside the pub. Matthew recognized some that had been laid off from the mill recently. Among them were hand-loom weavers and flax-dressers. Matthew grew nervous. Flax-dressers were kittle cattle. The job was to draw handfuls of flax over heckle pins to straighten the fibres, and the men were highly skilled. They were also argumentative and powerful enough to bring the mill to a standstill, if they had a grievance.

As a result, hackling was one of the first processes to be mechanized. Matthew had helped perfect a heckling machine, which could be operated by unskilled women. Men had been thrown out of work.

An angry shout went up as he was recognized. They gathered round.

'We've a bone to pick wi' you, laddie. You're the one that builds bloody machines that throw good men on to the streets.'

Matthew pushed Janet behind him for safety.

'If I won't work on the machinery they'll bring in someone who will. I'm sorry for you, truly I am, but what can't be changed, must be endured.'

'Save your breath to cool your porridge, blacksmith's boy!' one of the group cried furiously. 'Leave the mill, or you'll be sorry!'

Matthew put an arm round Janet and managed to push past. They let him go, shouting after him.

'Heed the warning, Macgregor!'

Matthew felt wretched. He knew mechanization was the way ahead, but had not taken into account the human cost.

'What should I do, Janet? Good men are thrown out of work because of me. How can I go on working with that on my conscience?'

She stood on tiptoe and kissed him.

'If God gave you skill, use it, Matthew. Those men are wasting their breath. Progress can't be stopped.'

She took his hand and led him towards the market stalls. Matthew followed.

Janet kissed me! He thought dazedly. She kissed me!

MPs thronged the Westminster corridors for an important debate. The Home Secretary stopped Alistair Ross.

'Several months ago, Alistair, you asked about a youngster named David Macgregor, a lad sentenced to transportation, did you not?'

Alistair could barely hide his excitement.

'Indeed I did, sir. Has news come from Australia?'

'Not Australia. If this is the youngster you're interested in, he never went there.'

Alistair was astounded. He'd searched for news of Davey in penitentiaries and reformatories in London and the Home Counties for months, without success.

'You mean he didn't leave Britain?'

He nodded.

'That's right. David Macgregor is a lucky young rascal. There was an amendment made in criminal law at the time. He was under the age of sixteen and escaped transportation.'

'So what happened to him?'

'He was sent to Parkhurst Prison on the Isle of Wight, for a course of hard labour and reform The prison governor sent a favourable report about the boy to my office recently, recommending he be set free.' The Home Secretary gave Alistair a speculative glance. 'After the release was signed, the name rang a bell and I recalled you'd shown unusual interest in the case. I thought you'd like to know he was released, about a month ago.'

Alistair was annoyed with himself. Parkhurst jail! Of course he should have thought of that. It had a reputation for hard cases, but youngsters were imprisoned there too.

'Where is he now, sir?' he asked.

'Reunited with his family in Scotland, I imagine.' The gentleman smiled and went on his way.

Fate plays cruel tricks, Alistair thought. Mary-Ann was on the high seas, and there was no way of contacting her. It was a sad state of affairs. His son would have nobody to turn to now . . .

Ah, how he longed to meet his son, the only child he seemed likely to have! Once he had looked forward to being a loving husband to Mary-Ann and father of her children, but that dream had come to nothing, through no fault of his own. Now he was just a middle-aged bachelor who sought solace in work.

But he still had a son! Alistair's spirits lifted. He could travel to Forfar and meet David. He could even apply to be the lad's official guardian, now Mary-Ann and Ewan Macgregor had left the country.

There was a spring in his step as he followed the others down the lobby. He was impatient to be gone, but first he must listen to Prime Minister Robert Peel's speech, take part in the following debate, and attend to the business of the House . . .

Davey Macgregor had no idea whereabouts in England he was at that precise moment, but guessed it was not too far north of Birmingham.

After leaving Parkhurst four weeks ago, Davey had met a man called Ryan O'Sullivan lounging at the dock gates, on the lookout for likely lads to work on the London to Birmingham railway line. It had taken just a little blarney to persuade David Macgregor to join the railway gang.

Ryan O'Sullivan knew young lads fresh from Parkhurst jail were tempted by the promise of rich rewards as navigators – a word Ryan used advisedly, since it had better connotations than just plain 'navvy'. The lads were tough, used to hard physical labour and eager to earn good money.

Davey Macgregor, with barely two and six in his pocket, had proved no exception.

At the moment, O'Sullivan's team were excavating a long underground tunnel. The railway track must pass through a very sizeable hill. When Davey had first viewed the project, he had deemed it quite impossible. He was wiser now.

They began digging from either side of the hill, while also drilling down from above and working outwards from within. The main shaft had gone downward with the help of a winding engine, a large steam-driven horizontal wheel which lowered men down on hawsers to burrow into the excavation and heaved large buckets of earth back up top.

O'Sullivan was banksman in charge of the wheel, and had positioned Davey precariously at the edge of the shaft. He was ordered to lean out over the abyss with a pole, steering buckets away from the sides of the shaft. Nobody had told Davey the fate of the lad he had replaced at the job, but he feared the worst.

His thoughts turned longingly to Matthew as he sweated over the dangerous, arduous task. Matthew would have worked out a safer method of aligning the swaying buckets. He vowed never again to scoff at his half-brother's ingenuity. Davey aimed a kick at an empty bucket, which did not do his new moleskin trousers and boots any good. He muttered curses.

O'Sullivan laughed.

'Sure, that's fine cursing, Davey lad. You'll make a navvy yet.'

That was Davey's ambition, in fact. He'd bought trousers, boots and waistcoat with his first fortnight's wages. He intended returning to Forfar in style when the contract with O'Sullivan ended. He expected substantial wages and bonuses if the work was finished on time. He planned to return home with a jaunty step, the past behind him, a rainbow waistcoat on his back and sovereigns jingling in his pockets.

However, it was not for selfish ends that Davey craved the trappings of success. He wanted his mother to be proud of him . . .

On the long, weary journey to Australia, Danny had kept a careful tally of the days at sea. Mary-Ann knew that this was the ninetieth day, and land had been sighted far off, the first since the Cape of Good Hope.

There was an air of great excitement aboard. It was agreed that it had been a good journey on the whole, with only one outbreak of typhoid and four deaths among the steerage passengers. After passing the Cape, the clipper had run fast before a half-gale under reefed upper topsails for several days, averaging an impressive 14 knots.

Abraham told the passengers the entrance to the Bass Strait was not far off and the Cape Otway landfall light had been sighted. God willing, they would be berthed in Sydney harbour in a few days time.

Mary-Ann gathered her children in the family cabin for a talk, now that arrival was imminent.

She cast an anxious eye over them.

Shona and Agnes had guarded a milk and roses complexion against freckles, and would pass muster in the best society, thank goodness. Danny was as brown as a nut. She prayed he would not be branded a convict's child. She warned them to say, if asked, that they were Scottish emigrants who had come to join a craftsman father.

'Remember, you must not tell anyone that Papa and Davey were sentenced to be transported.'

'Can we tell lies, Mama?' Danny asked, hopefully.

'Well, honesty is the best craft, Danny. Maybe it's best if you children just keep quiet,' she said.

Shona grinned impishly.

'That suits me. I shall remain a woman of mystery, Mama. Men love that.'

Shona was well aware of her charms by now, having been much admired on the voyage, and was eager to make new conquests ashore. Agnes was homesick and scared, and only wanted to be back home in Scotland.

'Will Australians not like us if they know the truth?' she asked woefully.

Mary-Ann hugged her.

'Of course they'll like us, dear, who wouldn't? But we'll take no chances.'

Mary-Ann went on deck in the cool of evening. It was the time she liked best, when the strange southern stars were shining in the darkening sky and the clipper heeled and dipped with a life of its own.

She leaned on the rail.

So the longest journey was almost at an end! It felt strange for a woman born and bred in the heart of the countryside to feel nostalgia for the open sea, but she knew she would miss it, when they reached land. Yet she was longing to reach Sydney. She was confident she would soon find her husband and son. They could make a new life for themselves, persuade Matthew to join them. It could be a prosperous new beginning for the whole family . . .

'Mary-Ann!'

The whisper came out of the darkness, startling her.

'Who's there?'

'It is I, Louisa. Don't be afraid.' Her friend stepped out of the shadows and looked around furtively to make sure they were alone. 'I've been wanting to talk with you, Mary-Ann. You were kind enough to offer help, and I was very touched by that generous offer, though I did not expect to trouble you. But – but as it turns out . . .'

Louisa paused uncertainly.

Mary-Ann smiled.

'I can guess, my dear. You've decided to be sensible and accept what help I can give.'

She clasped Mary-Ann's arm with a trembling hand. She seemed greatly agitated.

'I guess that you are a Scottish lady travelling in style, to be with your husband who is in business in Sydney. Am I right?'

Mary-Ann didn't know what to say. If only the poor woman knew the true state of affairs!

'Well, I—'

Her friend continued desperately.

'All I need is a loan, Mary-Ann. I will repay it in full one day, with interest.'

'How – how much?'

'Fifty pounds.'

She gasped. The demand took her breath away. She did not know what to say. There were gold sovereigns and silver coins hidden in secret pockets in her walking out costumes and sewn into the hem of her gowns, but the hoard had been intended to keep her and the children while they searched for Ewan and Davey. They would need every penny themselves, but it was hard to refuse! The poor woman was awaiting a decision with pathetic eagerness.

'Louisa, I – I . . .'

'Yes?'

Mary-Ann struggled with the dilemma. A promise is a promise, and she hated to break it. Her offer of help had been genuine. She had even been prepared to pay for Louisa's food and lodgings, till her friend found her feet ashore.

But fifty pounds! How on earth would they manage, if she loaned Louisa such a large sum, with little prospect of seeing any of it returned?

Nine

Mary-Ann had hesitated a fraction too long, and Louisa Polpatrick looked hurt.

'You don't trust me!'

'No, it's not that.'

'What then?'

The night was warm, the clipper running free before a steady breeze, carrying them closer to Sydney with every passing hour. Mary-Ann sighed. She'd been acting ladylike, but if you try to stretch above your reach, you're sure to tumble, she thought.

'I'm not a wealthy lady, Louisa dear. I've been living a lie throughout the voyage.'

'What do you mean?'

'I'm a convict's wife. My husband and son were transported for a petty misdemeanour and we are travelling to Australia to find them. I only have a little money from the sale of my husband's business, and we could need every penny when we arrive. I'm so sorry.'

Far from being dismayed, Louisa looked delighted.

'My dear, how wonderful! You and I are in the same boat, two women facing adversity. This creates a much stronger bond, and we should enter into partnership! The business I have in mind cannot fail. All we need is an outlay of fifty pounds.'

'What sort of business?' Mary-Ann asked warily.

Louisa's eyes gleamed in the starlight.

'Merchandise! Even as a child I loved playing shops, Mary-Ann. I could persuade my friends to buy all sorts of things they didn't know they wanted.'

Mary-Ann couldn't help laughing.

'Maybe so, but what on earth does one sell to Australians?'

Louisa glanced over her shoulder and lowered her voice.

'I made friends with the ship's carpenter when my poor dear husband died, and he told me a Cape Town merchant had ordered a large quantity of goods, hoping to equip an evangelist's camp

in the wilds of Africa. At the last minute the missionaries went
down with a fever and went back home, the venture was cancelled
and the merchant left with goods on his hands. Do you remember
a loud argument in the cargo bay, when we arrived in Cape
Town?'

Mary-Ann nodded.

'Yes, I mind there was a rumpus. But what was in the cargo?'
She ticked items off on her fingers.

'Six bundles of shovels, seventy-eight camp ovens, ten kegs of
nails, goodness knows how much rope, canvas and tent poles, fifty
straw hats and pairs of breeches, seventy umbrellas and four bales
of dark blue cloth to cover natives' modesty. Drums of liquorice
juice, isinglass and gelatin, half a hundredweight of arrowroot,
two gallons of cod oil, a drum of glue, one hundred clay pipes
and enough tobacco to smoke out a wasps' nest – not to mention
bibles and sixty copies of the Reverend Samuel Rutherford's
uplifting sermons, destined to enlighten heathens. And it could
be ours, for fifty pounds!'

'It – it *does* seem a bargain,' she agreed doubtfully.

'It's heaven-sent, my dear! The carpenter tells me the captain
accepted the lot and hopes to sell it when we reach Sydney for
the first offer of fifty pounds.' Louisa gripped Mary-Ann's hands
excitedly. 'You *will* join me in this, won't you? It's a wonderful
stroke of luck.'

It seemed more like a gamble, Mary-Ann thought. Louisa
believed that playing shops was an amusing game, but Mary-Ann
had known the hard realities.

'I have fifty pounds – and – and more to spare, but—' she
began uncertainly.

Louisa hugged her.

'Splendid! I have a diamond necklace and earrings hidden away.
You buy the goods, and I will sell my jewels. It will be a wrench
to part with them, but they are only stones, after all!' She laughed
gaily. 'We can use the proceeds to rent premises and set up shop.
Then we can begin to make a fortune, Mary-Ann!'

'Louisa, pause a moment, please!' Mary-Ann cried. 'I must find
my husband and son first. I have no idea where they are and
that may involve some travel. If so, my children must not suffer
hardship!'

'Australia is vast, my dear! Far better to remain in Sydney and seek for news of your loved ones, who will find you more easily there. That seems much more sensible than setting off on a dangerous quest, with your children in tow. So you see, you must have a roof over your heads and some means of earning money,' Louisa argued reasonably.

'Yes. You are right,' Mary-Ann agreed.

She had not looked forward to arriving with three children, to find herself alone and friendless in a strange town. This way, she would have Louisa, a purpose in mind, and hopefully somewhere to live.

Mary-Ann smiled in the warm darkness.

'Wasn't it Napoleon who said the British were a nation of shopkeepers?'

'The wretched man meant it as an insult, of course!' Louisa laughed. 'But for once, he hit the nail right on the head, my dear!'

Mary-Ann lingered on deck after her friend had gone down below.

Now that she had thrown in her lot with Louisa Polpatrick there was no going back. Once more, the boats were recklessly burned.

Thoughts of Alistair Ross entered her mind on this balmy moonlight night, making the warmth seem suddenly oppressive. What was the true motive behind her reckless dash to the ends of the earth? Had she honestly set out to find Ewan, or was she running scared from a love affair with a man she had loved and lost?

Abraham the steward loomed out of the darkness.

'Not long now, Mrs Macgregor, ma'am. That light you see on the port beam is Cape Otway. Many a ship's been wrecked sailing bass strait between Otway and Van Diemen's Land.'

She shivered.

'I've heard of that place. It has a cruel reputation!'

He laughed equably.

'Reefs and rocks can be crueller than reputations, ma'am. The strait betwixt New South Wales and Van Diemen's Isle cuts near seven hundred mile off the voyage, so us sailors looks more kindly upon it, than those poor devils incarcerated ashore . . .'

★   ★   ★

Ewan Macgregor had not looked kindly upon Van Diemen's Land, perched beside the woman driver of the buggy. Admittedly, the foliage was lush and green and the high hill rising behind Hobart had reminded him of Scottish peaks. The roadway leading out of town was wide and smooth and he couldn't help remarking upon it.

Miss Rose shot him a cold glance.

'It was built by chain gangs. Convicts built all our roads, Macgregor, and an overseer made sure the work was well done.'

Ewan was outraged.

'With the aid of whip and baton, I suppose!'

She shrugged.

'When needed, no doubt.'

She turned her attention to the horse, gloved hands holding the reins, and Ewan lapsed into silence. He had nothing to say to the cold-hearted bitch.

They had not gone more than a mile from town before the horse wheeled smartly down a narrow, leafy lane. The animal knew shelter from heat and flies was near, and took off along the lane at a fast trot. The vista opened out into fields planted with vegetables and fruit, all neatly tended. Beyond rose a rough hillside dotted with sheep. The rural scene caught Ewan by surprise. Well-tended farmland made him feel homesick.

Miss Rose stopped the buggy in front of a squarely built stone house. A bright-eyed little black boy came running. She tossed down the reins and he caught them deftly.

'See to Pegasus, Tooke.'

'I do him, Missie Rose.' He grinned.

She clambered down and waited while Ewan retrieved his bundle.

'Follow me.'

He obeyed. She led him along a path skirting a graveyard, the grass freshly clipped around old headstones. The church which had once dominated the churchyard was a tumbled ruin of weeds and blackened stone.

'What happened to the kirk?' he asked.

She paused.

'It burned down.'

She stared at the ruin. She had thrown back the fly veil from

her face. He could see fine lines and a host of freckles, like a
common bondswoman working in the Forfar fields. He wondered
what the hands hidden by white cotton gloves were like. The
dustcoat was patched, the toes of the boots cracked and scuffed,
yet she carried herself like a lady.

He knew her type. In a previous existence he'd dealt with stiff-
necked gentry just like her, with scarce two farthings to rub
together.

The pale eyes seemed too bright as she gazed at the blackened ruin. Was that a sheen of tears? He wondered. Was it possible
that this cold female had a heart?

She roused herself.

'Come along!' she commanded in a tone he had not heard
since schooldays.

Marching ahead, she led him to a timber building roofed with
shingles and shaded by trees. 'This is the bunkhouse, Macgregor.
You will sleep and spend your leisure time here. You will be on
probation for a month. Kooka, the stable boy's mother, will ring
a bell at seven o'clock prompt. Be sure that you are clean and
tidy, then assemble with the other men in the kitchen for supper
and prayers.'

He raised his brows.

'And the rest of the evening?'

'There is a bible in the bunkhouse – if you can read.' She
turned her back on him.

Ewan muttered angrily under his breath.

'Cheeky besom!'

'I heard that! Report to the house at six tomorrow morning
and I will tell you what is to be done.'

He watched her go off down the path, then shoved open the
door and went inside. The interior was spacious and cool. There
was a hurried scuffling from four occupants seated round a table.
They were all older men. Ewan caught a glimpse of playing cards
and dice swiftly swept under the table.

They studied him with interest.

'G'day. Are you the craftsman she's been lookin' for?' one asked
in friendly fashion.

'I don't know about that. I'm a blacksmith to trade.'

'Ahh!'

They glanced at one another, grinning.

The grinning annoyed Ewan. He dumped his bundle on an unoccupied bunk.

'I was promised freedom when I arrived ashore. This doesn't feel like it.'

They laughed quite kindly. A spare grey-haired man clapped him on the shoulder.

'You don' pay no heed to Government promises, Jock. They're smoke in the wind. Look at us, f'r instance. We're old crawlers who've served out our time years ago, yet we're still prisoners, one way or t'other.'

'True enough,' another said, nodding. He jerked a thumb at the speaker. 'Old Enoch here was sent down for fourteen years in 1830 for having two pops an' a galloper.'

The old man cackled as Ewan looked blank.

'Highwayman, I was! Just a sideline, mind, when building trade was bad. I carried two old pistols unloaded and rode an old farm nag, but I never hurt nobody.'

Ewan frowned.

'You're free men! Why work for this woman?'

They looked away, down at their boots, anywhere but at him. Nobody spoke. Ewan could hear an assortment of insects buzzing against a fly-screen.

'The tucker's good,' Enoch said at last.

The others growled agreement.

'Meat, veg and pudden every day. Bread, butter and ewe's cheese for supper. Miss Rose don't work us too hard neither. We're craftsmen, like you. She's been building a team of skills. You're the last.'

'Why aren't you working today?'

They stared at him.

'It's Sunday! Miss Rose don't hold with work on the Sabbath. Prayer meeting was only called off 'cause she had word of a convict ship just in, with craftsmen aboard. She don't venture out on the Sabbath usually, but she's been huntin' a blacksmith for months.'

'What does she want wi' a smith?' Ewan asked uneasily.

'You'll find out soon enough. Sufficient unto the day is the evil thereof,' said Enoch, virtuously.

And the four resumed the game of poker they had abandoned.

Ewan lay down wearily on the bunk. He wished he had a likeness of Mary-Ann to gaze upon, but he had nothing, not even a letter. He closed his eyes and imagined he saw her smiling at him. It was torture of a kind. Did she still care, or had she gone running to Davey's father? And what had happened to the lad? Hardly a day passed but he worried about him and loved him, like one of his own. Where was he?

Davey had been a constant source of trouble to the black-smith, but having met Alistair Ross, Ewan now knew that the boy was a bright and brilliant academic like the natural father. He had realized months ago you don't beat gold into a plough-horse shoe, no matter how malleable it may be.

So he lay and wondered, imagined the worst, and felt like weeping . . .

Mary-Ann and Louisa had reached Sydney harbour and stood on the quayside. They were flushed with more than success, for it was January and unbearably hot. Louisa was dressed in grubby finery, but Mary-Ann's walking-out gown and petticoat felt the lighter of a hoard of coins.

Fifty pounds worth of packing cases lay piled on the quay before the two women. Mary-Ann clutched a thin purse, mostly containing silver and copper.

Shona and Agnes, dressed in sprigged muslin and floral bonnets, stood a good distance off, trying to appear as if they did not belong. Danny loitered unhappily with his sisters, decently attired, socked and booted, cap in hand, hair pomaded. He wore a lace collar Agnes had crocheted specially for the occasion. Had Danny been a lesser boy, he would have howled.

Mary-Ann eyed the stack of boxes.

'Now what do we do?'

Louisa was in her element. She glanced around.

'You, boy! Come here!'

She beckoned imperiously to a young man lounging on the canvas-shaded driving seat of an empty wagon, the horse drowsing between the shafts.

He jabbed a thumb at his chest.

'Who, me?'

Her glare brought him over at a laconic saunter.

'G'day, both.' He touched the brim of a stained leather hat with a forefinger. All that could be seen of his eyes were two little sparks of bright blue.

'Is that wagon for hire?' Louisa demanded.

He straightened.

'It is now.'

'Load these packing cases, please.'

'Where d'you want them taken?'

That was a problem. Mary-Ann spoke up.

'We've just arrived, hoping to find lodgings and business premises. Our stock is in the cases. Do you know of anywhere suitable?' She allowed the coins in her purse to jingle. The shadowed blue eyes gleamed. 'And quite cheap,' she added hastily.

The young man fingered his chin.

'There is a place empty, north end of Macquarie Street. Shop with living quarters above. I could fix it with the owner, quite reasonable.'

'Could you? We would be so grateful, Mr—?' She smiled charmingly.

'Gideon Jones, ma'am.'

He yelled at two or three loafers taking their ease in the shade.

The men obligingly loaded the cart and Mary-Ann doled out more coins from the skinny purse. Gideon eyed the jaded travellers. The sun made its contrary journey northwards across a cloudless sky and the day was even hotter.

'The little 'un can ride with me, the ladies follow after, in a hire carriage.'

He let out a piercing whistle that earned Danny's admiration. A smart little horse and carriage appeared and Mary-Ann, Louisa and the two girls climbed gratefully under the fringed hood.

Gideon lifted Danny on to the driving seat of the cart and the little cavalcade set off.

Danny wriggled.

'Something snuffled my leg!'

'Just Kelpie, my dog. He's under your seat. Don' you fret, he don't bite.'

Danny was intrigued.

'Mama read to me about kelpies, they're water fairies.'

'My dog don' fancy bathing. So your ma reads you stories?'

'Yes. Does your mama read to you?'

'Never knew her, sonny. She ended in the women's peniten-
tiary at Parramatta, marshy place, means place of the eels in
Aborigine lingo, if you're interested.'

Danny immediately forgot Mary-Ann's warning.

'My papa's a convict. We've come here to find him an' my
brother.'

'That so?' He glanced down thoughtfully at the boy. 'Lucky
you have a pa to find.'

Danny put a hand under the seat and encountered a moist,
nuzzling nose.

'I hate wearing this soppy lace collar,' he confided to his new-
found friends.

'Things you don' like, you don' have to suffer,' Gideon said.

'Oh yes I do! My sister Agnes knitted it.'

And Danny sighed, resignedly . . .

Mary-Ann and Louisa were agreeably surprised, driving along
Sydney streets.

'It is quite civilized!' exclaimed Louisa, who had expected the
worst.

Tawny sandstone buildings would not have disgraced an English
provincial town, and terraces of houses with ironwork balconies
were all most reassuring. The road, if dusty, was wide and smooth.
Mary-Ann's spirits rose. She felt confident that she would find
Ewan and Davey quite easily, if they were here.

Gideon stopped the cart outside a stone building whose ground
floor consisted of a variety of shops, the upper storeys given over
to living quarters with wrought-iron balconies.

Gideon strolled across, having lifted Danny down. Trotting at
their heels was the oddest-looking dog Mary-Ann had ever
seen. Its sharp ears were alert, reddish coat thick and wiry. A
pink tongue lolled in a grin. It trotted along on strong, stubby
legs a plumed tail creating a friendly breeze. Danny patted the
dog.

'Mama, this is Kelpie. He don' bite.'

'Which breed is he?' she asked curiously.

Gideon smiled.

'Bit of this, that and t'other, plus dingo, which is native.'

He produced a bunch of keys and fitted one into the lock of an empty shop.

The women were surprised.

'Should you not ask the owner's permission, first?' Louisa remarked.

He grinned.

'I am the owner, lady. Profit I make from haulage goes into property.'

They followed him inside. The shop was quite large enough to display everything.

Upstairs, the living quarters were simply furnished but spotlessly clean. Mary-Ann remarked upon the fact to Gideon.

'Too right. Last tenant's wife was a house-proud English chum. Husband came out hoping to make a fortune, but they sailed off home in the wet, broke. Some folks don' take kindly to Australian ways.'

'Well, we intend to make a go of it, young man!' Louisa declared.

'Down to business then,' he said. 'Rent, five shillings a month, payable in advance, 'case you shoot through. Guinea deposit 'gainst damage and repairs, returnable if there ain't none. I won't charge haulage, this time. That's fair.'

Mary-Ann paid up and was left with a pittance. Louisa eyed the slender purse and spoke up in her loftiest tones.

'I would be obliged if you could direct me to an establishment where I might realize some assets, Mr Jones.'

He grinned.

'No sweat, lady. There's a pawnbroker down by the docks.'

He lifted the hat in farewell, revealing a thatch of tawny hair, eyes of startling blue, tanned skin and very white teeth.

Shona gasped and stared after him.

'Oh, Agnes, isn't he so handsome and dashing?'

'I couldn't see past the awful hat,' her sister said jealously.

Agnes had noticed the young man's frank appraisal of Shona's charms and had been favoured with a blue-eyed wink herself, but all Agnes wanted was to find Papa and Davey quickly as possible and go home to Scotland. She looked around their sparse new surroundings, and wiped away a homesick tear.

★　　★　　★

Alistair Ross had not left for Scotland as planned, after hearing that his son had been freed from Parkhurst jail. Affairs of state had intervened and Alistair remained in London until a few weeks before Parliament reassembled after the Christmas recess, in early 1850.

Queen Victoria's dislike of Henry Palmerston, which, given Her Majesty's passionate nature amounted to hatred, kept Alistair busy soothing fierce wrangles between a volatile Foreign Secretary and offended Queen. At last, Alistair could be spared for a few days, and set off for Forfar in keen anticipation.

He was in excellent spirits as he travelled through bare, snow-dusted countryside. He could hardly wait to meet his son for the very first time.

Leaving his baggage at the inn, he set out eagerly to walk to the smiddy. A damp chill struck him as he walked. Frosty rime rose mistily from the surface of the loch penetrating the fine cloth of a London overcoat. Shivering, he turned up the velvet collar and wished he'd had the sense to bring a muffler.

Of course the fine gentleman attracted attention. A bowler hat with curly brim had not been seen in Forfar, and word of the new fashion was soon carried into the nearest hostelry. Mangling Maggie met the handsome gentleman at the smiddy gate and recognized him as the man who had visited Mary-Ann Macgregor once. She dropped the man a curtsey and turned sharp right towards the laird's mansion, to pass on this interesting titbit of news to her second cousin Phyllis, the laird's housemaid.

Alistair paused in the yard. The big doors leading into the smiddy stood open beneath the sculpted stone horseshoe, which formed the archway overhead. The forge glowed red, sparks flew and the steady clang of hammer on anvil rang out sharp and clear. His heart beat fast. Had David returned, to follow the blacksmith's trade? He went inside.

Matthew looked up, and almost missed a stroke.

'You've a nerve, coming here!'

'I came to see David,' Alistair said.

He noted that the lad had grown into a powerful young man, big and handsome.

Matthew stared, frowning.

'Davey? But he isn't here.'

'Where is he?'

'Stop playing games with me, Mr Ross!' Matthew cried. 'Your son was transported, and serve him right. Davey was the ruin of my family!'

That jibe infuriated Alistair.

'At least he did not steal from his mother. You left her short of funds which she entrusted to you.'

'It – it was a mistake.' Matthew looked stricken. His mother's letter had made light of the matter, but his conscience remained heavy with guilt.

'What's done is done,' Alistair said, more leniently. 'But David never left these shores. He was imprisoned on the Isle of Wight, and freed months ago to make his way home. So where is he, Matthew?'

The lad shrugged.

'I don't know. He has not come back to Forfar. I honestly thought he was in Australia, with my father.'

Alistair believed him. Bitterly disappointed, he prepared to leave.

'When David returns, will you tell him I was searching for him? Ask him to please write to me at this address.' He handed Matthew his card. Matthew glanced at it briefly.

'I won't promise you anything.'

Alistair was enraged.

'For heaven's sake, Matthew, David's your brother!'

The young lad stared at him, coldly.

'No, sir. He's your son.'

Alistair left without a word, frustrated and angry.

Wullie strolled in. He had been bending hickory wood in the kiln for a racing sulky the laird's son fancied, in order to cut a dash in town.

'Thon's a familiar face that went glowerin' past. I could see there was something heavy on his mind,' he remarked.

Matthew grunted, putting in vicious effort with the bellows.

'Whatever bothered the man, I fancied thon bowler with the curly brim,' Wullie continued. 'I'll maybe step into Sturrock the draper and order one for mysel'. Sturrock kens the business of every visitor that stops at the inn.'

He lit a taper from the blazing forge and attended to his pipe. He cast a canny glance at Matthew.

'By the by, was it you that went into Sturrock's women's department, last weekend?'

Matthew blushed scarlet.

'I bought gloves for Janet Golightly. Her hands were freezing.'

Wullie raised his eyebrows.

'You'd ken, of course, after holding them.'

Matthew was left speechless.

Alistair decided there was no point lingering in Forfar, hoping that his son might arrive. He was desperately worried. It was months since David had been set free. Anything could have happened, the most likely being that he had fallen into bad company. Despite Robert Peel's efforts to establish an effective police force, the streets of London remained dangerous. Even fashionable Belgravia had been renamed 'Burglar-ia' by a wag. Alistair shuddered at the thought of his son being corrupted by criminal elements. The sooner he returned to the capital and resumed his search, the better.

But next day, he received an unexpected visitor.

Alistair had met the laird of Graystones in Edinburgh, while attending the St Clair wedding, the events of that day forever memorable, because of the meeting with Mary-Ann. He was pleased to find the spry old gentleman waiting for him after breakfast that morning. They greeted one another cordially and withdrew to a quiet corner to talk.

'To what do I owe the pleasure of your visit, sir?' Alistair asked.

The laird smiled, cannily.

'I was told you had shown an interest in the smiddy folk, Mr Ross. The reason for your visit has aroused speculation.'

'And my interest there is nobody's business but my own! However, I don't mind telling you my concern is for the two Macgregor lads, left without parents. David escaped transportation, and was freed from Parkhurst prison some months ago. There's been no word of him since, and I'm extremely worried.'

The laird's keen eyes fixed upon him.

'So you would be – naturally!'

Alistair stared.

'Sir, is it possible that – that you know—?'

The laird held up a hand, checking him.

'I'm a lawyer, Mr Ross. It's my business to form an opinion and keep it to mysel'. Don't fret. I'll do all I can to find your boy, if you'll just oblige me.' He reached into his pocket and drew out a long envelope, which he laid on the table.

'This document contains evidence which will ensure a full pardon for Ewan Macgregor. The man's only fault was overzealous protection of a young lass whose father was at death's door and a lad who tried to help them. It contains sworn statements from the lass and my repentant gamekeeper, a man well known for grabbing the wrong end o' the stick and using it.'

Alistair looked at the envelope, frowning.

'But sir, what can I do?'

The laird leaned forward and pushed the document towards him.

'Take it. You can bring the evidence to the Home Secretary's attention. I want Ewan Macgregor and his wife back in Forfar, where they belong. Never mind the cost, I will bear it. Scotland can ill afford to lose men and women of their stature!'

'But, sir—' Alistair began, desperately.

The old man's stern eyes seemed to bore into him.

'I judge you to be an honourable man, Mr Ross. You will do your utmost to make sure Ewan Macgregor is pardoned, and reunited with his bonny wee wife.'

How much did the wise old man guess, and what did he know? Alistair wondered uneasily.

He picked up the fateful document that would set Mary-Ann's husband free, and cursed the responsibility that had been thrust upon him.

Ten

In New South Wales, the travellers settled down in the strange new environment of Sydney. Town. Danny kicked off boots and socks in the attic room allocated to him and tore off the hated lace collar, safe at last from Agnes's wrath. Danny's room faced the main street and Mary-Ann had feared it might prove noisy, though Danny had been known to sleep through thunderstorms.

He loved this room. Danny lost no time opening the skylight and leaning out to view passers-by on the street. Wouldn't the girls be jealous!

'Ouch!' He soon leaped back inside. The metal was burning hot beneath a blazing sun.

Agnes was grousing about the other attic room that she and Shona shared. It overlooked a courtyard with communal well, row of privies and washing lines.

'Why can't we have the view Danny has?' she moaned.

Shona unpinned her hair, letting it fall around her shoulders. She studied the effect in the glass with pleasure.

'No doubt Mama had my honour in mind,' she said smugly. 'A lover could easily signal from the street, and Gideon Jones couldn't take his eyes off me.'

Agnes scowled.

'He's a flirt. He gave me the wink too.'

'He must've had dust in his eye and been half-blind.'

Agnes flung a hairbrush furiously, with accurate aim.

'Oww! You horrible little beast,' her sister howled.

Downstairs, Mary-Ann sighed. Her daughters were forever squabbling, and the rows threatened to become more heated the older they grew. It would have been wiser to separate the two, but she and Louisa Polpatrick occupied the two main bedrooms above the shop.

Shutting her ears to the quarrel, Mary-Ann returned to the

letter she was writing, seated in the parlour on the ground floor, behind the shop premises.

She had already written to Matthew, telling him they had arrived safely and found comfortable lodgings. She had ended the letter lovingly, with a confident assurance that Papa and Davey would soon be found and returned to the bosom of the family. She made no mention of money, or lack of it.

With that letter sealed, she had braced herself to write another, this time to Alistair Ross, as promised. She gave a brief account of the voyage, making light of storms, discomfort, a monotonous diet, and heat. She told him that they were well housed in Sydney and she had made friends with an amiable lady. She paused, wondering whether to mention the business venture, and decided against it. It would sound even more risky when set down on paper.

Instead, she wrote cannily: '*I plan to find employment to keep me occupied while searching for Ewan and David within the confines of the town. I may have good news for you in that direction, very soon . . .*'

After some hesitation she ended, '*I am, sir, yours sincerely, Mary-Ann Macgregor.*

It sounded cool and formal but what else could she write? Her true state of mind would make strange reading: *In tears, alone in a strange land, longing for a husband's comfort and strength, grieving for a first love's lost friendship. Confused and very lonely – Mary-Ann.*

Louisa's priority had been a thorough scrub in clean cool water with carbolic and a dash of sulphur. She unearthed a hip bath and dragged it into her room, then found two large pitchers, which she filled at the well. She could hardly lift them when full.

Changed days, my lady! She thought grimly. She had never shown a spark of sympathy for servant girls who had toiled upstairs to keep her scented bath filled, in happier times. Ah, but she was a much humbler, more appreciative person now!

A little later, Louisa emerged glowing from the bathtub. She discarded filthy clothes and stepped into an embroidered silk wrap in Japanese style, which she had grabbed on impulse when fleeing the country, mainly because it took up little space.

The cool silk felt wonderful against her skin, feet thrust into slippers, no corsets to pinch and itch, no crinoline cage to stiffen petticoats, no yards of material to hamper and hinder easy movement. Only a new lightness and heady freedom.

Louisa Polpatrick, new woman, opened the door boldly and stepped out into the future.

Mary-Ann joined her friend downstairs in the shop, later. Shona had discovered priceless treasure in the parlour when they arrived.

'A piano. Mama!'

It was a musical instrument of sorts, Mary-Ann thought with a smile, running her fingers over the keys. It sounded tinny and sadly in need of tuning, but provided her children with absorbing amusement. Shona had taken piano lessons at school and played well. Her lovely voice, Agnes's youthful contralto and Danny's choirboy treble sounded pleasantly in Mary-Ann's ears as she descended the stairs and found her friend busy with a claw hammer.

'What are you doing?'

'Examining the stock, my dear. Come and see.'

Louisa had prised open packing cases and the floor was strewn with a variety of strange objects.

This was Mary-Ann's first viewing of their purchases, and she was shocked.

'Lord preserve us! What a load of rubbish!'

'Nonsense! Useful articles every household should have!' Louisa declared happily. She held up odd-looking headgear for Mary-Ann's inspection.

'Pith helmets, dear. They are ever so cool, you know. Gentlemen wear them in the tropics. Come and give a hand with these kegs of nails and bales of canvas.'

Mary-Ann obeyed, but with serious reservations. She had hoped for straw boaters, ladies bonnets and dressmaking material.

'Louisa, we'll never sell this stuff!'

She looked astonished.

'Why not?'

'Because we're women! Men won't expect ladies to sell buckets, shovels and nails. It's not natural. They'll avoid us like the plague!'

Louisa sighed.

'Well really, Mary-Ann, I never thought that you, of all people, would be so staid!'

Mary-Ann looked indignant.

'I sold fire tongs and cartwheels when I was a working woman, Louisa, but you're a lady born and bred, and it shows!'

'Oh, fiddle de dee! Lady no more.' She laughed airily. 'I am not wearing corsets and it feels wonderful. I may never wear corsets again. You should try it, my dear.'

And Mary-Ann was left speechless.

Many miles away from Sydney, across the Bass Strait in Van Diemen's Land, Ewan Macgregor was far from happy. Miss Rose Bates had presided over an excellent supper, followed by prayers and bible readings – carefully chosen with a newcomer in mind, Ewan suspected.

She gave him a pointed glare before she read . . .

'Joy shall be in heaven over one sinner that repenteth, over more than ninety and nine just persons which need no repentance . . .'

It took much restraint not to growl, 'speak for yoursel', woman!'

Then Miss Rose prayed vehemently for the Almighty to show mercy upon poor misguided sinners given into her charge.

Ewan fumed with indignation, but his four companions in adversity did not appear to care, dozing peacefully throughout the long intercession and only rousing to intone a hearty

'A-a-a-men' which closed the proceedings.

Next morning, vigorous handbell ringing roused the bunkhouse. Enoch and the others crawled out of bed yawning and scratching, but Ewan was already up and about. He had slept lightly and wakened very much earlier. Always fastidious, he dressed and went outside to wash in the stream beside the bunkhouse. After, he washed his shirt and spread it upon rocks to dry in the sun. Bare-chested, he walked along the path towards the church. The desolate place had interested him.

When he reached the ruin, he stopped to examine it more closely. To his surprise, there was a sudden movement within, and Miss Rose stepped through the blackened archway that had once housed a doorway. She was as startled as he, staring with heightened colour at the bare chest and shoulders, and then looking hastily away.

She was hatless this morning and he noted her confusion with amusement. So his nakedness embarrassed her. Serve her right!

'Good morning to you,' he called.

She regained composure and approached. The cotton gloves were off, the hands red and roughened, though the fingers were long and shapely. Capable hands. He granted her that.

She became businesslike.

'A fortunate meeting, Macgregor. I can discuss what is expected of you without interruption. The shipboard report claims you are intelligent. That will be put to the test.'

'Oh, indeed?'

The insolence was not lost upon her. She met his gaze coldly.

'The report also notes that you are stubborn, puffed up with pride. Those vices are of no use to me, I warn you.'

He laughed.

'Good. I assure you I'm stubborn as a mule and proud as a peacock. I'll away and pack my gear right away.'

She ignored that, her attention returning to the ruin behind her. She was silent for a minute or two, and when she spoke, it was in a gentler tone.

'I want to rebuild the church, Macgregor. That is why I have gathered craftsmen here. When the work is finished you are all free to go wheresoever you please. That is a promise.'

Ewan was startled.

'What? It could take years of hard work to raise that heap of rubble from the ground, not to mention a rich man's fortune and many more good men than you have mustered!'

She shrugged.

'I have only the cash that can be spared from the farm and the wool trade. But dressed stones lie there for the using and there is ample timber to be had in the forest. Now that I have found a blacksmith, I have five carefully selected craftsmen. All that is needed now to rebuild the church is God's help.'

He stared incredulously.

'Woman, this is daft! I noticed fine spires in Hobart. Why rebuild this wreck?'

She hesitated a moment.

'My brother came to Van Diemen's Land twelve years ago, and I came from England to keep house for him. He had made this church a place of peace and sanctuary, before it was maliciously destroyed. He died in the fire, trying to save it.'

'You seem bitter, Miss Rose,' he observed.

She whirled to face him.

'I have every right! Those he tried to help started the fire deliberately. He wasted his life ministering to wicked, worthless convicts. This was the thanks he got!'

'So that is why you hate us!' he said, enlightened.

'Do you blame me?'

He shrugged.

'I pity you, but the work can't be done without us. That's your dilemma.'

'Save your pity for yourself,' she said coldly. 'I have only to lodge one complaint with the constables to have you imprisoned.'

'Just a minute!' he cried angrily. 'The others have served their time and are free men, and if I'm scunnered with you, I can leave. Exile from my native land was the price I paid for freedom.'

'Not if you offend me, Mr Macgregor!'

They glared at each other. It was an impasse. Miss Rose turned on her heel.

'Plans and working details are in the house. You and the others will study them after breakfast. Then you will make a start to clearing the site.'

She walked away. Defeated, he watched her go.

She held the trump card. The vixen!

Alistair Ross considered himself fortunate to have reached London before Parliament resumed after the Christmas recess. Winter storms had set in after his meeting with the laird, and roads were impassable.

Although by now he had returned to Westminster over a month ago, he had not handed the document to the Home Secretary, which would secure Ewan Macgregor's release. Alistair was not sure why he hesitated, but the envelope lay on his desk, unopened.

Today he was more concerned about a letter received from the governor of Parkhurst prison confirming David Macgregor had been released several months ago with sufficient funds to carry him home to Scotland. The governor understood that the missing youth had relatives in London. Perhaps they could help?

Alistair despaired. Casting his mind back to his courtship of

Mary-Ann, he could recall no London relatives. Her parents were dead, so where could he look? It seemed an impossible task, yet there must be something hidden in the past, which would give a clue to his son's disappearance.

He rose and went to the window. The cold was so intense there was frost in intricate patterns obscuring the windowpane. He traced a straight track abstractedly through the ice with a fingertip, and suddenly recalled that, from the 1820s onwards, Mary-Ann's father had worked as foreman overseer on the railway. Mr St Clair, who had invested heavily in the new project, had valued him highly. Indeed, that was why the St Clairs had taken Mary-Ann into their care as nursemaid, when she was orphaned at fourteen. Was it possible that the lad had decided to follow in his grandfather's footsteps?

It was an exciting thought. Somehow, Alistair did not think his son would turn to crime, but he might well have been ashamed to return home till he had made good. Work on the railway might seem a natural choice if the opportunity arose. Navvies could command high wages. They were strong, swaggering men, hard drinkers, but confident of respect, and that aspect of the job might appeal to a youth fresh from a humiliating spell in prison. It was a possibility, and a daunting one. The railway network was complex, and growing daily . . .

The tunnel north of Birmingham was a vast undertaking, nearly a mile of track burrowing through rocky hillside, and Davey Macgregor was still there. He had gained promotion after months of hard work. Another youngster had been selected to replace him on the freezing hilltop beside the winding engine.

David Macgregor was digging dirt, 90 ft down inside the earth.

They said it took a year to make a navvy, but he had short-ened the process, by popular demand. His grandfather O'Malley was still remembered and revered by older workmates, and after six months Davey was permitted to pay for the traditional two gallons of beer and accepted into one of sixty gangs of men working inside the tunnel. He was given a navvy name in a solemn ceremony, during which the two gallons were drunk. The name given was in deference to the young lad's undoubted brain-power.

David Macgregor became Professor, or Prof, for short.

Despite back-breaking work and harsh conditions, Davey was happy. He was well paid, sometimes earning eighteen shillings a week on six-hour shifts. He was careful with money, and took care not to become blind drunk, and open to thievery.

The gangs lived in shanty towns erected at both entrances to the tunnel, while burrowing through to a central shaft, from either end.

An old body named Peg, who earned a few pence for the privilege, tended David's hut. An orphan lass called Molly, selected at random from a Birmingham workhouse, had been brought in to do fetching, carrying and dirty work. Peg presided over a wash copper, lines of steaming washing draped above, and cauldrons of soup, boiled beef and porridge, kept well out of reach of packs of bull terriers and lurchers, much beloved by navvies.

It was an arrangement that suited everyone, including Molly the skivvy, bedded in a separate store shed with old Peg. The men treated the fifteen-year-old waif with rough courtesy and banter, which she returned in kind. On Saturday nights, navvies went on the batter, sending the surrounding countryside into a state of fear and alarm.

Forfar and Parkhurst seemed a lifetime away, and Davey did not dwell upon the past. He bought the best pick and shovel money could buy, a pair of fine quality moleskin trousers for best, and a rainbow-coloured waistcoat to flaunt beneath a blue velvet jacket. His latest acquisitions were a bowler hat with curled brim and a white-spotted red neckerchief. Stepping out on a Saturday night for a modest pint of ale, the Professor was a handsome dandy.

Davey was on night shift in the chilly month of February 1850.

Not that night or day mattered, when working underground. He whistled as he shouldered pickaxe and shovel. The arched entrance to the tunnel was completed in dressed stonework and he paused to admire it in moonlight. The tunnel mouth was like an entrance to Hell, lit by hundreds of lamps and fire-baskets slung along the length of the interior. It was satisfying to think he'd played a part in the marvellous feat of engineering. Grandpa O'Malley would have been proud!

The peculiar smell of the huge undertaking invaded his

nostrils as he stepped out of the chill night air – a smell compounded of burning tar barrels and smoking torches, hot metal, and the resinous smell of massive timber props shoring up the 25 ft archway. Added to that was the animal stench of sweating men and horses, and an overpowering smell of damp, disturbed earth.

A hideous din echoed down the completed section. Hammering, shouting and hissing of steam as he approached the central shaft deafened him. The winding engine groaned, squealed and clanked as it lifted tons of earth skywards, from the diggings below.

Davey picked his way past gangs of men stripped to the waist. He paid no heed to weird echoes and garbled commands, or water flowing past his boots in a steady, trickling stream.

A daunting scene, soon to be made worse! he thought as he reached his destination, an outcrop of rock at the head of the work-ings. He studied it with expert eye by the flickering light of torches. Four members of his own gang were clambering over the greasy rock face with the agility of monkeys. Davey joined them.

'Here's the Professor,' one of them grinned. 'A pint o' bitter all round if he don't tell us we've mined the blasted outcrop wrong.'

Davey studied the boreholes.

'So you have. If you study the rock strata and calculate the mechanics of this explosion, you can see the boreholes should be deeper to have greater effect upon the mass of rock. Another borehole here, and here, would be more advantageous.'

The judgement was greeted with hoots of laughter. The over-seer sighed.

'You could be right, Professor, but must you use words as big as your bloody head?'

At last each hole was charged with gunpowder, and the fuses run. Warning bells tolled and work stopped. All the men in the workings trudged back to the entrance, crouching behind safety barricades. An expectant hush fell.

'Wouldn't be surprised if this were the breakthrough, mates,' someone muttered.

Davey hoped so. There would be celebrations if the blast brought down the last remaining obstacle and two sides of the tunnel were united at last. Beer all round, and . . .

'I thought you'd welcome a flagon o' tay, Davey, as it's so cold.'

Startled, he looked round. The workhouse lass stood a few feet away in the passageway, unaware of the danger. She stood directly in the path of a huge blast that would send small rocks and large stones hurtling far and wide. The explosion, he reckoned, was imminent.

'Look out!' he yelled. And made a dive for her.

Even as he pinned her to the ground beneath him, the earth shook with a fearsome rumble and debris and flying stones engulfed them in clouds of dust. He felt a stunning blow on the back of the head and warm blood trickled down his face. He was not aware of pain, only the girl's faint whisper in his deafened ears.

'Davey, you saved my life. I'll never forget—'

And that was all he heard, as the scene darkened and faded.

February weather was having a devastating effect upon Forfar's linen trade. Mill dams froze solid and water-powered works ground to a halt. Bleaching linen was impossible. Deep snow filled every crevice and knife-edged snowdrifts blocked roads. Carts could not move, and orders went unfulfilled.

Atrocious weather meant coal wagons and carts could not get through from the seaport. That was a hardship for Forfar householders, forced to burn wood to keep warm, and a disaster for the smiddy. Matthew could not operate the forge, without special small coal from Fifeshire pits. He and Wullie were on an enforced holiday.

In the smiddy-seat, Wullie stretched out his feet to a log fire.

'Baxter's have laid off ninety spinners at Glamis, the lade's frozen, and machines lying idle,' he remarked.

Matthew was working at the table, drawing with T-square and set square. He had taught himself engineering draughtsmanship, and found he had a natural aptitude for it.

'Aye, and frost burst a boiler in the laird's mill, Wullie,' he said. 'Luckily nobody was hurt, but it could've been a disaster. I saw it coming and warned the millwright the metal was too thin and a side weld faulty, but the man paid no heed. The laird was nowhere to be found, or I would have told him, and something might have been done.'

Mrs Wullie paused, turning the heel of a sock.

'The laird's poorly. Phyllis says it could be inflammation o' the lungs.'

Her husband looked grave.

'We'll be in dire straits if that good man doesna recover.'

Matthew looked up.

'Why's that?'

'Because we'd be at the mercy o' the laird's son.'

'But he's well-liked. He's a fine young gentleman.'

'So he is. But he went to an English school and spends more time in London than Forfar.'

'That would change if he was laird.'

'Naw, it wouldna. He doesn't want the scunner of running an estate and would sell it to builders for housing plots. You'll maybe not have noticed while out courtin' that lass, but there's new houses springing up here, there and everywhere. Some folk are no' short of a bob or two and keen to put on a grand show.'

Matthew was shocked.

'What will happen to Janet's job, and the smiddy?'

'She'll be out on her ear and the smiddy will be the first to go, to make way for a rich man's dwelling. It's a braw site, handy for the town.'

Mrs Wullie resumed knitting.

'Aye, Forfar's prosperous, and growing fast. It'll maybe come true what's predicted years ago – Forfar will be Forfar still, when Dundee's all pulled down . . .'

Mary-Ann was dreaming longingly of snowy winters, that February. Sydney was in the grip of a heat wave. Working in the shop was hot and exhausting.

Not that business was booming, though!

Showing off an odd assortment of items to best advantage, had very little effect upon sales. She and Louisa had polished buckets and shovels to make them look more attractive, but they remained unsold. As for kegs of nails, rolls of coarse canvas and tangles of thick wire and rope! These defeated even Mary-Ann's ingenuity, and drove her to despair.

Pathetic pith helmets made a laughing stock of all their efforts at tasteful display. Sydneysiders would not be seen dead in them, despite blazing sun.

'G'day.'

Mary-Ann looked up to find Gideon Jones in the shop.

'Don' look like you ladies sold much,' he remarked.

She sighed and glanced across the shop, where Louisa was deep in hushed discussion with a female customer.

'Only medications, I'm afraid.'

Louisa handed over a small bottle filled with black liquid, which the customer swept furtively into her bag. Money changed hands, and Louisa smiled. 'If that doesn't do the trick, I have something guaranteed to move mountains.'

The customer scuttled out and Louisa strolled across. She wore a loose silken gown and looked quite cool and delighted with herself.

'Another two shillings, for a concoction of senna pods and liquorice juice. This town is in desperate need of an apothecary and we have means at our disposal to supply that need, Mary-Ann. Soon, I hope to have enough saved to order more supplies sent out from England.'

Mary-Ann frowned.

'We won't survive for long on proceeds from liquorice juice and camphor oil. We must sell everything, or go under.'

She felt hot, tired and irritable. She had hoped her daughters would help out in the shop to give herself and Louisa a break, but they'd rebelled. So she had packed them all off to school, protesting loudly. Shona was earning a small wage, teaching singing and piano, and Agnes and Danny were unwilling pupils. Mary-Ann could ill afford the fees, but the expense was worth it, for the sake of peace and quiet.

Gideon had been studying items on sale.

'If customers don' come to goods, take goods to customers, I'd say. Makes sense. Find yourselves a cart, get out of town an' go walkabout in the bush, where this stuff's more precious 'n gold.'

Mary-Ann considered the idea, which had merit. A pity it was impossible.

'No, Gideon. It can't be done. We don't know the country, and besides the risk would be too great for women travelling alone.'

'No risk if you hire my cart, ma'am, which is all fitted up for comfortable journeying. I'd drive you myself, if we can settle a fair price for hire an' percentage commission on sales.'

Louisa looked shocked.

'Out of the question! Your travelling arrangements are quite improper, Mr Jones. What would people think?'

He grinned.

'In the outback, ma'am, nobody would bat an eyelid.'

She turned to Mary-Ann.

'I've had my say and it's up to you, Mary-Ann, but I warn you, I'll have nothing to do with such a journey.'

Mary-Ann was in a quandary. She longed to accept Gideon's offer, which apart from boosting sales, meant venturing farther afield in the search for Ewan and Davey, which had proved fruitless so far. On the other hand, she did appreciate her friend's point of view.

It was a dilemma, and she was not sure what to do.

Eleven

Mary-Ann decided that desperate times needed desperate solutions. She would take the risk and go with Gideon.

'I proved that I can take care of myself on the voyage, Louisa. Now I have the chance to improve sales and widen the search for my husband and son. Gideon will be coachman and I will travel with him. It is just a business arrangement, after all.'

'That's not the point, my dear! We should be showing these uncivilized people a better example!' Louisa protested.

'Hey, ma'am, less of the—' Gideon began indignantly.

'Oh, be quiet!' she snapped. 'It's all your fault, encouraging wild Scottish ways.'

He took one look at Mary-Ann's angry expression and tried to calm the situation.

'Why don' I load the selling goods on to my cart, Mis' Mary-Ann, and you follow behind in a pretty little covered wagon with good-natured old horse, easy handled for lady-driving? Little more pricey, o' course, seeing how the wagon has every convenience for comfort, such as insect-screens an' driver's dust coat. Water barrels extra.'

Mary-Ann thought about the suggestion. She nodded thoughtfully.

'Surely you can't object to that, Louisa?'

'Indeed I do! Why doesn't Gideon go out into the wilderness himself and sell the goods, if he's so keen?'

He shook his head

'No, ma'am! I'm your man for real estate, houses, wagons and horses. I don' go selling little-bitty stuff.'

'Give me patience with the pair of you!' Louisa sighed.

Mary-Ann tried reasoning with her.

'We are all agreed that something drastic must be done if the business is to succeed, Louisa. Why don't I accept Gideon's offer and see how it goes? You could keep an eye on the bairns and tend the shop, while I'm away.'

She flung up her hands in horror.

'Oh no! I can't look after children. I never had any and would not know what to do with them. I'm sorry, Mary-Ann, but if you are determined to risk your life, limb and reputation, you must make other arrangements.'

This was the last straw.

'Then let's just forget the whole miserable business!' Mary-Ann cried in despair.

'Not so hasty!' Gideon said. 'I have an answer to the fix. Take the family with us.'

'But they're still at school!' she protested.

'There's no learning done in summer heat, Mis' Mary-Ann. School will be closing soon anyway, 'cause of fire risk in the dry.'

She considered the suggestion. It appealed to her. She did not think Shona would relish several days in the wilderness, but the younger ones would be enthusiastic.

'I shall have to consult the children first, Gideon,' she said.

'You do that, ma'am.'

Gideon grinned, quite sure the battle was won. What kid worth its salt wouldn't leap at a chance to skip school and go walkabout?

Mary-Ann put the proposition to her children that evening.

To her surprise, Shona was all for it, Agnes was not enthusiastic, and shuddered.

'There are insects and horrid jumping beasts out there. The girls at school told me so.'

Mary-Ann tried to smile confidently.

'They won't bother us, dear. Gideon says we shall have insect screens. I daresay jumping beasts will stay well away from wagons.'

'Kelpie is part dingo-dog. He can chase them,' Danny volunteered. What an adventure! He was desperate to go.

Shona lowered her eyes to hide a gleam of delight.

'I'm sure we'll be safe, with Mr Jones to guard us.'

'We'll vote on it,' said Mary-Ann diplomatically. 'Those in favour say aye.'

There was an enthusiastic chorus, but Agnes said; 'No!'

Shona glared at her sister.

'What d'you mean, no?'

'I'm not in favour. I'm not going. I hate travelling.'

'But Agnes dear, we can't leave you behind,' Mary-Ann said.

'Yes, you can, Mama. I'll stay with Mrs Louisa. I won't be any bother.'

Agnes did not relish the prospect of Mrs Louisa's company, but anything was better than watching Shona mooning over Gideon, or Gideon mooning over Shona. Besides, she hated this country and had no wish to explore it. She wanted to go home.

Mary-Ann sighed. She knew nothing would shift Agnes once her mind was made up. Louisa must somehow be persuaded to look after her.

'Very well, you can stay, Agnes, if Mrs Polpatrick agrees.'

Shona was secretly delighted. She would have Gideon all to herself now. Mama would be occupied with customers and Danny could be discounted as nuisance value.

'It's noble of you to offer to stay behind to help Mrs Louisa in the shop, Agnes,' she said sweetly.

'Yes, isn't it? Why don't you stay, too?' Agnes suggested wickedly, and was rewarded with a furious scowl.

Louisa was not easily persuaded to take charge of a thirteen-year-old lass, with whom she had exchanged only one or two stilted words.

'Agnes will be no trouble, Louisa, she's quiet and well behaved,' Mary-Ann assured her.

Louisa eyed the silent girl doubtfully.

'And she'll help in the shop,' Mary-Ann added.

That could be useful! Louisa thought. Now that she was resigned to Mary-Ann's journey, she could see benefits. With her friend out of the way, Louisa could experiment with ideas, which Mary-Ann would almost certainly veto. The girl assistant would be handy to hold the fort, while Louisa went out and about in town, ordering certain commodities she had in mind.

'Oh, very well. I daresay Agnes and I will get along.'

Mary-Ann hugged her.

'Oh, Louisa dear thank you!'

Louisa studied the girl. She was a solemn, dark-haired child. Agnes smiled under the scrutiny, but the smile did not reach her eyes.

Louisa sighed. She wished it had been the pretty, older one. Shona she might have understood. They could have discussed fashions and – oh, dear me, yes! – the advantages of creaming one's face under hot, skin-wrinkling conditions.

But Agnes! What on earth do I have in common with her? Louisa wondered . . .

In Van Diemen's Land, the men had started work upon the ruin under Miss Rose's strict supervision. Tangled undergrowth was cleared and the bare bones of the former building revealed. The inferno which had destroyed it had been so fierce that there was little left of the interior. When Miss Rose made her first tour of inspection after the clearance, she declared the devastation was much worse than she had imagined. She had lived with a vision of the church in its former glory, and the reality was heart-breaking. Ewan noted her cheeks were wet as she stood in front of the charred remains of altar and pulpit. Above their heads, the blackened roof gaped open to the sky. The weather had been warm and dry, but as if in sympathy with the woman's mood, dark clouds had gathered.

The men cursed, impatient to get started. They had been lucky so far, but it was midsummer, and rain was never far away in the summer months of January and February on this green island.

Ewan had been amused to see Miss Rose's authority gradually eroded by the very skills of the craftsmen she had picked so carefully. They were much more knowledgeable about the practicalities of building when studying the plans, and as a complete novice, she was forced to concede defeat on many points. Miss Rose was fast losing her grip upon the project.

The skies opened in a sudden deluge. They all scattered, running for shelter. Miss Rose headed for the entrance archway with Ewan following. In what remained of the entrance porch, she stared at the downpour.

'Rain is a nuisance, Macgregor. It will hinder work.'

'Is that all you think about?' he said. 'Personally, I welcome a torrent to refresh this God-forsaken place.'

'How dare you! This is holy ground.'

He laughed.

'Take off the blinkers, Miss Rose. It's a dismal heap of rubble.'

She turned on him passionately.

'God will never forsake this place! Every evening my brother came here, to pray for wretched sinners like you! Where you see ruin, I see the risen church. And it will happen, Macgregor! Enoch is a skilled stonemason, Isaac, Hayes and Charlie, carpenter, joiner and furniture maker. A new bell will hang in the belfry tower. Forging that bell is your main task. The other fell in the fire, and was cracked beyond repair.'

Ewan was startled.

'You expect me to cast a large kirk bell with the poor facilities you have here? That's impossible. I won't even try!'

'You will do as you're told, or wave farewell to freedom,' she said coldly.

He scowled, the hot Macgregor blood roused.

'There may be bats in your belfry, woman, but there won't be bells.'

Turning on his heel, he dived from shelter into the storm and was drenched in seconds.

Mary-Ann would have welcomed a cooling downpour as she drove the covered wagon, following Gideon's cart. Dust rose in clouds and engulfed her. The dustcoat Gideon had praised to the cloudless skies, gave little protection. Mary-Ann breathed dust; her teeth grated on it and her clothes were grey with it. The fly screens were dotted with dusty insects, dead or alive, which they had collected since she, Shona and Danny had waved farewell to Louisa and Agnes that morning.

Shona had withdrawn inside the wagon to guard her complexion, Danny had insisted on travelling with Gideon, and Mary-Ann's attention was concentrated warily upon Jagga-Jagga, the horse Gideon had assured her was suitable for lady driving. She had discovered Jagga-Jagga had an ill-natured side to his character and only understood commands in Daruk, an Aborigine dialect. `

The terrain had grown wilder as Gideon followed the old bullock cart trail out of Sydney, skirting the harbour's inlets and creeks. They had seen little sign of habitation all day, but towards evening a homesteader appeared out of the undergrowth, wanting bucket and shovel. After keen haggling, Mary-Ann settled for a shilling and a large fish newly caught in the creek, which Gideon said was worth its weight in pure gold for supper.

'We'll stop here tonight,' he said soon after, halting the wagons and unhitching the horses.

Mary-Ann looked around nervously. The chosen site was off the track, a clearing shaded by gum trees and eucalyptus. An evil chuckling broke the silence.

Shona peered out from the covered wagon.

'Who's laughing?'

Gideon smiled.

'Kookaburras. Harmless birds, so don' you fret. I always stop off here when I drive out with lady-folks. There's a spring nearby, or you can freshen-up in the billabong.'

'What's a billabong?' Danny asked.

'Just an itty-bitty pool.'

He lifted Danny down, the dog Kelpie scrambling after him. It immediately set off on the trail of a promising scent and the boy followed.

Mary-Ann panicked.

'Danny, come back! There could be snakes and wild beasts in there!'

Gideon was collecting firewood. He smiled.

'Don' you worry, ma'am, I warned him snakes shy off unless you happen on them sudden, and then they bite.'

The women did not find the information reassuring. Shona screamed and declared that nothing would persuade her to leave the wagon, unless Gideon lifted her down and accompanied her.

Later, they sat in the warm darkness around the campfire, after a supper of fish baked in aromatic leaves. Mary-Ann felt more relaxed and carefree than she had for months. It was as if she had left worries behind, when she entered the wilderness.

Shona knew firelight cast a flattering glow upon white skin and golden hair, and hoped Gideon had noticed. The dark trees surrounding the clearing suddenly reminded her of Scotland, and she began to sing, softly.

She sang about the rowan tree that had graced the smiddy garden, where they had played as children. The song was popular in Forfar, wistful and a little sad, and it suited her mood. She hoped the young man was impressed.

Mary-Ann hugged Danny and listened. It almost broke her heart. She joined in quietly, remembering contented, and uncomplicated years she had shared with Ewan when the children were small. Happy days gone forever, never to return.

Oh, rowan tree!

The women's voices faded into the silence of the night and Mary-Ann's cheeks were wet with tears.

Gideon's face was deeply shadowed beneath the hat's wide brim.

'I never seen – never heard – anything quite so beautiful, ma'am,' he said gruffly.

Davey Macgregor did not know how long he had lain insensible after the blast knocked him out. He moved his head painfully and groaned.

A girl's face swam hazily into his vision.

'You're alive! They said you were, but I wasn't sure. You looked dead.'

He tried to remember.

'You brought tea. The tunnel – the blast – Molly!'

She nodded.

'You saved my life. Nobody never bothered about my life before, an' you saved it!' She sounded awed.

He licked dry lips. 'I'm thirsty.'

'I'll make you a brew once the doctor's been. Overseer sent for him, case you die an' they need proof it were an accident, not a murder. They'll dock his fee off your wages, if you live.'

Davey closed his eyes and lapsed into semi-consciousness. When he opened them again, a grey-bearded gentleman was taking his pulse and a lurcher with sorrowful brown eyes was licking Davey's cheek.

'I'm alive!' he murmured.

'God willing,' said the doctor. 'What's your name and how old are you, son?'

Davey thought about it.

'David Macgregor – or – or is it Ross? I'm sixteen – or maybe seventeen. I lost count.'

The doctor probed Davey's bandaged skull gingerly. He addressed old Peg and Molly, who were hovering close by the bunk.

'Could be fractured. No way of telling, but we should know one way or t'other within twenty-four hours. If he recovers, he won't be fit to lift a pickaxe for at least a week and must take no part in the celebrations.'

'What celebrations?' Davey said.

'They broke through to the other side. The management has ordered kegs of beer for the entire workforce. There'll be more sore heads than yours, before this night's out.'

By the time Davey was back on his feet, there had been changes. He had enjoyed the enforced fortnight's rest, waited on hand and foot by the women. He had become quite fond of Pegasus the mournful stray lurcher. They walked together most days in the keen, frosty air. Davey began to long for home and family. He wanted to see his mother again. It had been a long time. Too long.

He was well enough to start work when the members of his gang began packing up.

'We're moving on, Professor,' they told him. 'Digging's done and it's up to bricklayers, masons and tracklayers to finish the job. We're off to start the next section. You coming?'

He thought about it.

'No. It's time I headed home.'

They laughed.

'Lucky to have one, Prof!' They gathered round to shake his hand. 'Been a pleasure working with ye, Professor. Maybe us'll meet again in Oxford Universitay.'

His mates left the hut, bellowing with laughter.

It was deathly quiet after they had gone. Pegasus pushed his sad nose into the palm of Davey's hand.

'You been abandoned too, old boy? We're in the same boat!'

He remembered that he had wages to collect, and felt more cheerful. He had been frugal, and was due a tidy sum. He would not go home in disgrace. He would be well off, well dressed and well muscled to deal with any who dared rake up the past.

The workhouse girl rushed in. She was dressed in shawl and bonnet.

'I'm ready to go, Davey!'

'Back to the workhouse, Molly?'

She laughed.

'Naw. They've been trying to get rid of me for years. I'm going to Scotland with you.'

'Wha–at?' He was astounded. 'Oh no, you're not!'

'But you saved my life!'

'Molly, I know you're grateful, but you don't owe me anything.'

She glared indignantly.

'Me, owe you? 'Tis the other way around! You owe me! I never asked you to save my life. So I'm your responsibility now.'

There was a certain mad logic to the argument that he could not counter.

'That's settled then,' she said happily. 'I'll help pack your gear.'

She reached for the velvet jacket, and the dog growled. She eyed it nervously.

'You're never taking that flea-bitten brute with us, are you?'

He looked at Pegasus.

'Oh, yes, I am!'

And there he was, lumbered.

It was Janet Golightly's afternoon off. She stood in the laird's kitchen warming herself before braving the March wind. A thaw had set in and snow lay wet and heavy in slushy brown ruts. Packhorses could now pick a path to Dundee along a track hewn through the heights at Lumley Den, which Mr Don's squad had dug at enormous expense. The mills were working again, and the busy music of hand looms was heard in Forfar closes.

Janet stood in the middle of a circle of seated servants, her hands held out to the fire. Life was easy in the laird's kitchen. There was only a frail old man to see to, with the young master away gallivanting in London.

'You look bonnie, love,' said Cook.

'Don't fill the lassie's head with smoke! Pride goes afore a tumble,' warned Phyllis, busy polishing silver with bath brick and cork.

Janet laughed.

'I'll watch out when I set foot on slush, Phyllis.'

She was happy today. A whole afternoon lay before her to spend as she wished. She sighed. Matthew would be waiting, and would be sure to have plans. They would argue, and she would probably give in. Still, she was lucky to have a steady lad like Matthew courting her. She still had nightmares about the weaving sheds and a dark, cheerless roadman's bothy filled with horror.

She shivered and pulled on her gloves. They were beautiful, warmly lined leather gloves, fit for a lady. They must have cost Matthew a fortnight's wages, at least. She had cried when he'd given them to her, because she'd never owned gloves before. He had taken her in his arms and she had kissed him for gratitude.

That was a mistake. Somehow the kiss had changed friendship into commitment, and that was not what Janet had intended.

Cook eyed the new gloves.

'Those are braw. Your lad must be keen.'

Phyllis laughed.

'Och, a'body kens that the lad that covers a lass's hand, never claims it.'

Janet was startled.

'Is that true?'

'It must be, or it wouldna be spread all round Forfarshire.'

They were teasing her. Janet tossed her head and made for the doorway.

'Old wives' tales!'

'Mind who you're calling old, my girl!' Phyllis shouted after her.

Janet hoped the afternoon would improve as she squelched along the laird's rutted driveway. When the master was fit and spry, a squad of unemployed men would be set to work and the driveway cleared in no time. Now there was a sad air of neglect about the estate.

The young master was to blame. He was nice enough, but his visits were infrequent, and he would never be the man his father was. Nobility without ability is like plum pudding without suet.

Matthew was waiting by the gate, as Janet had expected. He was grinning like the cat that had the cream.

'How d'you fancy going east, west, down the Spout, and home?'

'Not much. I don't fancy walking, except maybe as far as the baker's for a hot pie.'

Her hands were warm, but her heart was troubled. Did she want him to claim her hand? She was not sure.

He laughed.

'Who said anything about walking?'

He led her past the lodge gates. A smart green gig stood waiting outside, drawn by the smiddy horse. She gasped.

'Matthew! It's beautiful! Where did you get it?'

'From a farmer's midden! I've been working on it for months. I could hardly wait for the thaw to come, to try it out with you.'

She felt like crying, because she knew he'd done all this work just for her.

'Oh, Matthew, you're so kind. I do love you for this!'

He turned and stared at her seriously.

'You never said you loved me, before!'

She was dismayed. It had just slipped out unawares and it wasn't fair to give him hope, if nothing could come of it. Old wives' tales had a nasty habit of coming true sometimes.

Hastily, she grabbed his arm.

'Come on, Matthew. Let's cut a dash through the town.'

The gig was light and beautifully balanced. Squads of the un-employed had been out clearing slush from the cobbles, and the town was busy with a Saturday crowd. Everyone stopped and stared.

Matthew glanced at the sky.

'It'll turn to frost. I'll take you back to the smiddy before the roads turn slippery. Mrs Wullie will give us a bite of supper.'

Janet nestled closer. She was exhilarated and happy. He reached out and held her gloved hand.

Old wives' tales. What rubbish! Janet thought.

On the smiddy road, they came across a couple, walking. Matthew pulled up with a sudden exclamation.

'Davey! Is – is it you?'

Janet sat up. It was quite true! It was Davey Macgregor, but not the slightly built young lad who had once befriended her. This was a tall, handsome young man, broad-shouldered and well dressed, a curly-brimmed bowler set at a rakish angle on his fair hair.

'Davey!' she cried delightedly.

She climbed down and ran straight into his arms.

'Janet Golightly!' He hugged her and held her admiringly at arm's length. 'Let me look at you! You've grown into a lovely young lady. Where's the skinny wee lass I remembered?'

She laughed breathlessly.

'Gone forever, Davey, well fed in the laird's kitchen. Oh, it's so good to see you again!'

Matthew had climbed down. He stood holding the reins in one hand, his heart like lead. He had forgotten how dull and awkward he was in David Macgregor's presence.

Davey smiled at him.

'It's grand to be home, Matt. How I've longed for this day, brother!'

'You're not my brother!' Matthew said deliberately.

Matthew's beloved lass held Davey's hand, but that was not the real betrayal. Of her own accord she had run straight into his arms.

Davey was staring in shocked surprise.

'Matthew! What's wrong?'

Matthew clenched his fists.

'Our family's ruined, thanks to you, you filthy jailbird. Take your hands off my lass!'

They faced each other as Janet stepped hastily aside, horror-struck.

She and Davey had been through so much together; she had been overjoyed to see him safe and sound. She had not bargained on Matthew's jealousy.

At that moment she remembered the girl Davey had brought with him. There was a thin, shaggy dog as well, skulking close to Davey's heel. The dog had a possessive streak. It growled at Janet. The girl met her eyes in a challenging stare.

Janet saw it would not take much for the brothers to come to blows. Matthew would welcome any excuse to lash out.

'Please don't fight,' she cried tearfully. 'I'm the cause of your discontent, and – and I can't bear it!'

She picked up her skirts and ran down the road. Matthew would have followed, but Davey gripped his wrist.

'Let her go! We have a score to settle, you and I.'

Janet ran on, breath coming in gasping sobs. Frost was taking a grip and the going was treacherous. Once she fell all her length, scrambling up bruised and stained, the beautiful gloves muddied in freezing slush. At last she reached the laird's driveway and burst into the kitchen.

The servants were sitting round the table, eating. They looked up, startled.

'Mercy on us, lassie, what ails ye?' Phyllis cried.

Janet faced them wildly.

'I'm leaving this place, I have to get away!'

The kitchen was in uproar as they tried to calm her down, but she paid no attention. She hurried upstairs to the little turret room that was her sanctuary and lay down on the bed. She needed peace and quiet to decide what to do now.

One thought remained clear in Janet's mind. She would not stay in Forfar to be a bone of contention between two brothers. She had brought tragedy and trouble to the Macgregor family before. Enough was enough, and this time she had to go . . .

Twelve

The heat was sweltering.

Mary-Ann struggled to control the horse, Jagga-Jagga. It was in uncooperative mood as the covered wagon lurched down the awful bushland track.

'Whoa!'

She hauled on the reins, then lost patience and brought the slack down smartly on Jagga-Jagga's rump. She wondered if Gideon's docile horse for lady driving had somehow been replaced by the bunyip, an ill-natured monster of Aborigine folklore.

'Behave yourself, you wicked changeling beast!' she yelled.

The horse tossed its head at the touch of leather. It rolled its wicked eyes and considered kicking the dashboard to splinters, then thought better of it. Jagga-Jagga plodded sulkily through bottlebrush and eucalyptus, the wagon jolting dustily behind.

Mary-Ann lifted the insect-flecked fly-veil on her bonnet to wipe her brow. Her hands ached with constant pulling on the reins. Driving gloves, which Gideon had provided, had worn into holes within days and her fingers were wrapped in dirty cotton strips torn from a petticoat. She dreamed wistfully of cool, scented baths.

And yet she was surprisingly happy. There was an air of freedom in the lonely wilderness that was liberating.

Louisa would have hated it and Shona certainly did, although she endured hardships without complaint, much to her mother's surprise.

Mary-Ann had gained confidence. She would survive, even if Gideon were to be spirited away. She could light fires, feed the children and bring them safely home. She had haggled with settlers and sold everything one could imagine to lonely women marooned on sheep stations, whose only real need was Mary-Ann's sympathetic ear.

At the last homestead, while chatting to the settler's wife, Mary-Ann had her hopes raised in the continuing search for her husband and son.

'I heard tell there was a Scotchman in the last batch of convicts shipped in. He was assigned to a sheep station not more 'n ten mile away, south-west,' the woman told her.

A glimmer of hope at last, after months of disappointment!

Gideon had been reluctant when he'd heard she intended going there.

'South-west? Mary-Ann, ma'am, do you want us to perish?'

'Of course not. It's only ten miles, Gideon!'

He had looked at her with glinting eyes and shrugged, then turned the wagon into the bush. Mary-Ann soon discovered the hazards of real bushland, trackless and deadly dangerous, dense with high dingo scrub, bone dry and dusty.

And yet she remained in high spirits. She sang softly, for love of Ewan.

They were all exhausted when they reached the poor huddle of shingle-roofed shanties, which formed the outstation. The scenery was memorable. The Blue Mountains really were blue, Mary-Ann discovered. They rose into a pale evening sky, a cool backdrop to the dust-laden, milling scene that confronted her as they approached sheep-pens.

'Upwards of three hundred cross-bred merinos, by my reckoning,' Gideon told her as they climbed down and stretched aching limbs. 'We could be lucky. Assigned men are usually given shepherding tasks out in the bush, where it's certain death to try to bolt. I guess this flock has been brought in 'cause of dingo attack. Could be your Scotchman is home.'

A lanky man who seemed to be in charge strolled out of a nearby shanty and approached through the cloud of yellow dust. Shona clambered out of the wagon and stood watching. Danny was in Gideon's shadow, the dog Kelpie at heel.

The settler scowled at the dog.

'You keep that half-bred mutt under control, mister!' he warned.

Gideon grinned.

'No worry. He's sheep-trained and don' draw blood. I seen him run across the backs of a flock once, to get at a troublesome old ewe.' He indicated Mary-Ann with a thumb. 'Lady here looking for her husband, a Government man. We heard you had a Scotch-man assigned to you quite recent. Big fellah.'

The man nodded.

'He's big, sure enough.'

'Is his name Ewan Macgregor?' Mary-Ann asked eagerly.

'Jock. That's all I know. He don' speak much. Shipboard life and exile sent him real cranky. It does that to some, ma'am.'

She steeled herself to find her husband much changed.

'May I see him?'

He turned and bellowed.

'Jock! Get youssel out here!'

A powerfully built, black-bearded man came shambling from one of the shanties. He stopped and squinted at them suspi-ciously. The poor confused soul bore no resemblance to Ewan Macgregor.

The disappointment was so great Mary-Ann could not speak. Danny cried out tearfully. 'That's not my pa!'

The settler was apologetic.

'Sorry. He's the only Scotchman I know of, hereabouts.' He looked at the setting sun and rasped a thumb awkwardly across stubble. 'We got no overnight lodging for lady-folks, ma'am. My wife's been dead of childbed fever these two years.'

Gideon took control of the situation.

'No sweat. Mis' Macgregor's wagon is fitted out for lady-comfort. All that's needed is water and fodder for the horses. Tomorrow she'll permit a viewing of high quality goods carried in the travelling shop. Gift of mutton could help keep prices sharp.'

'I'll see to it, son.'

The settler hurried off. A shop was unheard of in this deso-late fringe of the outback. Such a welcome novelty was well worth the donation of a prime haunch of lamb.

Danny was inconsolable. He had been so sure their search was over.

'Oh Mama! It wasn't Pa!'

She hugged him sadly.

'Not this time, lovie.'

Kelpie snuffled Danny's hand sympathetically and boy and dog wandered off together. Mary-Ann made a move to follow, but Gideon caught her arm.

'No, ma'am, leave him be. When a boy needs comfort, a dog does it best. I should know. I've been there.'

Mary-Ann buried her face in her hands. 'And who can comfort me? Oh, Gideon, I was so sure it would be Ewan!'

'Aw, ma'am, please. Don' cry!'

He gathered her in his arms. It happened so naturally; he didn't have to think about it. One hand slipped around her waist, the other drew her head against his chest. They stood in the shadow of the wagon, till the crying stopped. She raised her head and looked at him.

'Gideon, I'm sorry—'

'No regrets, ma'am.'

Then he kissed her. Come to think of it, he'd wanted to do it since the travelling began.

Shona chose that moment to come round to the rear of the wagon looking for her mother. She saw everything, and was so horrified she thought she might faint.

Gideon had been attentive recently and Shona had been encouraged. They had walked and talked together, laughed at the antics of bounding beasts he called 'joeys', whose real name was kangaroo. He had escorted her to the billabong and turned his back discreetly while she bathed. She had noted his admiration as she returned to camp, freshened and glowing.

Gideon made no secret that he loved the wilderness, and although the untamed vastness and eerie night howling frightened her, she had not shown fear.

She had tried to be everything he wanted, and she need not have bothered.

It was Mama he held in his arms, Mama he kissed,

Mary-Ann stepped back hastily.

'I – I was upset, Shona dear, and – and Gideon—'

'I saw what he did. How could you, Mama?'

Shona turned and ran. She ran blindly, with nowhere to go. All around them was scrub and the white bleached skeletons of dead eucalyptus trees. Nowhere to run, nowhere to hide. The girl stood in the gathering dusk and wept.

Helplessly, Mary-Ann watched Shona running, hesitating, crying. She rounded furiously on Gideon.

'Now you've upset Shona! How dare you take such liberties? I'm old enough to be your mother!'

'I never knew my mother, ma'am,' he said.

She looked at him speculatively.

'Maybe that's the explanation. You've never known a mother's love. It was nothing more than that. We'll pretend it never happened.'

He sighed.

'No use pretending. It don' seem like mother-love to me, but what would I know?'

He turned on his heel and strode off towards the huddle of shanties and the company of men.

Mary-Ann was left alone, wondering what she had done to deserve this further complication.

Louisa Polpatrick had been busy since Mary-Ann's departure. Agnes took little interest in Louisa's activities at first, but curiosity got the better of her. The fine lady spent hours down in the basement, crouched beside a steaming cauldron suspended over one of the camping stoves. She was beetroot-red and sweating in the great heat.

'What are you doing?' Agnes asked.

Louisa did not welcome the interruption.

'Boiling oil,' she said.

Agnes wrinkled her nose.

'It stinks.'

'Of course it does. There's whale grease in there, among other things.'

'Was that the smelly keg you bought?'

Louisa nodded. The concoction was at a crucial stage. She wished the child would go away, but Agnes lingered.

'You were swicked, you know. Five shillings was too much for stinking oil.'

'This is special. Don't you dare mention the price to your mother!'

Louisa uncorked a vial of pale liquid and referred to a tattered recipe book. She carefully added the liquid to the brew. Agnes was at her elbow.

'What's that you put in?'

'Essence of lavender. I'm making soap.'

'Soap?' Agnes was interested. 'Mama made soap, back home. Hers didn't smell nice, though. There was soda in it for cleaning clarty claes.'

'More Scottish gibberish!' Louisa sighed. 'Can't you speak proper English?'

'Of course I can!' Agnes said indignantly. 'You don't like me, so I don't bother.'

Louisa couldn't help smiling.

'Well now, isn't that strange! I thought *you* did not like *me*.'

Agnes studied Mrs Polpatrick. She was ladylike, despite the free and easy dress she adopted, but her eyes were nice, a warm hazel-brown, and sparkled when she smiled.

'Maybe we can learn to like one another, if we are better acquainted, Mrs Louisa,' Agnes said.

Louisa was touched. The young girl's frankness was quite endearing.

Agnes's attention returned to the concoction, which Louisa had removed from the fire to cool.

'Why are you making lavender soap?' she asked.

'Because it is a luxury, my dear. I follow my mother and grandmother's recipes for fine soap, face creams and lotions. They were famous beauties, in their day. People need a little luxury in their lives sometimes, you know, and will pay sweetly for it.'

Louisa stirred the sweet smelling brew.

'Maybe we should strain it through muslin, Agnes. What do you think?'

She nodded.

'If it's luxury it has to be pure. We could pour it into baking trays to cool.'

'Good idea!' Louisa said enthusiastically. 'When it hardens we will cut it into squares and wrap each one in paper, fastened with a dot of sealing wax stamped with the Polpatrick crest. How fortunate that I still have my poor dear husband's signet ring, Agnes.' She wiped away a tear.

'I'm good at drawing, Mrs Louisa. Shall I fetch my paint box and paint sprays of lavender on the paper?' Agnes offered.

'That would be splendid, my dear!'

Having agreed the experimental marketing of their product, they stared at one another with shining eyes. Louisa felt quite emotional.

'Agnes, if this proves popular, do you realize we could ask as much as one shilling a cake? And there are dozens of recipes in the book for lotions, balms, hair washes and medicinal remedies for us to try.'

Agnes grinned.

'We'll be rich one day, Mrs Louisa!'

And they felt almost friendly enough to hug each other, in delight.

Miss Rose Bates was well aware that farm work was suffering on the few hundred acres of freehold outside Hobart. All because she had become so emotionally involved in the rebuilding of her dead brother's church.

The outer walls were rising high, the masons progressing well. She had set her heart on rebuilding the belfry tower, and that led to argument.

'If I'd known it were a cathedral you was after, I'd have backed out from the start,' Enoch grumbled.

'It need only be a simple tower, just a symbol to link earth and heaven,' she argued.

'And heaven knows the difficulty and expense involved!' Ewan chipped in.

Miss Rose glared.

'Nonsense! The original tower was quite modest.'

Enoch nodded grimly.

'I recall it was a wooden affair clad with lead, and burned like a candle that night. Molten lead poured from the gutters like rain.'

'I am not likely to forget the spectacle,' she said.

There was awkward silence.

Enoch sighed and scratched his grey head.

'If you've set your heart on a stone tower, we'll get no peace till you have one. You're an awful stubborn woman,' he said.

Before the start of this venture he would not have dared, but attitudes had changed.

They knew Miss Rose would never trust them, but sometimes she came close to liking them. She herself had found the situation confusing and went down on her knees repeatedly, asking God's help with the problem. She knew her own shortcomings only too well, yet these wicked, dangerous men generously forgave all her sins. Why could she not find it in her heart to forgive them? So far, the Almighty had vouchsafed no answer.

Miss Rose continued, ignoring Enoch's criticism.

'It's April, winter will soon be upon us. The main building should be roofed before then, but the tower could be left till last, I suppose.'

Ewan shrugged.

'We'll run out of cash long before we reach that stage.'

'Which reminds me, blacksmith,' she said coldly. 'Your task is to make the bell.'

'Find me a forge, first,' he retorted. 'And while you're about it, thirteen parts of copper and four parts of tin, to make bell-metal. That'll cost you!'

'The Lord will provide, Mr Macgregor. Go on with your work.'

She turned her back on him and walked away. Ewan leaned on the spade and watched her. Tall and spare, tough as old leather, the very opposite of all that he admired in a woman. Yet he found something admirable in her – attractive, even.

'What drives that woman, lads? Is it a worthy ambition to restore her brother's kirk, or revenge on convicts for killing him?' he said.

The others did not reply, bending silently to their tasks. That surprised him. They were men who held strong views, and were not afraid to voice them usually. Frowning, he stared down at a blackened stone block embedded in earth. Heat had split it clean in two.

'It must have been a fearsome blaze!' he remarked.

'Aye, it was,' old Enoch grunted.

Ewan glanced up.

'So you were there when it happened!'

'That's no concern o' yours, Macgregor,' Enoch growled.

Angrily, Ewan drove the spade deep into earth. He couldn't

wait to be shot of this place, with its cruelties and mysteries, but freedom depended upon the finished kirk.

And a kirk bell to peal in the belfry . . .

Janet Golightly had abandoned her free Saturday afternoons, although it was April and Forfar was enjoying mild spring weather. She knew the Macgregor brothers would be waiting for her to appear. If she did, she feared there would be angry words and maybe a sparring match. She had no idea how to cope with the situation, except by making herself scarce.

She'd had a good excuse as it happened, because the laird had been taken ill again. He had insisted upon going to hear a court case in which he was interested and ended up with a chill. Weakened by the bout of inflammation of the lungs in March, from which he had just recovered, they had nearly lost him. Only the staff's constant, dedicated care had pulled him through.

Now another Saturday afternoon was looming, the laird progressing well in spring sunshine, and Phyllis nagging at her to make peace with her lad. Janet had no alternative but to grit her teeth and go.

She dressed carefully, minus gloves, and set off in trepidation. She heaved a sigh of relief when there was no sign of anyone at the gate, but when she turned the corner, there was Matthew leaning against the wall, his expression dark as a thundercloud.

'I've been waiting here every Saturday. You've been avoiding me!'

'I haven't, I've been busy. The laird was at death's door.'

He looked concerned.

'I heard he was poorly. How is he?'

'Much better. He'll live to be a hundred, that one.'

They walked side by side. He took her hand.

'No gloves today?'

'It's much too warm, Matt!'

'Ladies wear gloves summer and winter.'

'I'm not a lady.'

'You will be one day, when I'm rich.'

She didn't know what to say. There was a grim determination about him. It had not been there before Davey arrived.

It made her wonder what had been going on between them in the smiddy.

'It was a cold welcome you gave your brother. I hope you apologized,' she said.

He gave her a withering look.

'Yours was a damn sight warmer than the scoundrel deserved.'

She whirled round angrily.

'Matthew, stop this! Davey will always be my friend. I was pleased to see him home.'

He kicked a loose stone viciously into the ditch.

'You'll be pleased to hear he's still here, making a scunner of himself.'

'I'd rather see him for myself, than hear ill of him!' she said angrily.

He shrugged.

'We'll stop by the smiddy-seat if that's what you want.'

They walked on, keeping a distance apart.

'There was a girl with him, wasn't there?' Janet asked presently.

He wrinkled his nose.

'A workhouse wench called Molly.'

Janet was not encouraged to ask for more information. They walked on in silence.

Davey was sitting at the table scribbling on sheets of paper, when they walked in. Mrs Wullie and the workhouse wench were in a huddle at the other end, discussing some problem with a lump of pastry. The shaggy dog lying on the rug growled, and Davey looked up. 'Janet! I was wondering when I'd see you again!'

He came towards her with outstretched hands. With shirt-sleeves rolled up, she could see how muscular his arms were. He was not so tall and broad-shouldered as Matthew but looked much more of a man. Suffering had left its mark.

Her eyes filled with tears. She had been responsible for that.

'Davey, there's something you should know,' she said, holding tight to his hands. 'I told the laird everything that happened the day you and your father were taken. It was all my fault. I should have owned up from the start.'

He smiled.

'Don't be daft! You would have ended up in the jail, with us.'

'No, the laird said if he'd known the facts he would have ordered your pa to pay for the deer and given it to the game-keepers, and that would've been an end to it. He's written to the Home Secretary, asking him to consider a pardon for you and your father.'

Davey shook his head sadly.

'Too late. Our family has been torn apart.'

Arriving home to find the smiddy sold, his mother, sisters and wee Danny gone, had been a shattering blow. He couldn't blame Matthew for hating him.

Molly had been listening with avid interest.

'So you went to the nick to save her! Proper little hero, ain't you, Davey?'

She had been getting on his nerves.

'Hold your tongue!' he growled.

Mrs Wullie wagged a finger at him, and hugged the girl.

'There's no call for rudeness! Don't you mind him, love!'

Mrs Wullie had taken the orphan lass to her heart. She and Wullie had lost their one and only tiny baby, fourteen years ago. It was a girl, and they'd laid her sorrowfully in the Kirk yard. The moment the workhouse wench walked in the door, it was as if heaven had relented and restored Mrs Wullie's daughter.

Welcomed, hugged and mothered, Molly could hardly believe her good luck.

Davey turned to his brother. He had been working upon a peace offering.

'I calculated the stresses for those gear castings, Matt. You should increase the overall tolerance by one sixteenth.'

Matthew shrugged dismissively.

'I worked that out by rule o' thumb, three days ago.'

Davey sighed.

'I can't do anything right, can I! Why can't we work as a team, you and I? Cooperation can move mountains. I've seen it in prac-tice, working on the railway.'

Janet seized enthusiastically on the plan.

'That's a wonderful idea. I can see the name above the smiddy door already, Macgregor Brothers and Co.!'

Matthew glowered.

'Of course you'd take Davey's side, wouldn't you?'

Her heart sank. Matthew's jealousy knew no bounds. Her enthusiasm was enough to set him dead against the plan, even though it could be the saving of them. It was an impossible situation.

'You're a fool, Matt. Leave her alone,' Davey said sharply.

'A fool, am I?' He clenched his fists.

Janet had heard enough. She shouted at them furiously.

'Two fools in this house are a couple too many!'

She whirled round and ran outside.

'And good riddance!' Molly said complacently.

Matthew gave the girl a venomous look and hurried to the doorway, but Janet had already rounded the corner and was out of sight.

He leaned against the wall, tearfully.

The moment Davey Macgregor had set foot in Forfar again, things had gone wrong. If only he would pack his bag and go, and take the workhouse slut with him! But Matthew knew his half-brother intended to stay. It would take something really drastic to shift him.

Matthew straightened suddenly. The solution was so simple; he couldn't imagine why he hadn't thought of it before.

He went inside and up to his room. Then he settled down to write a letter.

<u>To the Right Honourable Mr Alistair Ross, MP</u>

Dear Sir,

It is my duty to inform you that David Macgregor, the person for whom you were searching, is now abiding at his home address in Forfar, and may be contacted there . . .

The laird took an afternoon nap in his favourite sheltered spot in the garden, when the weather was clement. The April afternoon was as balmy as summer that day, and he dozed pleasantly on the lounger, dreaming of the tray of tea, scones and butter and his favourite raspberry jam, which would arrive punctually at three thirty. He enjoyed being pampered and was having an excellent convalescence.

'Please sir! May I speak with you, sir?'

The urgent young voice roused the laird. His inner clock,

usually remarkably accurate, told him it was not yet time for tea. He opened an eye warily and focused on the girl standing before him.

'This had better be important, Janet Golightly,' he warned grimly.

'Oh, it is, sir, terribly!'

He sat up, prepared to listen.

The whole story came pouring out in an emotional torrent. It was a common enough tale of two brothers fighting over a lass, but in this instance it meant further disaster for an already divided family. When she'd finished she stood twisting a corner of her apron miserably between her fingers, struggling with tears.

'What do you propose to do about it, Janet?' he asked kindly.

'I was hoping you'd tell me, sir.'

He smiled.

'I gave up giving advice, years ago. Nobody heeded it. But have you ever heard tell of woman's intuition?'

She hesitated.

'It's doing what your heart says, not what other folk tell you.'

'I couldn't put it better myself. So what does your heart say?'

'Leave Forfar. The Macgregor family has suffered enough because of me. I won't stay and add to their grief.' She looked down at the ground. 'Matthew Macgregor bought me gloves, sir, do you think he will claim my hand?'

'Do you want him to?'

'I don't know. I don't want to break his heart. That's why I must go.'

She was young and troubled and he pitied her, but the decision to leave was sound. She needed to distance herself, in order to see the situation more clearly. In her present state she was no match for strong-willed Macgregors.

'Where will you go, Janet?'

'Dundee. To the mills,' she answered promptly.

His heart quailed, though he gave no sign.

'You'll maybe allow me to arrange lodgings and employment for you?'

She smiled.

'Oh, thank you, sir, that's kind. Please don't tell Matthew or Davey where I am, though.'

He was weary now, his eyelids drooping.

'I promise I'll keep quiet as a mouse.'

Janet hesitated. It was a terrible liberty to take, but she bent swiftly and kissed his cheek. The laird didn't seem to mind. He was smiling as she stole quietly away.

Thirteen

Mary-Ann returned to Sydney before winter rains reduced bullock tracks to rutted mud.

She was barely on speaking terms with her dear daughter, and Gideon remained dour and silent. Her only comfort lay in bare shelves in the travelling shop and a heavy money bag strapped round her waist. She had not counted the proceeds, but there was much more than she had expected. Despite the bitter disappointment of finding no trace of her husband and son, Mary-Ann decided the venture would be repeated when the weather improved.

Alone, if need be!

She brought Jagga-Jagga to a halt outside the shop and was surprised to find a queue of women awaiting entry. She tethered the horse to the trough rail to drink and patted Jagga-Jagga's neck warily. He rolled a warning eye at her but did not bite. They respected one another.

Mary-Ann headed for the shop door, only to find the way barred by indignant women.

'Here, you! Get to the end of the line. Wait your turn.'

The door swung open, and Agnes hurried out.

'Next six ladies, if you please.'

She gave a whoop of joy when she saw her mother and flung herself into Mary-Ann's arms. 'Dearest Mama, you're home!'

'What's happened, dear? Why the crowd?'

Agnes grinned.

'Mrs Louisa advertised a new batch of peaches and cream complexion milk in the Gazette. That's our best seller, Mama, apart from eucalyptus oil and camphor, which is only seasonal. There's winter coughs and sneezes going the rounds this April an' we've been rushed off our feet.'

She disentangled herself. 'Sorry, Mama, must go. There are customers waiting.'

And off she scuttled, after ushering more eager ladies inside.

Louisa could be seen behind the counter, giving advice. Satisfied customers emerged, each clutching a brown paper bag and struggling with crinoline hoops, which jammed in the doorway. The queue shuffled patiently forwards.

'Well, I'll be darned! Mis' Louisa's hit on somethin' profitable!' Gideon muttered, pushing his hat up his forehead.

Mary-Ann sighed.

'It'll take more than peaches and cream to sort my complexion, after this trip.'

'Y'know, Mis' Mary-Ann,' Gideon said thoughtfully, 'sheep-shearers have lovely soft hands. They have crook backs and faces like wallaby hide, but their hands are soft. I've heard tell oil in the fleece does it. I daresay the same could work for women-folk. Wonder if Mis' Louisa knows.'

Shona entered the discussion. She gave her mother a scornful look.

'Thank goodness my skin is soft and white. It's vulgar to be brown, like a convict.'

The remark was hardly tactful, and Gideon responded angrily.

'You're only a pampered girl, missy. You don' live in the real world!'

Shona ran into the shop, blinking back tears, mortified.

Mary-Ann understood her daughter's problem only too well. Shona was in love with Gideon, and one foolish, stolen kiss had destroyed trust between mother and daughter and ruined a pleasant friendship. She turned to him.

'Shona admires you, Gideon. You were unnecessarily cruel.'

'It's a cruel world, ma'am.'

'Next time I travel to the outback, I travel alone. Understood?' she said coldly.

He shrugged.

'As you please, ma'am.'

He pulled the hat down over his eyes, clicked his tongue to Jagga-Jagga, and led horse and wagon away, whistling.

'Mary-Ann dear. Welcome home! Did you have a successful trip?' Louisa called.

'Oh yes. We sold everything.'

Mary-Ann was travel-stained and weary and in sore need of

a bath. Louisa hid apprehension behind a radiant smile as she greeted her business partner. Would Mary-Ann approve of the new venture?

The shop was crammed to overflowing with ladies. The whole place rustled with poplins, crapes and silks, the creak of whalebone, and one or two ominous rips as customers craned to catch a glimpse of the newcomer. Louisa made the introductions.

'Ladies, Mrs Macgregor is our intrepid traveller, selling goods to settlers in the outback. In months to come, you will note how effectively Polpatrick preparations will preserve Mrs Macgregor's glowing complexion.' She caught sight of Mary-Ann's hands and recoiled, then recovered swiftly. 'Pay particular attention to Mrs Macgregor's hands, dear ladies, deliberately ruined by carriage-driving, in order to demonstrate the wonderful benefits of Polpatrick hand balm. Customers are invited to visit the shop to observe the improvement for themselves.'

'Louisa, I'd be obliged if you will explain!' Mary-Ann said grimly.

'It's good business, Mama,' Agnes intervened. She put a colourful bottle into a paper bag, which she closed with an expert twirl. 'Mrs Louisa makes lotions, face creams, scent and soap from old English recipes.'

One of the customers nodded enthusiastically.

'We never had such luxuries till Mrs Louisa came. Menfolk don't consider womenfolk's needs.'

Louisa smiled and handed Mary-Ann soap and a bottle of yellow liquid.

'Here, my dear. Lotion with a hint of sulphur to remove any – er – *livestock*, when you bathe. By the by, letters arrived in your absence. I put them on the mantelshelf.'

Letters!

Mary-Ann hastened upstairs to the living quarters. There were two. She examined the writing on travel-stained envelopes. Her heart missed a beat as she recognized Alistair Ross's hand. The other was from Matthew. She opened that first.

He had written on receipt of her letter on arrival in Sydney, and it was rather restrained in tone. He told her that the bothy was now under the laird's ownership, and he employed Matthew. He assured her that he was well, Mrs Wullie presided over the smiddy-seat and he and Wullie were in partnership, making spare parts for the mills. He made no mention of his hopes and fears for the future. It was a letter completely devoid of any emotion, ending your dutiful son, Matthew Macgregor.

Mary-Ann felt oddly let down.

She held the second letter in her hands for a few moments. The familiar handwriting brought back memories of innocent first love, mostly painful. Opening it, she noted that he had written immediately upon receipt of her own cool note. His was written in similar vein, but the letter contained startling news.

> . . . I have discovered that David was not sent to Australia. Instead he went to Parkhurst prison on the Isle of Wight for a course of correction, because of changes in the law affecting young offenders. I have confirmed that your husband Ewan Macgregor did sail for Australia to complete his sentence under the Government exile scheme, having first served a period of hard labour. Records are incomplete and I have been unable to find the name and destination of the ship. On the other hand, I have learned that David was released from prison some weeks ago, but has not returned home. You may rest assured that I will make every effort to locate the lad, Mary-Ann . . . A hint of warmth, but the ending was formal.

She sank down upon a battered chair, imported by one of their predecessors. Dear Davey, lost and alone, and herself thousands of miles away! What would he do when he arrived at the smiddy and found her gone? Matthew will be there, she thought uneasily, but that could only be a recipe for trouble.

Mary-Ann despaired. With hindsight, leaving Scotland had been a grave mistake, and she should never have sold the smiddy. Now there was no work for Ewan to come home to, and the family was divided.

From April onwards winter set in, and Sydney experienced sudden torrential downpours.

The shop prospered despite the weather. Male customers were few, and sales of shovels, buckets, coarse canvas and kegs of nails

declined. A huge demand continued from the female clientele
for herbal remedies and cosmetics.

Louisa had found a reliable supplier of locally grown herbs,
and storerooms smelled muskily that winter of thyme, rosemary,
lavender, fennel, mint and many others hung drying in bunches.

Agnes had left school and was working in the shop with great
enthusiasm. She obviously idolized Mrs Louisa. Mary-Ann lay
awake at nights and worried. She had lost the respect of one
daughter, was she about to lose the love of another?

Round about Christmas, demand for lotions, creams and soap
increased and the two women decided they must have help to
encourage male custom, which had dropped away to nil. Mary-
Ann had hoped that Shona might volunteer, and her pretty face
would do the trick, but when school resumed her daughter had
returned as a fully-fledged music teacher, earning one shilling
and nine pence a week. Shona offered to contribute to household expenses but Mary-Ann refused, urging her daughter to
open a savings account.

A serious mistake, as it turned out.

So advertisements for a male shop assistant placed in the Gazette
yielded results and Mary-Ann and Louisa settled upon a suitable
applicant. Norman Wilberforce was a swagman who had given
up tramping the trails with a pack of saleable goods on his back.
Louisa was sure his sales expertise would encourage male custom
to the discreet area round the back where shovels, buckets and
nails were displayed.

Mary-Ann was intrigued by the name Ada tattooed upon the
man's forearm with the aid of needles and gunpowder. This hinted
romantically at a lost love, since there was no Ada Wilberforce in
evidence and he was homeless. Wilberforce was granted permission to spread his swag in a basement cellar next door to the
kitchen, and appeared satisfied with the arrangement.

Mary-Ann kept a meticulous tally of profit and loss, and was
surprised when stocktaking at the end of 1850 revealed that their
enterprise was providing a decent living for themselves, schooling
for Danny and employment for others. Apart from their single
employee Wilberforce, a glass-blower manufactured bottles and a
carter, Gideon or his protégé, brought shipped goods from the harbour.

★   ★   ★

Mary-Ann decided to venture out with the travelling shop when the weather improved. Gideon provided transport, with a gleam in his eye she mistrusted.

'Cart's all fitted out for comfort, Mis' Mary-Ann.'

'With a gentle horse for lady-driving?'

'Oh, yah. Jagga-Jagga.'

'I might have known.' She sighed and met his eyes squarely. 'I will travel alone this time, Gideon.'

'Uh-huh. Hope you don't meet up with bolters, ma'am. Escaping convicts are desperate men. Be sure to make plenty of flat-footed din in the bush, to frighten off snakes.'

'You can't scare me. Besides, I don't intend to venture very far from Sydney. I'll establish a round on the outskirts of town, so that customers can depend upon regular visits.'

He laughed uproariously and slapped his thigh.

'Well, strike me down! A swag lady!'

He loitered around to see her off with more shouted advice, as she gee'd up Jagga-Jagga.

'Keep an eye open for funnel-web spiders. One bite, an' you're dead.'

She had gone off alone, to prove to herself she could do it, and to her delight had stayed away several days without incident and established a round of reliable customers. She was very well received, and met not the slightest hint of unpleasantness from man, beast or insect. On the contrary, she had found nothing but kindness and wonderful hospitality. She had enjoyed herself enormously and the expedition had been profitable. She returned home with a new sense of independence and confidence in her own ability.

Until she was faced with Shona, who was seething with jealousy.

Shona had watched Gideon's comings and goings for weeks, with an aching heart. When he visited the shop he spared only a casual word for the lovelorn girl. After Mary-Ann had insisted upon travelling alone, Shona's highly coloured imagination began working, and she became convinced her mother and Gideon had arranged a secret assignation, in the bush.

When Mary-Ann returned from a perfectly innocent business trip, Shona glowered so fiercely her mother was alarmed.

'Mercy on us, Shona dear! What ails you?'

'You know fine, Mama. It's Gideon!'

Mary-Ann sighed.

'If he has been unkind, my dear, it is not my fault.'

'Oh, but it is!' she burst out passionately. 'Mr Ross drew in his chair at our table, after my father went to prison. You flirted with Mr Ross, and now you are behaving just as badly, with Gideon.'

'Shona, that's not true!'

'Yes it is. You swore we'd find Pa and Davey, but Davey never came here and nobody knows where Pa is. Maybe you knew you wouldn't find him and you could get yourself another man. Maybe that's why Matthew didn't come. You planned it that way, thinking daughters would be easily fooled. Well, think again, Mama!'

Mary-Ann was badly shaken.

'How dare you speak to me like that?'

'I dare because I don't care any more.' Shona wept. 'One day I'll find my father and when I do, I'll tell him what you've done. I'll make sure he knows the truth.'

With that she ran sobbing from the room, leaving Mary-Ann trembling.

The thought of leaving Sydney to find her father took root in Shona's mind. She began to investigate the procedure secretly, but it soon became clear she would need help. She knew where to find it.

Gideon was surprised when Shona turned up at the livery stables. He was cleaning a harness when the girl arrived.

'Where do you think my father could be?' she demanded, without preamble.

He pushed his hat up his forehead.

'Melbourne, maybe. I heard tell convicts went up the Yarra River 'bout the time your pa came out.'

She looked at him with disgust.

'And you let my mother search the bush, when you knew it was pointless!'

He shrugged.

'Yah – well.'

She stared at him. Strange, but she did not love him any more.

'You never expected her to find him, did you, Gideon?'

He breathed gently upon the leather.

'I'm a kind-hearted fellah. I don' destroy hope.'

'Only reputations!'

He shot her a quick, angry glance.

'What do you want with me, missy, apart from aggravation?'

'I want to go to Melbourne to look for my father. I want you to fix it for me.'

'Why should I?'

'Because I swear I will find him one day. He's a big, strong man with a tremendous temper. When I tell him you and my mother were kissing, he'll blacken your eyes and throw my mother out into the street.' She leaned closer. 'But if you will help me get to Melbourne, I give you my solemn promise I'll keep quiet.'

Gideon buffed the leather thoughtfully.

'Shipping an' lodgings cost a deal of money, missy.'

'I have plenty of savings, and the talent to earn more, if I have to.'

'What'll I tell your ma if'n you go?'

'Nothing. Chances are she won't suspect you.'

He eyed her with grudging respect. She had it all figured out.

'There's a steamer carrying passengers and freight bound for Melbourne next Wednesday, leaves Sydney morning tide. Ten shillings, steerage,' he said.

'Perfect!'

'Promise me you won't make trouble for your ma, if you find your pa?'

Shona smiled.

'I promise. Cross my heart an' hope to die!'

'Yah − well,' he nodded, uneasily.

Matthew Macgregor had waited eagerly for the postie to climb the brae to the smiddy, bringing Alistair Ross's response to his letter. He kept an anxious eye on arrivals by coach and train, but no letter came, nobody arrived, and weeks passed. Matthew was bitterly disappointed. Perhaps Davey's father did not want to claim a jailbird son.

One Saturday, Matthew stood waiting patiently at the laird's gate for Janet. He waited a long time, stamping his feet and nursing his fingers under his oxters to keep warm. It was one of the cold days Forfar can drum up, even in summertime, a wind whistling from the east with a bite of the cold German Ocean in its teeth.

At last he became so chilled and anxious, he marched up the driveway and tugged the doorbell. Phyllis answered.

'Och, it's you!'

'Where's Janet?'

'Janet's gone.'

'Gone?' he repeated blankly. 'Gone where?'

Phyllis shrugged.

'How would I know? She packed her bag and left. Cook and me wasna taken into her confidence.'

'Did – did she get the sack?'

'Not her! Janet Golightly and the laird are as thick as yesterday's porridge.'

'He must know where she is!'

'If he does, he's keeping mim as a mouse.'

'Let me speak to him!'

'No fear! The old man's so frail a puff o' wind would blow him awa'. Then we'd all be oot o' a job. Besides, the laird's a slippery customer. You'd find it easier to pull salmon frae the Esk than get satisfaction frae him.'

He stared at her, near to tears.

'What'll I do, Phyllis?'

She was sorry for the lad. Janet's departure had upset the whole household. The lass was well liked. She patted Matthew's arm.

'Go back to the smiddy-seat, son. If I hear any news, I'll send word.'

He nodded and retraced his steps. By the time he had reached the smiddy, misery had hardened into anger. He found his half-brother sitting in the living room, on his own. Mrs Wullie and Molly had gone off to town to buy the workhouse wench decent clothing.

Matthew suspected Davey had forked out money to busk the girl. Davey had learned about the bank account in his name and had offered Matthew a handout. Matthew told him what to do with it. He wouldn't soil his hands.

Davey had his nose in a book, dry as dust science. Matthew brought a fist down upon the tabletop.

'Janet's gone, and it's your fault!'

Davey jumped at the crash. He looked astonished.

'What are you blethering about? I never spoke more than a polite word to the lass. I wouldn't dare, with you ready to punch my head in.'

'There's neater ways to send you packing than punching!' Matthew threatened ominously.

Davey sat up. Violence he could handle, scheming was something else.

'This is my home, Matt. I've no intention of leaving.'

'That's what you think.'

Matthew sat down and folded his arms. Davey watched him warily.

'Where has Janet gone?' he asked.

'I don't know. Nobody knows except the laird, and he's not telling.'

Prison cultivates speedy awareness of another's moods, and Davey detected real heartache behind his half-brother's aggression. He felt sympathetic. Janet was a winsome lass. He'd been fond of her himself when she was just a bairn, till Fate took a hand. He gave Matthew a comforting glance.

'Forfar tongues wag far and wide, Matthew. Sooner or later, there will be news.'

'Aye, news for somebody that least expects it, I shouldn't wonder,' Matthew said dourly.

He stood up and went out into the workshop. Davey stared after him, frowning.

Now what the devil does he mean by that? He wondered, uneasily.

I've grown soft! Janet Golightly thought.

She'd been taken on at Baxter's Dens Works in Dundee, not long after leaving Forfar. She could have tried for a job with Cox's or Gilroy's, but those mills were experimenting with a foreign Indian fibre called jute.

Janet knew all about spinning flax and weaving linen, so she'd settled for Baxter's.

Forfar weaving sheds had never been like this factory, though! It was huge, and growing bigger, five more storeys being built along Princes Street.

The foreman introduced her to a noisy hackling machine, in charge of an older woman called Connie, who yelled at her to feed the clawing beast with stricks of flax to comb and straighten the fibres. The consignment of flax that had reached Dundee from the Baltic that year was soft and towy. Fibres floated in the air and tickled Janet's nose, lint obstructed her breathing and made her cough. She paused and doubled up with a fit of coughing, while the machine thundered on relentlessly.

'Come on, lass, keep your end up!' Connie shouted above the din.

But Janet still coughed and choked. Connie was alarmed.

'My Goad, it's no' the cholera, is it?'

'If it is, I'm past caring,' she groaned weakly.

Connie quickly fed the machine, and then thumped a fist between Janet's shoulders.

'Och, they all cough at first when they're taken on. Your lungs'll get used to lint. We're making fine canvas for sailors' breeks. Is that no' a braw prospect?'

She dug Janet in the ribs and cackled.

Janet smiled and wiped the back of her hand across her mouth. It tasted of linseed oil. She spread more stricks on to the combs. Her head ached, her back ached, her throat felt raw.

Aye, she'd grown soft in the laird's mansion, walking on thick carpets in peaceful quiet! Tripping out on Saturdays with gloves on her hands, like the lady she was not and never would be.

By the end of the long day, she was so exhausted she was fit to drop. Her whole body ached, and when she reached the lodgings the kind laird had secured for her, Mrs McConachie's rich, fatty cooking ensured that her stomach ached, as well.

Of course, as days passed, she got used to it. She had time to think as she fed flax on to the mechanical beast's claws. She thought mostly about the Macgregor brothers, Matthew and Davey, and her heart was troubled. Matthew was kind and devoted and very dear to her, but she could not forget reckless, attractive, exciting Davey, her first childish love. If it came to making the choice between them, would it be a case of first come, first chosen, or slow and steady wins the race?

What a quandary! No wonder she had lost courage and fled.

Connie hated long faces. She gave an encouraging shout.

'If the work's getting ye down, lassie, just remember. Sailors' breeks!'

Alistair Ross had been one of a deputation making a lengthy survey of the powerful Russian empire, in his capacity of under-secretary for Colonies and War. In due course the British deputation moved on, to study events in the crumbling Turkish Ottoman empire. The two were neighbours whose bad-tempered border spats threatened the fragile European peace. The situation, in Alistair's view, was a powder keg waiting to erupt.

He was overjoyed to find Matthew's letter in the House of Commons' rack on his return to London, containing the news that his son David had arrived home safely in Forfar some months ago.

Alistair was preparing to travel north with all speed when a tragic event drastically changed his plans. Sir Robert Peel was thrown from his horse on June 29th and died of his injuries a few days later. His influence on law and order had been immense and the establishment of a regular police force, known as 'Bobbies', had been a master stroke. His loss was keenly felt throughout the land. Queen Victoria was reported to be inconsolable.

Turbulence resulting from Peel's death rocked the Government and there were rumours and resignations that kept Alistair in London for several months, till the situation was resolved. Christmas had come and gone before he felt free to leave London and travel to Scotland.

He sat in the corner seat of a first-class rail compartment staring out at the winter landscape without seeing it. His thoughts were fixed upon a staff vacancy, which had arisen in Government House in Sydney, New South Wales. Alistair knew the position could be his, if he wanted it. If the meeting with his son went off as planned, he had made up his mind to offer Davey the chance to come with him, to have a fresh start in a new land where the lad's past would have little significance.

Alistair leaned forward and cleared a patch in the misted windowpane, to hide his exultation. Imagine Mary-Ann's delight when he turned up in Sydney with their beloved son! Her grateful arms would be around his neck, her kiss warm upon his lips . . .

* * *

But kissing was far from Mary-Ann's thoughts at that very moment. She was standing on the dockside at Sydney Rocks, blistering summer heat burning through the thin soles of her shoes. A harbour official in peaked cap and reefer jacket was sweating uncomfortably as he faced her.

'But if you checked the passenger lists, you must have seen the name Shona Macgregor!'

He sighed patiently.

'I check lists of passengers, crew, ships' manifests and bills of lading every day till I'm cross-eyed, ma'am. One name in partic'lar ain't likely to stand out, specially if she went steerage.'

'Please think!' she begged desperately. 'She's tall, very pretty and very young, though she looks older than her years.'

The man fingered his chin thoughtfully.

'Pretty little sheila, you say? Well now, there was one I noticed on the quay, a cut above the rest.'

Mary-Ann clutched his arm, full of hope.

'Where was she bound?'

'I couldn't say for certain she's your daughter, o' course, but this little maid went steerage, to Melbourne.'

'Melbourne? Is that far?'

'A fair distance, ma'am.'

Tactfully, he kept mercifully silent about the unsavoury reputation of the runaway's destination . . .

Fourteen

Mary-Ann worked with Louisa and Agnes in the shop, but work did not ease the grief of Shona's departure. Mary-Ann blamed herself for the disaster. She knew Shona had fallen in love with Gideon, whose ridiculous courtship of her mother had driven the sensitive girl to run away.

Mary-Ann went walkabout with Jagga-Jagga and the cart several times to combat her anxiety. Women living on the fringe of town welcomed her visits with open arms. Sydney ladies frowned upon those with a convict connection, but lonely settlers' wives were not so fussy. They were only too pleased to sit down and pass the time of day, even with a felon's wife.

Mary-Ann had dragged information unwillingly from Gideon. She now knew that Shona had fled to Melbourne, hoping to find her father.

Melbourne was unknown to Mary-Ann, and everyone she questioned gave vague and unsatisfactory answers. She lost count of the number of times she heard the tale of a Sydney woman who had four children, two living, and two in Melbourne. This was accompanied by hoots of laughter from Sydneysiders. Mary-Ann was not amused.

As time wore on without further news, it suited her frustrated mood to remain in the workroom with pestle and mortar, pounding Louisa's medicinal clays to powder and crushing dried herbs to scented dust. Her days were spent boiling, infusing, mixing and bottling, with Louisa's delicate nose hovering critically over the bubbling brews.

The most popular product with customers was undoubtedly face cream, a mix of boiled water, glycerine and lanolin, which Gideon procured from sheep farmers. To this was added a liberal portion of essence of roses and a dash of neat alcohol, then the mixture was beaten with whisks till their arms ached. The result was a rich, delicately scented cream that sold in tubfuls.

Mary-Ann approved of the cream, in this land that bred freckles and wrinkles as a matter of course, but had reservations about rouge and lip colour. Louisa was experimenting with both, using Australian red clay, which contained harmless oxide of iron in varying rosy shades. Mary-Ann remained doubtful.

'Isn't it rather wicked, Louisa?'

Her friend laughed.

'Certainly not, my dear! It's a valuable aid to bring bashful beaux up to scratch.'

Wicked or not, women clamoured for the cosmetics. More ladies forced their way into the shop, crinoline cages helped through the doorway with a hefty shove from Agnes. In inclement weather, muslins and silks gave way to mud spattered serge and damp worsted. The grasshoppers' song ceased in the wet chill of April.

Increased trade gave Gideon an excuse to visit the shop with deliveries, always lingering longer than necessary. His infatuation was embarrassing, but Mary-Ann was powerless to stop it. She was forced to endure the unwelcome attention, flattering though it was.

Agnes had been upset by her sister's sudden departure. She missed Shona more than she would admit, and worried about her constantly. Shona was tall, slender, beautiful and talented, everything Agnes was not. Her own strength lay in the possession of good plain common sense. Goodness only knows what evil mantrap impulsive Shona might fall into, without Agnes on hand to haul her out.

And she knew whom to blame for this sad state of affairs!

Agnes was waiting for Gideon when he arrived in the back yard with a fresh delivery. He reined in the carthorse, braked the cart and jumped down, spending a few idle moments watching Kelpie race around, chasing his tail.

Agnes stepped out of the shadows.

'I've a bone to pick with you!'

He grinned.

'Give it to the dog.'

She ignored the little girl teasing. He'd soon find out it was misplaced.

'Did my sister run away because of you?'

He thought about it. His thoughts ran to Mary-Ann, and one stolen kiss, which Shona had observed.

'Well – yah. Probably.'

'So what will you do about it?'

He shrugged.

'Nothin''

She doubled her fists.

'If I were a man, Gideon Jones, I'd make you sorry!'

He shielded his chin, playfully.

'Don' hit me! I arranged everything safe and comfortable for her. Shona wanted to go find your pa. She thinks your ma don' try nearly hard enough. Maybe she don' want him back.'

'Do – do you think so?' Agnes asked tremulously.

'Don' matter what I think about that, missy. I'm a tender-hearted fellah. Couldn't refuse to help a young lady go find her pa, now could I?'

She recovered and lifted her chin.

'Oh yes, you could! I bet you made a huge profit on the deal. Shona had plenty money saved, but she couldn't leave Sydney without help. The carter told me you take a hefty percentage on every passenger fare you arrange with Edison Cargo line.'

He glared.

'Too true! A man has to live.'

'And you live very well, Mr Jones! It's your duty to make sure Shona arrives home safely. If she comes to harm, my father will know whom to blame and will have your guts for garters. So think about it, and good day to you!'

She turned on her heel and bounded up the steps to the apartment, affording him an entrancing glimpse of frilly cotton pantaloons.

Gideon pushed his hat up his brow. It appeared he was for it, when Mr Macgregor arrived in Sydney.

If he ever did, o'course.

The raging remnants of a far-off typhoon came screaming in from the sea. Gales howled across the scrubby heath of Botany Bay, which, contrary to popular belief, had never sustained a convict settlement. Torrential rain lashed South Head, creeks, inlets and broad reaches of Sydney harbour seethed with white foam and monstrous waves.

The storm struck the town in the darkness of early morning.

Mary-Ann was roused with a start by drumming rain and a shrieking gale, which shook the building to its foundations and rattled unshuttered door and window.

Louisa's screams and Agnes and Danny's yells of 'Mama!' brought her out of bed and running through corridors in the candle's guttering glow. Mary-Ann collected Agnes then hurried to the front of the house from the rear attic room, to find the full fury of the storm beating like fists upon Danny's skylight window. She scooped the terrified boy out of bed as a loose shingle crashed against the glass.

Danny buried his nose thankfully against his mother's shoulder and recovered his courage. 'I'm brave, aren't I, Mama? I never cried, but Mrs Louisa screamed.'

They found Louisa downstairs, buried beneath the eiderdown. Holding hands, the four made their way to the basement.

Wilberforce appeared, holding a lantern.

'Are you folks all right? It's one of the worst howlers I've seen. Better stay in the basement, ma'am, while I secure storm shutters. It's safer below ground.'

It was snug in the basement kitchen with a kettle singing on the fire. Mary-Ann brewed strong tea liberally sweetened, and even Louisa relaxed.

Mary-Ann took the chance to survey Wilberforce's living quarters curiously. The cellar was very tidy, but devoid of any personal touches. It contained only a chair, a bed and makeshift washstand with an enamel basin and jug, razor, leather strop, a comb and a cake of soap. The only other evidence of occupation was a bible on a shelf beside neatly folded clothing. The man himself remained anonymous.

He appeared at that moment, putting the lantern on the kitchen table.

'No damage upstairs. One or two cracked panes, easy sorted tomorrow.'

He took the cup Mary-Ann poured and settled down on the floor, back to the wall. He smiled around the gathering.

'It's real nice, having company.'

Mary-Ann wondered about him. He could read and write and seemed well educated.

'Have you always been a swagman, Mr Wilberforce?' she asked.

'Oh no, ma'am.' He took a slow sip of tea, considering. 'I was a farmer, once. You probably heard there was a scheme to attract free settlers, to improve the penal colony's reputation. I bought two hundred acres of New South Wales for five pounds. But when my wife and I trekked out to claim our plot, we found nought but barren hillside, gum tree stumps, rocks and dingo brush. Still, I cleared the land, burned the trees and mixed ash with earth to improve the soil. In time I planned to raise crops, increase the holding, breed cattle and sheep, make a fortune like others have done.' He paused and drank deeply, then wiped his mouth and stared at the fire.

'So what happened, Mr Wilberforce?' Louisa asked.

'Ada died.'

'Your wife?'

He nodded, looking away.

'Didn't seem much point going on, after. So I went walkabout, as the black fellows say.'

'I'm so sorry,' Mary-Ann said.

She guessed that only the strangeness of the night had loosened this reticent man's tongue.

But for the storm, Mary-Ann might never have known Norman Wilberforce's background, and that ignorance could have meant disaster.

The storm had hit Van Diemen's Land, and passed on without doing damage to the restoration of Miss Rose's church.

By now, Ewan Macgregor had enough material to construct a small foundry, and a considerable quantity of copper and tin ingots, needed to make bell metal. Miss Rose had procured faithfully everything he had demanded, and Ewan suspected she had emptied her coffers in the process.

Bracing and strainer arches had been made ready to receive bell tower and steeple, but weeks had passed with no sign of a tower. The rest of the church was roofed, but tarpaulins covered a gaping hole at the western end. Chippy, Enoch and the rest of them had been put to work on the church interior, and a bonny job they were making.

'What about the bell tower, Miss Rose?' Ewan demanded.

'Time enough to start that when the shearers come and we sell the fleeces,' she answered airily.

'It'll take more than fleeces to raise a steeple.'

'The Lord will provide!' she said piously, ignoring his sceptical glare.

It took all Ewan's skill to construct the foundry from scratch. Enoch helped him put final touches to the brickwork. Somewhere in Enoch's past was a history of charcoal burners and he had memories of iron smelting, carried out in primitive clay kilns.

'I can smell the wood smoke reek yet,' he said, breathing deep. 'There are forests hereabouts. We could easy make charcoal, Ewan, and that's hot enough to smelt metal.'

'Miss Rose tells me she has ordered Port Arthur coal.'

Enoch scowled and spat on the ground.

'Man, that's sparky, stony rubbish, mined by convicts working in the dark, a hundred feet below ground. Are you not ashamed?'

Ewan shrugged.

'Shame doesn't enter into it with Rose Bates. She believes all convicts should burn in hell.'

The old man flung down the trowel in a fit of anger.

'It weren't convicts burned the church!'

He was startled.

'Then who did?'

'It weren't us, anyroads,' Enoch grunted, avoiding Ewan's eye uneasily.

He picked up the trowel and began dourly slapping mortar on bricks.

Ewan watched and wondered. Enoch was a self-confessed thief, liar and cheat. Who could believe a single word he said?

By the end of the day the miniature foundry was complete, furnace and flue constructed, the crucible in place and ready to receive molten ingots. However, before it was ready for use, fires must be lit, the heat within the structure gradually increased until the firebricks and mortar fused to withstand the tremendous heat required. It was necessarily a slow process.

Meantime, Ewan set to work clearing weeds and soil from the site where the old church bell had fallen. Miss Rose approached the excavation. She carried shears, and was smiling.

'You have a fine head of hair, Macgregor, will you donate a lock or two to help strengthen plaster on an ornamental frieze?'

She so rarely smiled. It transformed her. He laughed.

'If this is the trick Delilah played on Samson, to steal away his strength, I need all mine for digging, Miss Rose.'

She shared his laughter and somehow it was a rare moment, a meeting of eyes, and recognition of admiration, of liking. Maybe more. She glanced away hastily.

'What are you doing?'

He tapped the remains of the half-buried bell with his boot.

'I need to see what state this is in. Do you know?'

'Quite intact, apart from a crack which renders it useless, of course.'

He nodded, well pleased.

'I must make clay moulds to cast a new bell. That's tricky, and the problem's been exercising my mind, till I remembered the old bell. If it's not distorted, it'll serve as a template.'

She stood on the edge, eager as a child.

'Can I help?'

'Thanks, but it's no job for a lass.'

She stared at him tearfully, and he was concerned.

'I'm sorry. I have offended you,' he said.

She shook her head sadly.

'Lass is such a pretty word, Macgregor, and – and I am not pretty.'

'Pretty fades, Miss Rose, but beauty endures.'

He meant it. At that moment, she did look beautiful to him.

Startled and confused, Ewan drove the spade with all his might into the earth. The bell broke free with a dull, metallic clang. Miss Rose cheered as he bent to examine it.

'Well done!'

A sudden disturbance down by the track made him look up. Miss Rose whirled round, shading her eyes against the glare.

Fieldworkers were running from all corners of the land, spilling out on to the track, following a rider who came galloping from Hobart, shouting at the pitch of his voice. The man flung himself off the lathered horse and ran towards her.

'Gold, Miss Rose, Gold! They've discovered a huge goldfield, west of Sydney!'

News had travelled from the mainland swift as a bush fire, stupendous news that would change many lives – not always for the better.

★   ★   ★

Alistair Ross's eager anticipation at the prospect of meeting his son at last, cooled to apprehension when he reached Forfar on a cold, frosty gloaming.

His muscles ached after the long train journey, and he elected to walk to the nearest inn, carrying his bag. The town lies within a hollow beside the loch, and rime lay thick within it, gathering the yellow reek from a thousand chimneys.

Shivering, he turned up his collar and dreamed of warmth and sunshine. He had only to say the word to Earl Grey, and life in Australia could be his. It could be his son's future, and Mary-Ann's, should Ewan Macgregor never be found.

Next morning dawned brighter, with a freshening breeze as Alistair stood by the open window of his hotel room, watching the passing scene. He admitted he was scared. The boy had every right to reject him, and Alistair knew that his son's rejection would be heartbreaking. That was the risk he had to take, as he shrugged on his overcoat.

Mrs Wullie's jaw dropped when she opened the door to find a well-dressed gentleman on the doorstep. She thanked God she'd scrubbed the step that morning.

Off came his hat as if she were a lady, not a wifie in an apron.

'The name is Alistair Ross, ma'am. May I speak with David Macgregor, if he is at home?'

She stood aside to let him enter.

'I'll call him for ye, sir.'

He stood for a minute staring round the big kitchen. Mrs Wullie thought he looked sad. She ushered him into the little-used parlour. It was hung with dark brown velvet, and so crammed with unbending furniture nobody but the minister, lawyer or the laird's factor ever sat down at ease in it. She seated him in an armchair reserved for distinguished guests, and withdrew.

Molly was busy making scones. The workhouse wench was a dab hand at baking. She glanced up.

'Who's the toff?'

'A gentleman to see Davey.'

'What does he want with him?' she demanded sharply.

'I wasna taken into his confidence, hen,' Mrs Wullie said. She crossed to the smiddy doorway and shouted. 'There's a Mr Alistair Ross to see you, Davey, in the parlour. Quick now!'

The two brothers were working upon machinery for the mill. Matthew had been obliged to depend upon Davey's grasp of mathematics to calculate the various tolerances.

When the interruption came he glanced up guiltily and met his half-brother's eyes. Davey had turned pale.

'You fixed this, didn't you?'

'Aye. So I did.' Matthew said defiantly. But suddenly he felt ashamed. He knew his motives did not bear scrutiny.

Davey left him without a word.

So Matthew had summoned Alistair Ross in a bid to get him out of the house! Davey thought. He was reluctant to meet the man who had shamed and deserted his mother. He washed face and hands under the pump and ran a comb through his hair. He felt no emotion, not even curiosity.

When he entered the kitchen the two women were standing as motionless as herons by the waterside. He crossed to the parlour doorway and went inside.

As the door closed, Molly came to life and darted across, putting an ear to the door panel.

'Think shame, my girl!' Mrs Wullie said righteously.

Molly frowned, disappointed.

'Och, the door's too thick, I can't hear a word!'

'Try the keyhole, lass,' suggested Mrs Wullie, eagerly.

Alistair Ross rose to his feet when Davey entered, but a welcoming smile faded when he saw his son's expression. They stared at one another.

'Do you know who I am, David?'

He nodded brusquely.

'Yes. I hoped we would never meet. I suppose Matthew wrote and told you where I could be found. It was not my wish.'

A silence fell, cold and awkward. Alistair's brow felt clammy.

'I take it I'm not welcome?'

'What did you expect?'

'I didn't know, to be honest, because I suspect you don't know the facts. I had arranged to marry your mother, but she never received the crucial letter. I thought she did not love me. It was heartbreaking.'

'That's easy said!'

'I have never married. I could not!'

Davey shrugged.

'So you chose to remain single. What has that to do with me?'

'Everything. You are my only child. Without you, I have no future.'

Davey didn't know what to say. The man seemed sincere.

Looking away in perplexity, he saw the reflection of father and son reflected in the mirror above the mantelshelf. The resemblance was so striking, he realized the blood link could never be denied, it was there, and would not go away. It would be with him for the rest of his days.

'Why did you come? What do you want with me?' he demanded despairingly.

Alistair reached into his pocket and drew out a folded document.

'The Home Secretary quashed Ewan Macgregor's conviction and severe sentence. Both of you have been granted an unconditional pardon. You have your friend the laird to thank for that.'

The young man cried out in agitation.

'Too late! Mama is thousands of miles away searching for us now. This is tragic!'

Alistair took a hesitant step towards him.

'I wrote to her. She will know you never left this country, but you could still be reunited—'

He paused, he did not know what his son's reaction would be to what he had to say next, but the future hung upon it.

'I have the offer of a government position in Australia. I'm begging you to come with me, David.'

He stared in angry astonishment.

'Why should I? You've never cared tuppence what happened to me, till now!'

Alistair was just as angry.

'Confound it, Davey, give me some credit! I love your mother and was devastated when I heard she had married Ewan Macgregor. But I would never ruin her reputation as a respectable married woman by making claims upon you.'

'So why bother now?' his son said bitterly.

'She could need help. I worry about her, a woman alone in a strange land without a husband.'

'What if she never finds him?'

He hesitated.

'I don't know the answer. Come with me to New South Wales, Davey. Help me find out.'

Davey turned away. With the Queen's pardon he could start afresh in Australia. It was the chance of a lifetime, the past wiped clean.

But prison had left scars. Home was dear to him. He had planned to settle down in Forfar with a lass, find work, raise a family, cling to security.

'I need more time. It's a weighty decision,' he said.

Alistair nodded.

'Of course.' He picked up hat and gloves, preparing to leave. 'I'm going north to visit Lord Aberdeen on a constituency matter, and will be back in Forfar in two weeks. It will give you time to decide, Davey. Agreed?'

They looked at each other, hesitating, and then on a sudden impulse, father and son shook hands. As they left the parlour, Davey could see Mrs Wullie and Molly standing exactly where he'd left them. They bobbed a respectful curtsey towards the London gentleman.

He escorted his father out into the yard and watched him go on his way, but did not feel inclined to return to the smiddy to face questions. Lost in thought, Davey walked up the road towards the roadman's bothy. It was a sorry sight, rapidly falling into ruin. His thoughts turned to Janet, wondering where she was. He missed her. Janet would know what he should do. Even as a child she had been braver than most, and now he was afraid and uncertain and could not make up his mind.

Mrs Wullie turned eagerly to the girl the moment the men had gone outside.

'What were they saying?'

'The door's thick. I couldn't hear.'

Molly had heard every word, but decided to keep the information gleaned to herself. She was not shocked by revelations surrounding Davey's birth. Tangled webs were commonplace in the workhouse and she had already noticed the brothers did not resemble one another in the slightest. The truth was no surprise.

Mr Ross's plans for Davey had alarmed her, however. He aimed to take his son thousands of miles away, across the sea, and that threatened Molly's future security. Something must be done about that.

Mrs Wullie was frustrated.

'You must've heard something!'

'Just a word or two. I think the gentleman had decided we're in sore need of charity, with Davey fresh out o' jail.'

She knew this would raise Mrs Wullie's hackles like a cat facing a ferret, and was not disappointed.

'Charity?' screeched Mrs Wullie, 'Could the man not see the quality o' furnishings in this place and sniff good meat stew simmering on the hob? What cheek! I'll give the blackguard a taste o' charity, if he sets foot in my kitchen again!'

And much more, in similar vein.

Molly meekly fetched scones from the oven. They were done to a turn.

Fifteen

Sydney was no stranger to gold fever. In 1848 Australian prospectors had flooded across the Pacific to join the Californian gold rush. But this was mild compared with the frenzy that hit Sydney in 1851.

Bathurst, where the gold had been found, was less than 200 miles away.

Gideon Jones had wind of it earlier than most, from his friends the aborigine stockmen. He hurriedly sought out Mary-Ann.

'We should load the wagons and get on the road to Bathurst,' he advised her.

'I've more sense, Gideon! I refuse to be stuck axle-deep in mud just because you've caught gold fever.'

'Never entered my head,' he protested. 'There's more ways of getting rich than grubbing in earth. Buckets, shovels, tent canvas and pans are worth their weight in gold to a digger. You have a store of 'em.'

'Good. We'll sell them in the shop.'

'For a fraction of the price you could ask at the diggings? That's not good business, ma'am.'

'Maybe not. It's called fair trading.'

He sighed patiently.

'See here. You can sell the goods in the shop an' make a small profit. Or you can load a cart and head along the Western Road across the Blue Mountains, to where office workers are tearing at the earth with soft, bare hands. You offer them a shovel, and you shine like an angel – whatever the price. Ain't that fair enough, after all your trouble getting there?'

Gideon had made hugely inflated prices sound like a positive blessing to mankind, but Mary-Ann wouldn't yield.

'No. It's out of the question,' she decided.

All the same, she was sorely tempted. She revelled in the freedom travel gave her. Australia had brought her an undreamed-of independence.

Gideon tried another angle.

'There's a good chance you'd find Ewan at the diggings, y'know,' he coaxed her. 'Every government bondsman in the colony will want to try his luck.'

Mary-Ann shook her head.

'Not my husband. He doesn't trust to luck, he has more sense.'

He eyed her shrewdly in silence for a moment or two.

'Strikes me you don't want to find him, Mis' Mary-Ann. Maybe you value your freedom too much.'

She gave him a furious glare.

'Get out of here! I have work to do,' she cried.

Gideon left, as silently as he'd arrived.

Mary-Ann had been bookkeeping when he'd burst in with the news. She sat for some time idly, with the pen poised over the ledger.

Maybe Gideon had hit on a truth she hardly dared consider. The neat figures blurred before her eyes. It had grown hard for her now to visualize Ewan's face, and her memory could not recall the sound of his voice

If she did find her husband, would she find herself married to a stranger?

Gold fever emptied Sydney faster than a tidal wave.

'Sales this week have been terrible, Mary-Ann,' Louisa grumbled a few days later. 'With the men away, the women have nothing to spare for luxuries. We can't go on making losses like this for long.'

Secretly, Mary-Ann was annoyed with herself for not acting on Gideon's advice. But how could she have foreseen this disaster?

'There's a ship leaving for Glasgow this week. I'll send in an order for more tools and canvas for tents,' she said. 'By the time those goods are delivered, there'll be fortune-seekers pouring into Sydney from all over the world.'

Louisa snorted.

'That's all very well, my dear. How on earth will we survive till new customers arrive?'

Gideon appeared in the doorway, adept at turning up at crucial moments.

'I can tell you, ma'am. I'll load a cart with buckets, shovels an' tarpaulins from the shop, an' head for the diggings. Prices will go sky high there.' He caught Mary-Ann's eye and added hastily, 'I'll only take a small percentage on the sales, seeing as how you ladies're in a fix.'

Mary-Ann frowned. She was trying to work out why he was being so obliging.

'Will you go alone?'

'I'll take Wilberforce. He has a map.'

'A map? Of what?'

Now she was doubly suspicious. The vast continent was far too new to be reliably charted.

'Of his land,' Gideon said calmly.

'Wilberforce was a swaggie, Gideon! He doesn't own any land,' she protested.

'Oh yah, he does. He never sold it, 'cause his wife's buried there, atop a hill.'

She was suddenly anxious. Wilberforce would be putty in Gideon's scheming hands. She gave the young man a warning look.

'Gideon, I promise you will answer to me, if you dare cheat that poor old man out of his claim!'

He looked deeply offended.

'Do I look like a man who would go crook on a mate, ma'am?'

'Yes, you do,' she said, grimly.

The gold rush affected all the Macgregors, even young Danny. His tormentors at school seized on it at once, as a weapon.

'Your pa's big an' strong, ain't he Dan?' they said.

'Aye. He's a blacksmith, and the strongest man in Forfar.'

They danced around him, laughing.

'They'll put him in the chain gang, breaking stones, y'know. Your pa will be wearing irons this a'ternoon, Danny, not making 'em!'

'That's not true!'

Danny's friends came to his aid and, after a very satisfactory battle, his persecutors fled.

Tobias, Danny's best friend, put an arm round his shoulders.

'Don' you mind 'em, Dan. I bet your pa's gone to the diggings
if he's so strong. I bet he'll've dug hisself a big heap of gold,
right now.'

That comforted Danny, but he couldn't forget the chained
men he'd seen clanking along Pitt Street once, their ankles
rubbed raw and bleeding. He hated to imagine his father suffering
like that.

He cried for Pa that night, head buried beneath the quilt.

But Agnes heard and came in to sit on the bed and make
matters worse. She'd overheard what Gideon had said to her
mother, and it had worried her so much she had to discuss the
problem with someone. Danny was an obvious choice.

He listened aghast to what his sister had to say. The bed was
warm but he felt chilled.

'Do you really think Mama doesn't want to find Pa?'

Agnes nodded sadly. She had agonized over the matter for
some time.

'It looks awful like it, Dan. You see, she can give orders now,
without asking Papa's permission. And she can go off on her
own, whenever she wants to. Maybe that's why she doesn't want
him back. She's been different since he left, you know.'

Agnes felt much better after unburdening herself. Danny
looked miserable, though. She was sorry to have upset her wee
brother, and hugged him contritely.

'Never you mind, Dan. I'll tell you a story about goblins and
bogeymen. You love that, don't you?'

'Aye,' he agreed, rather hesitantly.

But that night he slept badly, and by morning when he awak-
ened he had a plan in mind. He knew that today it had been
agreed that Gideon and Wilberforce were to set out for the
diggings forthwith. Already they had the covered wagon drawn
up to the shop doorway, and Kelpie was running around, barking
excitedly and getting in the way.

Danny put on his school clothes and made the bed, his
morning chore to save his mother work.

Then he took his slate and slate pencil and wrote a labori-
ous message. He left it propped up on the dressing table, stuffed
some clothes into his satchel along with his china pig money-
bank, and went innocently down to breakfast.

He ate as much as he could stomach, stuffed his pockets with bread without anyone noticing, and left by the back door as usual, with a cheery 'G'bye!'

But he didn't go to school. He crept into the storeroom and looked around while Wilberforce and Gideon were out at the wagon.

Rolls of tent canvas lay ready to be uplifted, and Danny unrolled one and lay down on it. By holding one end and rolling over and over, he became tightly cocooned in canvas.

Next came the hardest part. He lay quiet for what seemed like hours, until someone came, heaved the canvas containing Danny on to his shoulder, and headed for the wagon.

Kelpie wasn't fooled. His whines gave the hidden Danny some anxious moments, but fortunately Gideon just yelled at the dog to get away, and Danny stifled a yelp as his roll of canvas hit the wagon floor.

Mary-Ann didn't miss her son till well after school came out. She was irritated by the lateness, but not unduly worried.

Danny often wandered home via the Rocks, a labyrinth of houses, shops, sail-lofts, chandlers and warehouses. Its inlets and creeks provided endless interest and delight for a small boy.

But she prayed Danny had stayed out of the Argyle cut. The long tunnel was a risky place, with a reputation for lurking thieves and cutpurses.

The worrying thought made her seek out Agnes.

'Have you seen Danny, dear?'

'No, Mama. Did he go straight to his room? He sneaks in there very quietly, if he's been playing in mud, and thinks he's in trouble.'

But Danny's room was empty and tidy when Mary-Ann inspected it. But – what was his slate doing there? With a sudden chill, she picked it up and read the message written in Danny's round, childish hand:

> *Gone to the diggings hid in Gideon's cart to find my Pa.*
> *Yrs faithfully Daniel Macgregor.*

Mary-Ann sat down suddenly on the bed.

'Agnes!' She called. 'He's run away – to search for Papa.'

'No!' Agnes stood in the doorway, white as a sheet. 'Oh, Mama, what will we do?'

'I must go after him and bring him back—' Mary-Ann said worriedly.

But even as she spoke, a torrent of rain suddenly hit the windowpane. She looked out at darkening skies in despair.

She daren't risk leaving town in this weather, and by the time conditions improved, Gideon and his small stowaway could be miles away, along the Great Western Road . . .

After Davey Macgregor was called from the Forfar smiddy to meet his father, Matthew had attempted to concentrate on the tricky job in hand. This was an important improvement he hoped would lead to increased speed and efficiency of spinning machines in the mill. Wullie and Matthew had completed the exacting task of making templates and forging intricate metalwork. Grudgingly, Matthew had been forced to admit that Davey's mathematical calculations had been invaluable at that stage. Wullie expelled the breath he'd been holding for the last few moments, as Matthew assembled and operated the mechanism. He punched the air.

'That's it, Matt, you've done it, laddie! A grand invention, these new gears.'

Matthew smiled.

'Improvement, you mean, Wullie! Inventors don't die rich, but improvers will. The machines will run faster and smoother now we've changed the tolerance of the gear teeth.'

Wullie reached for his jacket.

'Your heid's screwed on, my lad. Talking o' teeth, I'm away to the Croft market to have a tooth pulled. It's been giving me gyp.' He gave Matthew a cheery wave and went out.

At last Matthew had time to wonder where his half-brother was. It seemed hours now since Alistair Ross had left the smiddy yard, and Matthew had caught sight of Davey heading up the road towards the old bothy as if the Devil himself was on his tail.

What had his father said, to send him off in the middle of a working day in such a troubled state?

Matthew satisfied himself that his half-brother had not

returned to the living quarters, then went and stood in the doorway, looking in the direction Davey had taken. Where had he gone?

He frowned. Surely Davey would not have the brass neck to pay a visit to the laird, would he . . . ?

But that was exactly what David Macgregor had in mind.

There was only one man in Forfar who knew where Janet Golightly was, and Davey knew he could not make the final decision about his future without first seeing and talking it over with Janet. After a few minutes of indecision outside the abandoned bothy, Davey had set off with determined step, towards the laird's driveway.

Answering the doorbell, Phyllis the housemaid, was deceived by the quality of the visitor's velvet jacket into bobbing the young gent a curtsey.

'Good day to ye, sir. What can I do for ye?'

'I want a word with the laird, please. Tell him it's David Macgregor.'

She gave a shriek of recognition.

'Heaven preserve us, another Macgregor! Just when I thought we'd got the auld man back on his feet.'

Intuition warned him not to mention the real reason for the visit. He smiled disarmingly.

'I must speak to him, Phyllis. I want to thank him for securing a pardon for me and my father.'

She was relieved.

'Aye well, that's good news for once, I must say. The laird's awa' for a wee walk round the walled garden, seeing it's such a braw afternoon. Maybe he'll come to no harm talking to ye for five minutes. But no longer, mind!'

It was pleasant in the sheltered garden, even though the high stone walls reminded him horribly of Parkhurst Prison.

He found the laird sitting in a leafy arbour, and introduced himself. The old man gave him a long, shrewd look.

'Well, well!' he said.

Now that he knew the facts surrounding this young man's birth, the laird could see the resemblance to his natural father Alistair Ross, plain as day.

'I am very pleased indeed to see you, David'

'I'm greatly indebted to you, sir. The pardon was unexpected.'

The laird nodded kindly.

'I was uneasy from the first about the harsh sentence. A stern warning would have been much more fitting. I acted fast when Janet Golightly came forward with the true facts, but not fast enough, alas.' He sighed and shook his head, saddened by the disruption of a fine family.

Davey met the old man's eyes.

'Sir – I need to speak to Janet. It's very important, and I believe you know where she is?'

Frowning, the laird considered the request.

'What is this matter of great importance?'

'I've been offered a fresh start in Australia and a chance to join my family out there.' He hesitated for a moment, and then went on. 'I'd welcome a word with Janet before making such an important decision, sir. We – we were good friends once, you see,' he finished lamely.

The laird's lawyer's mind read with ease between the lines of this intriguing situation.

So the youngster's father was urging him to emigrate! he thought. Now there's a solution to everyone's problem – Mary-Ann's reputation saved, and the two half-brothers, at daggers drawn over a bonny lass, safely separated by many miles of ocean.

The only obstacle was a solemn promise to Janet that he would not reveal where she was living. The laird pondered deeply, and reached a compromise.

'She's in Dundee, working in Baxter's Dens Works, in Princes Street. That's all I'll say. The rest is up to you, my lad.'

But it was enough.

'Thank you, sir. Oh, thank you!' The sunshine seemed brighter, the air warmer, and Davey smiled.

'Aye well. Awa' you go, afore I break any more of the promises made to that bonny lass.'

Davey would have wrung his hand in gratitude, but didn't dare. He backed away, bowing and grinning like a gowk. The laird called after him.

'I wouldna tell Matthew where she is, if I was you, David

Macgregor. At least, not till you've spoken with the lass. And good luck to ye!'

Janet Golightly was hardened now to work in the mill, though she missed blue skies, green fields and fresh country air. In time she had become accustomed to the noisy clatter of machinery, the heavy smell of engine oil and linseed, and even lint fibres floating in the air, making the operatives cough.

But that wasn't to say that she enjoyed working there. She suffered it. She had a loom to herself now, a relentless machine that demanded all her concentration. It was all too easy to make mistakes. Fortunately, her neighbour, Lizzie Gibb, seemed capable of minding her own weaving and keeping an eye upon Janet's as well, and under Lizzie's expert tuition she soon learned to control the woven linen smoothly enough to pass the critical eye of the examiner.

The foreman was pleased with her rapid progress, although he never said so.

He had no need – the other weavers had read his mind, and beamed approval on Janet.

She had passed the test. She was a weaver, one of an elite sisterhood and a cut above the rest.

When winter came, bringing with it a poisonous yellow city fog, and ice and snow lay slushy on streets and pavements outside, Janet didn't mind the mill too much, but the gentle warmth and freshness of a Scottish springtime was hard for a country lass to bear, penned as she was inside the mill. She was glad obscured glass in the high windows gave no views to taunt her.

One evening, released from the mill after the late shift, she came out on Princes Street among a tide of womenfolk, all exhausted and work worn, but still cheery and ready to joke.

'You watch out for that foreman, Janet hennie!' one of them warned her, grinning. 'I never seen the grumpy auld deevil smile afore, but sure enough he did, stopped aside your loom, giving you the eye.'

She went or her way with the rest, cackling.

Janet stood aside from the flood for a moment, her face raised to the evening sky, taking deep breaths of pure air. A hand touched her arm.

'Janet, is it you?'

She had to look twice before she recognized the young gentleman.

'Davey!'

He'd turn any woman's head, so he would, dressed in fine English cloth, shirt and stock white as snow. On his curly head was a neat, fashionable bowler, which he doffed politely for her, though she was certainly not an object to command respect.

Beside him, Janet felt dirty, the mill smell greasy on her skin, her old shawl covered in lint fibres and dust. Yet he was obviously delighted to see her. She stared at him, puzzled and brusque with embarrassment.

'How did you find me?'

'Never mind how. I have to talk to you.'

He took her arm, and steered her away from curious eyes.

'Listen, Janet, I've been waiting outside a fair while, and don't have much time before the train leaves. I wanted to tell you the good news. The laird's done it. I've been pardoned – and so has Pa!'

Her eyes shone, and she clutched his arm.

'Oh, Davey, I'm so glad for you!'

Smiling, he looked down at the hand on his sleeve.

'That's not all, my dear. I've a rich relative – a – a benefactor. He has offered me the chance of a new life, far away from here, in Australia.'

There was a chill in the air of a sudden. She withdrew her hand and clutched the old shawl closer, moving away.

'I'm pleased for you, Davey. It was civil of you to seek me out to say goodbye.'

He stopped her, holding her arm

'Goodbye is not what I had in mind, Janet. I want you to come with me. I need you. In fact I believe I've loved you since the day I helped a brave, skinny wee lass clear a blocked culvert, for her father's sake. Don't you remember?'

She gazed at him, her tall, broad, handsome Davey, who had once been a kindly, reckless wee lad. Recklessness had been his downfall, alas!

'Aye, I remember,' she said softly.

He drew her closer, and this time she did not resist.

'Listen, dear. This benefactor of mine has been offered a position in Australia, and wants me to go with him. I feel it's too good a chance to be missed, but I would be leaving too soon to arrange for you to come with me. Once I'm settled, I can send word and book a passage for you, Janet. Will you come? Oh, please, my dearest, say you will!'

She looked at him gravely.

'Are you asking me to marry you, Davey Macgregor?'

'Yes, of course I am. Will you?'

He was eager and impetuous, as ever, she thought fondly, he would never change! Janet sighed. Dear reckless Davey, acting without a care for others involved.

'But what about Matthew?' she said.

He raised his eyebrows in surprise.

'What about him?'

'I will not break his heart, Davey.'

He laughed.

'Och, it'll mend.' He glanced anxiously at his pocket watch. 'Come, sweetheart, walk me to the station.'

In a daze, she went with him through the April evening. Heads turned as they passed, and scandalized tongues wagged. A young man finely turned out, his arm around a lass straight from the mill floor.

When they reached the East Station, he held her by the shoulders and looked deep into her eyes.

'You haven't given me an answer, Janet. When I send word, will you come out across the seas to marry me?'

There were tears in her eyes.

'How can I tell, when I don't know my own mind yet?'

'Will this help?'

Regardless of onlookers, he took her in his arms and kissed her with a passion that took her breath away. Then he stepped back, still holding fast to her hand with the train on the brink of departure, carriage doors slamming, all along the line. He released her reluctantly and swung himself aboard, as it started moving.

'Remember, my darling!' he shouted.

Aye, I'll remember, my dear lad, she thought tearfully, as she watched him go.

She knew the memory of his kiss would linger on, long, long after the train had gone into the gloaming.

Ewan Macgregor received news from England at last. It reached him as he worked in ferocious heat in the home-made bell foundry.

Miss Rose Bates brought him the envelope. She stood outside and watched him open it, her eyes guarded.

He drew out an official document, and read it through with heartfelt relief.

'It's from the lieutenant-governor's office, Miss Rose,' he said, wiping sweat from his brow and stepping out to join her. 'There's an official pardon for me, signed by the Home Secretary. In short, I'm free to go home, all expenses paid.'

'I'm pleased for you, Macgregor,' she said quietly.

He looked at her sharply, with raised brows.

'I've heard you sound cheerier! If it's the church bell you're worried about, the moulds are in place and ready and the alloy's melting this moment. You shall have your bell once the metal cools, Miss Rose. It takes a while, mind. Maybe four to five weeks for a bell this size.'

Her face gave nothing away. She nodded.

'Good. So Enoch can proceed with the bell tower.'

He snorted.

'Och, away, woman! You've no money, and don't tell me the Lord will provide, because He's taken long enough to think about it!'

'I've arranged a mortgage loan on my house and land, Macgregor. It's just enough to complete the church.'

He was aghast.

'You haven't!'

'Why should you care? Your work's done, your innocence proved. You can go.'

Maybe there were tears in her eyes as she left him standing there, staring after her. But he couldn't be sure . . .

News of Ewan's good fortune spread fast. Enoch caught up with him in the bunkhouse.

'So you're packing up, mate?'

'Aye.' He went on collecting his possessions, rolling them in his folded blanket.

The old man's eyes gleamed.

'Heading for the goldfields?'

'Maybe.'

'I'd go myself, but Miss Rose has a bad enough opinion o' the convict breed already. I'd not make it worse by deserting her now.'

Ewan straightened his back and looked at him.

'I hold the woman in high regard, Enoch. So do you.'

He tamped baccy in a clay pipe with his thumb, embarrassed.

'I've never met another like her, nor a finer man than her brother,' he said gruffly.

There was silence in the bunkhouse apart from a fly droning in the screen. At last, the old man sighed.

'I may as well tell ye, since you're leaving. It weren't convicts burned down the church, it were the Reverend hisself.'

Ewan sat down on the bunk, stunned.

'Her brother?'

'Aye. He drank whisky in secret, y'see. We convicts brought it for the poor tormented man, but Miss Rose never knew. She idolized her brother. He was chaplain in Port Arthur jail for some years afore she came out – goodness only knows what terrible inhumane punishments and awful suffering he was forced to witness there. It'd be enough to turn any merciful man to drink. Whisky would help dull the memory, I dare say.' Enoch sighed and shook his head. 'She believes he went to the church every evening to meditate and pray. Aye well, maybe he did pray hard, but he also drank hard. It's my belief that night he knocked over the lantern. The place was well alight afore me an' my mates could get to him, and when Miss Rose ran out, she saw a crowd o' us round the church, and thought we'd done it, the poor soul.'

'You should have told her the truth!' Ewan cried. He considered an appalling injustice had been done to innocent men.

Enoch shrugged.

'Should I? She loved her brother. In her eyes, he was a good man who did his best for us poor sinners. I wouldn't take that comfort away from a poor sorrowing woman, would you? Our backs are broad and scarred, Macgregor, what's a lash or two of contempt, to the likes o' us?'

Ewan was deeply moved. He put a hand on his shoulder.

'You have my respect, Enoch.'

The old man shrugged off the hand, and grinned.

'Respect an old crawler? Don't be cranky, mate!'

But all the same, he looked pleased.

Miss Rose was waiting next morning when Ewan came to say goodbye. She stood straight-backed, the straw hat set square on her brow, dustcoat over her gown, very much as he had seen her that first day.

He remembered he had thought her ugly then. But that was before he knew her better and learned to appreciate her rare, austere beauty.

'So, Macgregor. Enoch tells me you're off to search for gold. Greedy for material goods, like all the rest!'

'You told me the Lord would provide, and He has. I'm a free man now, Miss Rose. I can follow my own inclinations.'

She held out a parcel to him, a little awkwardly.

'At least I can provide some decent clothing. They were my brother's. You and he seem much of a size.'

He took it from her humbly. It was a generous gesture, knowing how much she had revered the man. He thanked her and held her hand. It felt rough and work worn, the slim fingers trembling in his.

'I'll be back to see the bell hung in the bell tower one day, I promise,' he said.

She gave a sad little smile and shook her head.

'If you're wise, you'll sail for home straight away. Why should you come back here?' She pulled her hand away. 'Don't make promises you can't keep, Macgregor! I thank you for your diligent labour and wish you well in the future.'

She lowered her head in a frosty little bow that hid her eyes, then turned and went into the house, shutting the door.

Ewan stood undecided for a minute or two, then went back to the bunkhouse and put on the Reverend's fine white shirt, dark jacket and breeches. It was bliss to wear fresh clothes, to feel a free man again after all this time in convict canvas.

He pulled on the bush hat Miss Rose had thoughtfully provided, and set off.

He caught the Hobart coach at the road end, clambering up to a rooftop seat.

At last he breathed the fresh air of freedom. Somewhere, far away across the seas, Davey, the lad he still thought of as his son, would also be pardoned and free, and reunited with his mother

Mary-Ann!

As the coach jolted past houses and inns that could just as well have been part of the England he remembered, he thought of his wife for what seemed like the first time in weeks. He could remember how she looked, but felt nothing, and that scared him.

Once I loved her more than life itself! he thought sadly. What has happened?

There had been nothing to keep Mary-Ann's memory alive, no likeness, and no letter, not even a lock of hair. And now her memory had grown dim, because it had hurt too much to remember. Besides, he was no longer the man he once was, a quiet Forfar craftsman cursed with a quick, unruly temper. Prison had cured him of that, but it had also given him long, lonely hours to reflect upon a love he had never really trusted.

Now that he was distanced from Mary-Ann, it had become clear to him that her love had been born of duty, a mere act of gratitude. That was not what he wanted from a woman he had loved, and made his wife!

Rain had begun to fall, a light shower drizzling the outside passengers. He pulled the hat well down over his brow and was thankful for it. Wet trails dripping from the wide brim hid secret tears trickling down Ewan Macgregor's cheeks.

When the coach reached Hobart, impartial officials in Government House arranged free passage for Ewan on a cargo ship bound for the mainland, across the strait, sailing on the top of the tide.

He was given a pass entitling Ewan Macgregor to leave Australia for his homeland at the expense of Her Majesty's Government, and a sum of money that would barely keep body and soul together, while he did it.

Ewan did not care. All he wanted was to cross the strait, far away from the shame of Van Diemen's Land.

After a cold, stormy voyage as deck passenger on the evil-smelling cargo ship, Ewan soon discovered the less pleasant aspects of the Mainland.

A flood of exiles had disembarked in Port Phillip Bay from Van Diemen's Land at the first hint of a gold rush. Inhabitants of the mainland town in which they found themselves, could barely contain their disgust at the unwelcome influx of 'Demons' from Van Diemen's island, and made little attempt to hide it.

Trudging from the docks with a damp bundle on his shoulder, Ewan found himself an object of suspicion. No decent lodging was prepared to take him, and he was so chilled by the plummeting winter temperature that he took shelter in a charity dosshouse.

At least here he could be sure of a plate of broth, a hunk of bread and a space on the floor to lay a blanket.

'Heading for Clunes, are ye?' his floor companion asked. 'Diggin' gold?'

'Maybe.' He turned his back, too weary to talk and too afraid of thieving to trust anyone.

He'd heard on the boat of the find at Clunes. It was only a hundred miles away from the port, they said, nothing in this land of vast distances.

Ewan had secretly planned to dig enough of the Lord's golden provenance out of the earth to build Miss Rose's bell tower, and save that dear, proud woman from ruin.

Refreshed after a good night's sleep and a wash under the pump in the yard, he set off to find his bearings and explore the city.

His blacksmith's eye relished cast-iron verandas that adorned the bigger houses of prosperous citizens. But Ewan felt more at home in rundown areas nowadays. He turned away from the broader streets and larger shops and plunged into a warren of dark and seedy wynds and alleyways, skirted by mean little shops and crowded, grubby alehouses. Shawled women stood by, eyeing prospectors with bold, hopeful eyes.

By now, Ewan's empty belly rumbled with hunger and he

looked around doubtfully for a more wholesome establishment to break his fast.

He had wandered far through the bewildering maze, when a thin, haunting, familiar melody came drifting faintly to his ears. At first, he thought he was imagining it.

'And fare thee weel, my only love . . . !'

He stood still, straining his ears to listen in disbelief.

'. . . And fare thee weel a while!'

It faded almost to a whisper. The well-remembered tune brought tears to his eyes and an incredulous ache to his hammering heart.

'. . . And I will come again, my love, though it were ten thousand mile!'

The love song Mary-Ann used to sing on peaceful evenings in the smiddy-seat, her eyes meeting his, tenderly. Ewan put a hand to his head. He must be dreaming this. Maybe hunger had made him delirious. Surely it was Mary-Ann's own lovely voice he was hearing?

But Mary-Ann was in Forfar, ten thousand miles away!

Ewan pushed his way roughly through the crowd, dodging handcarts and wagons, disregarding blows and vicious curses. He followed the elusive sound of a pure, beautiful voice, so out of place in this evil, stinking neighbourhood.

The sound led him at last to the door of a small eating-house. He burst in so suddenly, the customers stopped eating and turned to glare at him.

The girl standing by the piano was the image of Mary-Ann, as he had first known her, the pretty face too young and innocent to belong in this iniquitous den. Ewan stopped and stared in bewildered confusion. He could not trust his eyes, or his sanity. The singer had not seen him yet.

'. . . So fare thee weel, my only love, and fare thee weel, a while . . .' she sang again, so very sadly.

And then he knew her. This was no longer the bonny wee lass he'd left behind in Forfar, but he knew her. It seemed a miracle he could hardly comprehend. Dazedly, he held out his arms to his daughter.

'Shona!'

She stopped singing abruptly and stared in amazement for several long minutes. Then she ran and hurled herself into his arms with a wild cry.

'Papa! Pa, dear, I've found you!'

Ewan could not speak. He hugged his daughter to him.

'Ah, Shona!' he muttered brokenly.

He had found gold, sure enough, right here in the strange city of Melbourne . . .

Sixteen

'Oh, Pa, how did you find me?' Shona asked, laughing as she wiped away tears.

'I followed your beautiful voice, my dear.'

Ewan held his daughter at arm's length, studying her with delight. Shona was a young lady now; though still with the innocent look of a young lass, thank God! He frowned, looking round the rundown place, the air heavy with smoke and the smell of frying onion.

'Shona, dear, what are you doing here?'

The pianist stood up and came forward. He was young and beardless, foppishly dressed.

'She's working for me, mister,' he said.

'Not any more! I'm taking her away,' Ewan replied grimly.

The young man laughed. Not a pleasant sound.

'You can't, mate! Shona signed a legal contract with me. If she breaks it, I'll have the law on her, and you!'

Shona shrank closer to her father. Ewan's arm went around her shoulders, reassuringly.

'She's my daughter, mister. Do you think I care a button for your contract?'

'You'd be wise to heed what I say. The law's on my side. I'm her manager,' the young man warned.

Cedric Cunningham was determined not to lose the girl. Her looks and voice were better than a gold mine in the alehouses they visited.

Shona was terrified. Pa mustn't lose his famous temper now and start a riot. He was a convicted man, and they'd have him back in jail. But Shona had learned cunning since she had left her mother's side. She forced a winning smile.

'Please, Cedric, can't I spend just a little time with my father? I told you I came here hoping to find Pa, and by a miracle, I have found him.'

The young man pondered a moment, and then nodded reluctantly.

'Very well. But if your father were on his way to the gold-fields, I'd urge him to leave quickly. Melbourne don' welcome Demons.'

Shona glanced up at her father nervously.

'You're not one of them from Van Diemen's Land, are you, Papa?'

He smiled.

'Maybe I was, lass, but I'm a free man now. Your brother and I have been pardoned.

'I can bide in Australia or go home to Scotland, whatever I decide. No matter which, you are going with me.'

Cedric Cunningham's eyes narrowed. Shona's presence had put more money in his pockets in six weeks, than her predecessor had in a year. Something must be done, he thought artfully. He sighed and shook his head, in a show of sympathy.

'Such a pity about the contract, Shona! Should you break your bond, a court will uphold my rights, y'know. It will go very badly for you and your pa, if he disobeys a court ruling and tries to take you away.'

Ewan saw through all this wicked nonsense. However, this man and his scheming weren't worth bothering about. The important thing was to get Shona out of here.

'I certainly don't want more trouble wi' the law, sir!' he said equably. 'All I ask is an hour or two o' my dear daughter's time afore I go to dig for gold. If I strike it rich, I'll make it well worth your while to release my lass.'

Cedric studied the man. He was a big, strong fellah, and this was no mean boast. Even penniless tramps could become million-aires overnight. Mr Macgregor might well end up a very wealthy man indeed. In which case, he would then discover that his dear lass was literally worth her weight in gold.

Cedric usually guarded his precious white fingers from contact with dirty tramps, but he shook Ewan's hand.

'Should you be lucky, dear sir, I'm sure we could reach a friendly agreement.' He turned to Shona. 'Why not show your father the sights of our fair city before he moves on, my dear? Take your time, and I'll expect you back for the evening performance.'

★   ★   ★

Safely outside, Shona was exultant.

'Four whole hours before I need go back, Pa! Why, if only Sydney were not so far away we could tell Mama you were found!'

He stopped in his tracks, astounded.

'You mean your mother's here, in Australia?'

She laughed delightedly.

'Aye, she is! Of course, you wouldn't know, would you? Communications are so bad! She crossed the seas to find you and Davey in New South Wales. Agnes, Danny and I came too. Of course, we didn't know then that Davey was sent to an English prison and never came here at all.'

Ewan drew a deep breath.

'Thank the Lord he was spared transportation! I knew the law had changed, but I've had no word of him since.'

Shona hung on his arm.

'We had no idea where you were, Pa dear, so of course we could not write.'

Ewan walked on, trying to come to terms with this amazing news. There were many unanswered questions buzzing in his head. He frowned.

'Where did your mother find money for fares? She was left with little enough when I was taken.'

Shona hesitated.

'She – she sold the smiddy.'

He stopped dead.

'She what?' he cried wrathfully. 'Not the smiddy!'

All these long months and years the only hope Ewan had clung to, was the thought of the smiddy prospering in Matthew's capable hands, helped by Wullie Ogilvy. He could have wept.

'You mean that my business – our home has gone for good?'

Distressed, Shona did not know what to say.

'It – it was when Mr Ross visited us, I think. Maybe Mama heeded his advice and decided to leave just after that.'

'What was Ross doing in Forfar?' her father demanded sharply.

The situation went from bad to worse, as Shona was forced to give her own version of events.

'Well – I believe that Mr Ross admires Mama. She told us he was an old friend. He – he seemed a good, kind man, Pa, but

Matthew came home and found him sitting in your chair and was furious, so – so he threw poor Mr Ross out of the house. We were sent upstairs, but I heard Matthew quarrel with Mama. It – it was horrid!'

Ewan was silent. Could it be that Matthew knew the truth of that relationship?

Shona lifted her chin defiantly.

'Anyway, *I* think Mr Ross is a proper gentleman, Pa. He came all the way to Newcastle to bid us goodbye. Fortunately, Matthew wasn't there this time. He'd stayed behind in Dundee at the very last minute, and kept most of Mama's money.'

This beggared belief! Ewan thought in astonishment.

'Are you saying he stole from your mama?'

'Oh no, Pa,' she assured him hastily. 'We'd sewn all of Davey's money into Matthew's jacket, and I expect Matthew forgot he had it when he ran off, just before the ship sailed. At least, that's what Mama thinks.'

Her father groaned.

'Davey's money withdrawn from the bank? Heaven help us!'

Ewan walked on in a daze with Shona scurrying anxiously by his side. Presently, his pace slackened, and he glanced down at her.

'As for you, my lass, I cannot even guess how you came to arrive here all on your own, working for that scheming young scoundrel. And, oh Shona! I hope the wretch did not molest you?'

She smiled faintly. This city had taught Shona a great deal about life.

'Do not worry, Pa. I was quite safe with Cedric. He is not interested in women.'

Ewan was scandalized.

'I can't imagine your mother approves of any of this! Does she even know where you are?'

'N–not exactly.' Hesitantly, she explained about meeting Louisa on the ship, and renting the store when they arrived in Sydney. 'Then, you see, Pa, this man Gideon Jones suggested we'd do better if we travelled to the outback with the shop. Mama decided to go with him and Danny and I went too – hoping to find you.'

She paused. The next part would be painful, but had to be told.

'Then I caught Mama kissing Gideon in secret, behind the wagon—'

'You what?' He stopped in his tracks.

Tearfully, Shona told her incredulous father her own colourful version of the eventful journey. Ewan listened in horrified despair.

'My God! What has come over her?'

'She's changed, Papa. We've all noticed the difference,' Shona said earnestly. 'I think she enjoys her freedom.'

'Freedom from me, you mean,' Ewan declared bitterly.

Shona eyed her father nervously. He sounded angry and saddened and she was sorry for him, but what else could she do? She'd told him nothing but the truth.

'Anyway,' she went on bravely, 'I decided to come and find you myself. I made Gideon help me. He arranged the voyage and gave me Mrs Cunningham's address – she is Cedric's mother and runs a lodging house, you see. When Cedric heard me sing, he offered a five-year contract. It – it seemed a wonderful opportunity at the time.'

She daren't tell him how much Cedric and his awful mother scared her with their bullying threats. Pa already looked fit to murder someone.

'Right!' he growled grimly. 'Show the way to your lodgings and collect your belongings, Shona. We're going on a journey.'

'But Pa, the contract—!' she wailed

Ewan glanced down. At the sight of his daughter's frightened face, his heart turned over. The poor lass was scared out of her wits. He summoned a smile and put an arm around her shoulders.

'It's not worth the paper it's written on, my dear. Cedric knows that, even if you don't!' he said cheerfully.

Arriving at the lodgings, Ewan took great pleasure in putting the fear of death into Cedric's unpleasant mother. Afterwards, Shona walked beside him with a lighter step, hanging on his arm, smiling again, ready to follow him anywhere.

'Are we going to look for gold now, Pa?'

He laughed a little grimly.

'Aye, but not the sort that vile woman and her son would understand!'

He headed deliberately into the wind blowing from the sea. It brought a chill, and Shona shivered.

'Pa, this road leads to the harbour.'

'Aye. When my ship arrived yesterday, I heard there was a vessel leaving for Sydney tonight. We will be on it, my lass.'

'Sydney?' Shona said weakly.

He nodded.

'Your mother and my family are worth more than gold, to me.'

Now she regretted telling him about Mama and Gideon's sordid affair. Pa's anger was slow to rouse, but greatly to be feared. She dreaded to think what would happen when Pa walked into the shop and confronted her mother. All she knew was, she didn't want to be there . . .

Davey Macgregor had also embarked on a voyage. But as the privileged son of a member of the colonial staff, he travelled in luxury.

At that moment he and Alistair Ross were leaning their elbows on the rail of the mail packet *Lady Muldoon*.

They had been at sea a good few weeks now and were heading for coaling in Cape Town. The rigging creaked in a lively wind as the ship heeled. A black plume of smoke from the funnel was whipped sternwards.

'I'm glad we had time to visit the Great Exhibition before we sailed, son,' Alistair was saying. 'You enjoyed it, didn't you, and all credit to Prince Albert for its success. The Queen was so delighted to have all his critics proved wrong! Smug is the word that comes to mind, the day we saw Her Majesty visit the Crystal Palace!'

Davey had been left unmoved by the sight of the motherly little woman who was his sovereign, but had been greatly excited by exhibits on show, especially in the engineering section.

'I never saw such huge crowds!' he enthused. 'There must have been thousands there. And all those new ideas . . .' He paused, eyes shining. How wonderful to be a skilled engineer, able to take one's ideas forward into practice. His fertile imagination began conjuring up the fantastic ships he would design one day, faster than the mail packet and taller than cathedrals.

His father watched him with amusement.

'Day-dreaming again, Davey?' he said at last.

Davey started and met his father's smiling eyes.

'Och, you're teasing me!'

Davey grinned, and lifted his tanned face to the wind.

It was strange, but he had found mind and heart in tune with his father's. Whatever happened when they reached Australia, Davey knew he would always remember this long voyage and his father's companionship, with great affection. Prison and Forfar seemed like another existence, best forgot.

In fact, not long after they'd left home waters, Alistair had revealed with some amusement that Molly, the workhouse girl, had approached him in Forfar High Street to stake a claim as Davey Macgregor's ward.

'The cheeky wee besom had no business doing that! I – I'm sorry,' Davey had burst out indignantly, seriously embarrassed.

But his father had only laughed.

'She had a proposition to make. She wanted me to set her up in a tea room in Forfar, Davey, and that was easily done. Apparently she is a dab hand at baking. You must applaud her enterprise!'

'Her impudence, you mean! She has no claim on me!' Davey growled.

Alistair's eyes had twinkled.

'Ah, but she had reason on her side, my lad! She reckons you are responsible for her well-being and she had found out that I was proposing to remove her support.'

Davey had been furious.

'Responsible, me? I saved her life, but if I'd known the trouble she'd make . . .' He broke off, fuming.

'Molly says she never asked you to, so you alone are responsible for her being there. Quite logical reasoning, I must say. That young woman will go far, Davey. I feel assured her Forfar tea room will do splendidly.'

Then Davey had seen the funny side, and had grinned sheepishly.

'Well, good luck to her, and I hope she stays far enough away from me . . .'

But today, leaning to the sway of the ship, Davey's thoughts had turned to Janet Golightly. Truth to tell, she was seldom far from his mind.

He was well aware she hadn't given him an answer to his proposal, before they sailed.

He would send for her when he was settled in Sydney, but would she come? After all, back in Forfar there was Matthew to be reckoned with. Matthew, faithful, loving, and with a promising future ahead, earning an honest, steady living just a few miles away from Dens Mill in Dundee. With Forfar gossip being what it was and Matthew's connection with the mills, it must be only a matter of time before Matthew found out where Janet was working. And then what?

Davey sighed. Even half a world apart, he and his half-brother were still rivals, still at loggerheads, over one unique, bonny lass.

On parting, they'd shaken hands formally, and then stared awkwardly at one another for a minute, before embracing with a sudden tearful surge of warm affection.

Davey found himself uttering a silent prayer as the brisk wind hurried the packet onwards to the Cape.

Dear God, please don't let me break Matthew's heart!

When the weather had improved for the better, Mary-Ann had set off after Danny. She had asked at the stables for a fast light wagon suitable for lady driving, and the horse Jagga-Jagga. After all, she and the sullen beast did share a grudging respect. As an afterthought, she had loaded the last of the shop's remaining stock of shovels into the tail of the wagon as ballast.

She found the horse's fiery temper invaluable as the wagon joined a stream of ox-carts, buggies, traps and drays trundling towards the diggings.

Although she was alone, Mary-Ann felt safe. Jagga-Jagga's wicked, rolling eyes and strong teeth deterred many a footsore digger looking for easy transport and pleasant company.

At night, she could tether the horse to the wagon, confident that Jagga-Jagga would lash out viciously at intruders.

By day, she screwed up her eyes against dust and mist and anxiously searched the crowded road, but there was no sign of Gideon's cart ahead. As days passed with no news of Danny, she became increasingly worried.

Once the goldfield came in sight, however, she reined in Jagga-Jagga abruptly, while others around her yelled and shouted and charged ahead. She had never imagined a scene like this.

Nearly every inch of available ground for miles around the creek, and even up into the scarred hillside, had been trampled into bare red soil, and was covered with makeshift canvas shelters.

Higher up, above the nightmarish landscape, stood more sturdy shanties, tents, grog shops and Heaven only knew what other evils.

Further along the creek, rocks and gullies swarmed with men working in a human chain, digging, shovelling, cradling earth in the icy water, hoping to spot shining particles gleaming in the sand.

How could she possibly find Danny in the midst of all this frenzy?

'Mrs Macgregor! Hey, Mrs Macgregor!'

At first she didn't recognize the man who came panting towards her.

'Morris Abel, ma'am. You must remember me, surely? From the bank!'

Then it dawned on Mary-Ann that this was the teller who had regularly checked the shop's takings. The change from formal smart attire to mud streaked overalls and filthy boots was so marked, she almost laughed.

He was in deadly earnest, however.

'I say, ma'am, have you a spade for sale? Mine's broke.'

She smiled.

'Yes, I have brought a few.'

His face lit up with joy.

'I'll take one. Here.' He dragged a small canvas bag from his pocket and threw it on the buckboard at her feet. She picked it up gingerly. It felt like sand, but when she looked inside it glittered. She gasped.

'Gold? But I can't accept this, Morris!'

He looked worried.

'Oh dear! Is it not enough, Mrs Macgregor? State your price, ma'am. There's plenty more where that came from.'

'It is far too much,' she protested. 'It's only a spade, after all!'

'Only a spade?' He looked amused.

'Ma'am, when word gets around that another wagon has arrived this week with tools aboard, you'll be showered wi' nuggets.'

Mary-Ann leaned forward eagerly.

'Did – did you say *another* wagon?'

'Too true, ma'am. One came through four, five days ago. Young fellow, an old swaggie and a boy. They pressed on westward though, I believe. There's rumour of fresh strikes down that way – I may go myself now I have a good spade.'

She presented him with the best she had.

Once word spread, Mary-Ann was inundated with buyers. Soon the wagon was bare of all but her own pack, and that night she sat by the lamp and counted more notes, coins and canvas bags than she had ever dreamed of seeing.

She smiled shamefacedly as she locked away the takings in the strongbox. What Gideon had told her was perfectly true – there were easier ways of gaining gold than grubbing for it in the ground.

Next morning, Mary-Ann also headed west, in a dour, damp early morning. The terrain was wilder, and the road worse. She shuddered to think what would happen if the wagon lurched and broke a wheel or axle.

Weary and chilled to the bone after a day of relentless driving, she was not paying much attention to oncoming vehicles when she heard a familiar yell.

'Well, strike me down! Mary-Ann! I mighta knowed you'd follow!'

'Gideon! Oh, Gideon!' she cried out thankfully.

He reined in, jumped down, plucked her off the wagon and hugged her.

'Danny? Is – is he safe?' she asked breathlessly.

The young man laughed.

'Asleep in the cart with Kelpie, after more'n his fair share of bacon 'n' eggs!'

'Thank God!' she said, and drew back, looking at Gideon. She had never been so glad to see anyone. 'Thank you for taking care of him, Gideon. I've been quite ill with worry.'

He nodded sympathetically.

'It was a shock when the little 'un popped up, a day or so out from Sydney. He'd hid hisself in a roll of canvas and was hungry as a bolter.'

A liberal coating of mud couldn't disguise the quality of Gideon's elaborate waistcoat and new leather bush hat. The clay-plastered boots also looked new, and a selection of fine Havana cigars stuck out of his shirt pocket.

'Have you struck gold?' she asked.

He grinned.

'In a manner o' speaking.'

She looked around, her suspicions aroused.

'Where's Wilberforce?'

'Here I am, ma'am!'

He clambered from the wagon and shook hands warmly. Mary-Ann studied him anxiously. He seemed different, somehow.

'We reached my land, Mis' Mary-Ann. Gideon took me there,' he announced, beaming.

Gideon had strolled off to settle Jagga-Jagga, lest the horse took it into its contrary head to bolt. He caught Mary-Ann's accusing glare and laughed.

'You got a real nasty mind, ma'am. I could tell right away there's no gold on Wilberforce's land. It's the wrong sort of rock, for one thing.'

He extracted a cigar from his pocket, snipped the end and lit it.

'Made a fortune selling tools, tack and canvas in the outback, though.'

Wilberforce nodded.

'We found my old shack in good repair too. There's shepherds using it reg'lar, for shelter,' he told her. 'An' do you know, ma'am, they've been tending my Ada's grave real nice, all these years. The grass was cut, her name still writ bold upon the cross, and a sprig of sweet-smelling flowers beneath.' The old man wiped tears from his eyes before he went on.

'My Ada was a kind woman, y'see ma'am, travellers were always welcomed to our table for food an' shelter, and folk remembered. It means a lot to me, Mis' Mary-Ann, knowing my darling's not left lying there, alone and forgot.'

She pressed his hand gently. She could see now where the difference lay. Wilberforce's lonely heart had found peace.

The canvas at the back of Gideon's wagon parted at that moment, and a sleepy face peered out.

'Mama!' Danny's yell of delight sent Kelpie into a frenzy of excited barking. Her son climbed from the cart and hurled himself into her arms.

'I'm sorry I ran away, Mama. I didn't find Pa. It's an awful big country.'

'Yes, darling. I know.'

Mary-Ann held her son close. There were tears of relief on her cheek. At least the youngest member of her scattered family was safe, and now she could turn around, and go home . . .

When Shona and her father arrived in Sydney, she led him in silence to Louisa and Mary-Ann's shop. He paused and stood eyeing the handsome frontage for what seemed to Shona, was far too long.

'Your ma's done well for herself,' he remarked. He sounded anything but pleased, she thought nervously.

A young face appeared above the door curtain, studying the new arrivals curiously. The shop door opened, and Agnes peered out.

'Pa?' she ventured uncertainly. After a few moments of stunned disbelief, she let out a howl and flung herself at him.

She hugged Ewan until he was breathless, and then covered her sister's cheeks with kisses.

'Shona, you found him! I can't believe it! Oh, Pa!'

Ewan would not have recognized his roly-poly little daughter if they'd met in the street. She was taller, slim, graceful, and lively as a bellbird.

Mrs Louisa came hurrying to see what all the commotion was. She was so obviously a lady that Ewan doffed his hat and bowed.

'Pleased to meet you, I'm sure, ma'am.'

Agnes covered her mouth and giggled.

'Oh, Pa, you don't need to treat Mrs Louisa like the queen! She's poorer than us. We had a cabin coming over – she travelled steerage.'

He was shocked by such disrespect, but the fine lady laughed.

'Your younger daughter always tells the truth, Mr Macgregor. Personally, I find it most refreshing.' She stood back. 'Now please come inside, out of the sun.'

As Ewan walked in, he expected his wife to appear at any moment, and his heart was hammering like a clapper in Miss Rose's kirk bell. He paused and looked around.

'Your shelves are a mite empty, ma'am,' he remarked.

'We loaded the last of the stock on to Mary-Ann's wagon before she left for the diggings.' Louisa explained. 'Every fit man in town is there, so we're hoping her journey will help reverse our fortunes.'

He frowned.

'You mean my wife isn't here?'

Ewan wasn't sure what to think. It was a dangerous time of year for such a long, hard journey. The Mary-Ann he knew would never have risked such a thing.

There was an awkward silence. Agnes took a deep breath.

'Mama had to go off after Danny, Pa. He ran away, and she went to look for him.'

Ewan grew cold and Shona let out a cry and clutched her father's arm.

'Danny's lost? Agnes, this is terrible!' he cried.

Agnes hastened to reassure them.

'Not really lost, Pa! The wee devil went to look for you because he thought Mama wasn't bothering. He hid in the cart when Gideon set off for the diggings. Gideon will look after him.'

'Gideon again!' Ewan roared, his temper was still under control, but rising. 'Who *is* this Gideon fellow?'

Louisa intervened hastily. She sensed trouble.

'He is the young man who runs a haulage and cargo enterprise here in Sydney, Mr Macgregor. He owns this property, which we rent. Gideon has been a good friend, since we arrived in town.'

'To my wife in particular, I believe!' he said bitterly. 'My children seem to think she has not tried too hard to find me.'

'That's not fair!' Louisa glared angrily at Shona. 'I can guess what you've been told, and I would advise you to take it with a pinch of salt, till you are reunited with Mary-Ann.'

'And when's that likely to be?' he demanded.

There was a pause before the loyal lady answered smoothly.

'Difficult to say for sure, Mr Macgregor. This is a big country, you know.'

He watched Agnes and Shona exchange glances. It was plain from the look on their faces that his wife would be with this man Gideon, and the lovers would take their time coming home. Ewan felt suddenly old and defeated, too tired to be angry or even jealous. He just felt numb, sighing wearily.

'Aye, that is so. A man, or a woman, can easily lose the way in such a vast, uncharted land. I've heard that excuse afore, ma'am.'

They gave Ewan Danny's room, while Louisa and his daughters waited for Mary-Ann's return, with trepidation.

As Ewan had noted, the shelves were empty. Gideon had loaded most of the stock on to his wagon, Mary-Ann had taken the rest. The ship had not yet arrived with replacements. Louisa looked around anxiously for some other outlet. Sydney was like a ghost town. Many small shops were putting up the shutters, their owners gone to try their luck at the diggings.

But some men were returning home, having found more wealth than they had ever imagined – and eager to spend it lavishly on wives, daughters and mistresses.

Then Shona remarked that two of her favourite shops were putting up the shutters. One selling jewellery, the other ladies' mantles, and immediately Louisa's infallible instinct came to her aid. With a small bank loan and a few words with the shop-keepers' wives, Louisa's shelves were soon stocked with showy gold rings, baubles, necklaces and bracelets, and a discreet room laid aside for the display of stylish ladies' mantles and evening wear.

Trade picked up, and Louisa and the girls were kept busy.

However, Ewan had little to occupy his time and plenty of empty hours in which to brood. He was dreading seeing Mary-Ann again. Three years had passed since they had been parted – three years, which he knew had changed him beyond imagining.

From all he had heard about Mary-Ann, those lost years had changed her almost beyond recognition, also.

What would happen when they set eyes on each other again? He worried. Were they to meet as strangers?

She came on an afternoon warmed by the hint of a fickle Australian sun. Ewan was in the shop, helping to sort a shipment of tools and canvas newly arrived from Britain. The store was in chaos, with Louisa and the girls attempting to attend to eager customers. She was already considering a move to larger premises.

The wagons arrived in the midst of this, with a jingle of harness and a sudden bustle of noise and excitement.

Ewan heard familiar, merry laughter before he realized she was there, outside the shop. He set down his roll of canvas and straightened, just in time to see his wife stretch out her arms to a tall young man.

Gideon! – Ewan assumed it must be Gideon – lifted her effortlessly from the wagon. Did he hold her in his arms longer than was needed? Ewan wondered jealously.

Mary-Ann came into the shop like a breath of fresh air, laughing, free as the wind that had tousled her hair to a wild tangle. Her step was light, eyes bright, her clothing as mud-stained as any Forfar farm lass fresh from the fields.

He could see no hint here of the dutiful wife. This was a confident woman, beautiful, mature, yet looking so young she made him feel old.

The girls, busy serving customers, had frozen with apprehension as their mother appeared. Louisa went to them and put an arm round each of them.

'So. You're back,' Ewan said, his voice carrying across the shop.

Mary-Ann had been too preoccupied with the changes made in her absence, to notice her husband. She looked at him, and the laughter faded.

'Ewan?' she said uncertainly. 'Ewan!'

She would have run to him, hugged him, but his arms were folded across his chest, forbidding contact. She crossed the room and laid a tentative hand on his arm.

'Oh, my dearest, how I have missed you!'

'Have you?'

Anger had risen hot and bitter in his chest, at sight of her. Fortunately, the young man Gideon entered the shop at that moment, accompanied by an older man and a skinny boy.

Ewan stared.

'Danny, is it you?'

Could this really be his wee boy? He laughed incredulously.

'You've been doing some growing, my laddie!'

Danny let out a yell and hurled himself at his father.

'Pa, you're found!'

Tearfully Ewan caught his son up in his arms and hugged him, before setting him back on his feet. At least one member of this family was glad to see him! He looked at his wife. She had not moved a muscle.

Till this afternoon, Mary-Ann had believed that she knew all there was to know about her husband. She hardly recognized this disciplined stranger with cold, accusing eyes.

What had they done to him in prison? she wondered uneasily.

Why did he stare so accusingly? She had been faithful, she had longed for him, prayed for him, wept for him. Her only failing was a new-found confidence in her own ability – if that were a sin?

Their eyes met over Danny's head, and she saw the tears. He looked away quickly, but the sight had given her hope.

Agnes and Shona came forward to greet their mother and little brother. Danny found himself something of an unlikely hero with his sisters, and made the best of it, providing a distraction which Mary-Ann and Ewan found welcome.

Gideon, eyeing Ewan's muscular arms speculatively, disappeared quietly to see to the horses.

It was late evening before Mary-Ann and Ewan were left alone together in the parlour behind the shop. Louisa had sent the children off to bed, and tactfully withdrawn to her own room. Ewan sat on the piano stool, idly coaxing a tune from the old piano.

'Ewan, we must talk,' Mary-Ann said.

'What about?'

He twirled the stool to face her. Still impassive. Still cool. It almost broke her heart.

'Oh Ewan!' she cried in despair. 'We seem like strangers now. And you are glaring at me as if I have –' she swallowed and stopped for a moment – 'as if I have been unfaithful to you.'

'Haven't you?'

'Of course not!'

The bitterness surfaced, and the anger. He leaned towards her accusingly.

'What about your fling with the young Australian? Shona told me all about that. What about Alistair Ross, who persuaded you to sell my livelihood and my home, so that it was not worth my while to return to Scotland.'

She stared at him, and slowly shook her head.

'Ah, Ewan! Gideon imagines he is in love with me, but he is not. I am sure Shona's imagination has made much more of his foolish infatuation. Gideon is just a lonely youngster, who has never known a mother's love.' She sighed. 'As for Alistair, he is a good man who has been denied the wife and family he longed for, and yes, I believe he hoped to step into your shoes. Can you blame him, when he knew how contented I was with you and the bairns?'

She crossed the room and knelt beside him.

'I would not let it happen, my dear, and told him so, but it seemed wiser to remove temptation. It was I who decided the smiddy must be sold if I had any hope of crossing the seas, to find you. So I sold it to the laird. I knew the lease would be safe in his hands. He agreed to keep Wullie on, and let Mrs Wullie rule in the smiddy-seat. Matthew and Wullie will tend to the smiddy diligently, Ewan, and Matthew writes that he has become a full-fledged millwright.'

She looked up at him, her gaze warm and steady.

'Everything is left just as you would wish it, my dearest. And if you find me changed, I swear it is for the better.'

Some of the tension left Ewan. He took his wife's hand in his. She is so beautiful in the lamplight! he thought longingly. Her hair was shining. He had always loved to touch her hair.

Mary-Ann moved closer.

'Please Ewan, let's go home to Forfar and make a fresh start,' she said. 'We made a handsome profit selling goods at the diggings. More than enough to pay for our voyage home and leave Louisa with substantial working capital. Oh, please, my darling, let's go home!'

He longed to agree, with all his heart. But he had made a promise to another, and Ewan Macgregor was not a man to go back on his word. He sighed and shook his head.

'Mary-Ann, I cannot go. I promised someone that I would return to Van Diemen's Land, and I will not break a promise.'

She rose abruptly.

'Someone? A woman?'

'Aye, but she's not—' He paused, frowning. How on earth could one describe Rose Bates?

Mary-Ann had never felt so hurt, angry and betrayed.

'A woman!' she said bitterly. 'And you dare to accuse me!'

He looked at her in despair for a long hard moment.

'Ah, Mary-Ann, it is clear to me that we cannot trust one another, and what is a marriage without trust? Perhaps it was not a sound union from the very start. No matter how much I loved and admired you, I have always accepted that marrying me was only a safety net for you, and you were trapped in it. Best to end it, now.'

'If that is what you want, Ewan,' she agreed, standing very straight. 'Maybe it would be best for both of us, as you say. Out here it can be done easily and quickly, and without any scandal.'

'Good,' he said gruffly. She seemed so calm, while he was broken-hearted.

Mary-Ann turned quickly on her heel before he could note her distress.

'Very well. I will see to it.'

She walked to the door and left him alone.

Ewan sat for some time after he had heard her bedroom door close, waiting till he was confident she would be asleep. Then he tiptoed into Danny's room and bundled together his few belongings. Before he left, he stood looking down fondly at the sleeping child. Wiping his eyes emotionally, Ewan bent down and kissed his son's brow.

By the time the household stirred next morning, Ewan Macgregor was already miles away. He had a promise to keep.

Seventeen

Mary-Ann had tossed and turned all night, acutely aware of Ewan's presence in the house, so close, yet so far away.

She wakened next morning with a fresh determination to save her marriage. Ewan came back to me, she told herself as she lay planning the next move. Maybe this other woman made him promise, but first, he came back to me.

Then she heard Danny cry – such an anguished cry that she rose in an instant and clambered upstairs, bursting into her son's attic room. He was in tears, shivering.

'I dreamed that Pa kissed me and went away!'

She hugged him.

'It was only a bad dream, lovie. Come Danny, we will get dressed and go find Papa.'

Danny wiped his eyes furtively, as he hastily dressed himself. It was a while since he had cried. Not since he had lain in Gideon's cart for hours and hours, pinned down by stifling rolls of canvas, hungry, scared, and very thirsty.

Kelpie had known he was there. The dog had whined and barked and made such a fuss that Gideon had finally lost patience and shut Kelpie in the rear of the wagon in disgrace. It had not taken the dog long to sniff Danny out, and with the aid of teeth and paws, to nose aside the canvas to free him. After he had been found, the rest of the journey had been an exciting, dusty and wonderful adventure that Danny would not have missed for all the gold in the diggings. And to make it perfect, when he and Mama had returned, there was Pa!

Only – the nightmare of losing his father again so soon, had seemed frighteningly real.

With the help of Louisa and the girls, Mary-Ann and Danny searched the living quarters. Then with a sinking heart, Mary-Ann looked for Ewan in the shop, storerooms and yard. Her husband could not be found anywhere.

Wilberforce volunteered to go further afield, to the town

and harbour, and came back with the news Mary-Ann had dreaded.

A man answering Ewan's description had been seen late last night boarding a cargo vessel heading upriver. The ship had sailed in the early hours. Mary-Ann was in despair. She could hardly comprehend that her husband had chosen to return to the other woman, without a single regret for the life he and his wife had shared for so many contented years.

Struggling with tears, she had to admit that perhaps at first Ewan's love *had* been a safety net in time of trouble, but over the years that had changed. She had grown to love him very dearly, and now that he had set her free, freedom had lost its attraction.

Mary-Ann left her worried children and hurried down to Circular Quay, buoyed up with the hope that somehow Wilberforce was wrong. All around the quayside lay Sydney's magnificent, bustling harbour. A bewildering forest of masts lay at anchor; a flurry of sail and steam was coming and going on the sparkling blue waters. She stood in the midst of it all, and saw none of it. He was not there. He had left her forever.

But she would not stay to mourn the death of a marriage. Ewan's children must be comforted. They had been overjoyed because their father had returned. How could she explain the reason for his sudden departure?

When Mary-Ann returned with dragging steps to the shop, they were waiting.

'Have you found him, Mama?'

'No. Wilberforce was right. Your father was seen boarding a ship last night. It sailed this morning.'

'But why?' Agnes sobbed. 'Don' he love us any more?'

Mary-Ann sighed.

'He loves you all dearly, but I fear he does not love me.'

Shona glared angrily.

'Why didn't you stop him? You should have stopped him!'

'It is all your fault, Mama!' echoed Danny, tearfully.

Agnes had her arm protectively round her brother, Shona held her sister's hand. They were all in tears, accusing her.

As if this disaster is all my fault! Mary-Ann thought. She had not asked Ewan to desert his children, that was his decision, and his alone.

'How could I stop him, when he had made up his mind to abandon us?' she cried angrily. Mary-Ann lifted her chin and asserted her authority.

'We must go on with our lives, without him. Danny, you will go back to school. I will arrange for you to have extra home-work, to make up for the lessons you have missed.'

Danny gave a howl of protest, but his mother's expression reduced him to silence. She turned to her daughters, whose tears had dried, quite miraculously.

'Agnes, you can go on helping Mrs Louisa in the shop mean-time. Shona, I believe the choirmaster of St James's in Macquarie Street is looking for a lady musician to lead the choir. Would you care to volunteer?'

'We-ell,' Shona considered the prospect doubtfully. It meant remaining in Sydney, of course, but it would be pleasant to sing in a beautiful church, after the cheap alehouses Cedric had frequented. She shivered and felt quite sick, at the mere thought of Cedric.

Shona nodded agreeably.

'Very well, Mama.'

'But what will *you* do, Mama?' Agnes asked anxiously.

Mary-Ann squared her shoulders.

'I have not the faintest idea. But whatever happens, my dears, you may be sure that *I* will not desert you!' she said.

Alistair Ross and his son Davey arrived in Sydney to find the town basking in sunshine. A carriage and horses, and an equerry from Government House, were waiting to greet them.

Alistair's heart thudded with elation. He had not felt so excited, since he was a lad. A sideways glance at his son revealed Davey shared his feelings.

'Welcome to Sydney, Mr Ross.' The equerry shook hands. 'I am to escort you to your quarters, sir. The Governor-General said to waive formalities today. He will be pleased to receive you officially tomorrow morning.'

'That is kind of Sir Charles.' Alistair put a hand under Davey's elbow and drew him forward. This was a moment he had been planning, throughout their long voyage.

'May I introduce David Macgregor, my son?'

Davey glanced at his father. This was unexpected. Aye well, that's thrown down the gauntlet and no mistake! he thought. The resemblance between them was so marked it could hardly be ignored, but Davey had been prepared for more discretion when they arrived in Sydney. It would seem that his father did not wish to be discreet.

The equerry's smooth smile did not waver as he shook hands with the young man, though his eyes betrayed an interest. Mr Ross, he knew, was a bachelor.

Sir Charles Fitzroy would want to know about this. The equerry felt it would be time well spent to have a word or two with the ship's captain, concerning Mr Alistair Ross's reputation, over a friendly glass or two . . .

The driver from Government House gave Alistair and Davey a short tour of Sydney before taking them to their house, west of George Street.

Davey was impressed.

'I must say, it's all more civilized than I had expected,' he remarked when he and his father had time to look around the gracious house, set in its own grounds.

'Yes, thanks largely to convict skill,' Alistair said.

'And I will make sure everyone remembers the debt.' Davey looked grim, and his father eyed him warily.

'I would keep those thoughts to yourself, if I were you, Davey.'

'Why should I? I'm a free man now.'

'Yes of course, but it is a sensitive area, and it might be wiser not to stir up trouble.'

Alistair watched his son shrug, and felt anxious. He had grown to love him dearly, and wanted nothing but his future happiness and success. But had it been altogether wise to bring outspoken Davey to this land, where memories of the worst days of transportation were fresh? From talk aboard ship, Alistair had discovered that prejudice and suspicion thrived just as much here, as in London drawing rooms.

Davey broke into his thoughts.

'When can I see my mother and sisters, and wee Danny?' he asked eagerly.

'Tomorrow, perhaps.'

Alistair's heart raced at the thought of seeing Mary-Ann again, and yet he hesitated. Her last letter had been cool and formal, telling him nothing about her true feelings. He carried the letter with him everywhere. He took it out of his pocket now and studied the address.

'First we must find out where this is, and hope that your mother is still there.'

Next morning, at Government House, Sir Charles Fitzroy greeted Alistair warmly.

'It is always a pleasure to welcome new faces and fresh minds, Alistair, and best of all, of course, to have news of what is happening at home.'

Seated in armchairs with a cool drink to hand, the two men talked politics for some time. Sir Charles, aware of Alistair's recent experience, led the conversation to events of unrest in Turkey and Russia, and then went on to the lighter topic of the Great Exhibition.

'You're fortunate, Alistair, I wish I could have seen its marvels for myself,' he said wistfully.

'Yes, but do you know what impressed me most? The exhibition was attended by many thousands of the working classes and their families, very decent men and women. We have lost all our fear of mobs in Britain today, Sir Charles.'

'Maybe.' Sir Charles studied the contents of his glass. 'But you must remember that we expatriates still have great regard for dignity, and one's station in life.'

Alistair frowned.

'I do not follow your meaning, sir.'

'Then I must make it plain. You are a bachelor. Yet you have brought a son out with you, I am told. Now, this lad made it known on the voyage that he intended visiting his mother in Sydney.' The Governor-General glanced up, fixing Alistair with a keen eye. 'A woman who followed her husband overseas after he was transported for a serious crime.'

Alistair was incensed.

'A crime for which he has since been pardoned. Forgive me, Sir Charles, but this is no concern of yours!'

'You are quite right,' the Governor-General said gently.

'Had this woman been at her home in Scotland, it would be no concern of mine at all. But she is living in Sydney, I understand. If you were to resume your – er – association with this woman, I must warn you it would reflect badly on Government House, and that does concern me. People do like to talk, you know.'

He sat back and studied the younger man with some sympathy.

'I assure you that in coming here I only have my son's future in mind, sir,' Alistair said stiffly. 'This is a land of great opportunity for a clever young man.'

Sir Charles nodded agreement.

'Indeed it is. And the discovery of gold will change things. I can see an end to all transportation very soon. And then there will be a great demand for clever young men to settle here, to help us forget an unhappy past.'

Alistair firmly believed Davey's future lay here, but he had no desire to involve Mary-Ann in malicious gossip. He loved her – he always would.

'What should I do, Sir Charles?' he asked soberly.

'By all means let the lad meet his mother, but *you* must exercise great discretion, for the lady's sake, if not your own.'

Alistair considered this in silence. He had a feeling he knew what the Governor-General would advise. He looked up and met the older man's eyes.

'And then?'

'Then it might be best for all concerned if your son departed, say, for Melbourne. Or, better still, if his mother could be persuaded to return home.'

It was the solution Alistair had feared most . . .

Mary-Ann had been working hard since Ewan had left. Hard work helped to ease the pain of rejection. Encouraged by better weather, she had begun stocktaking, to put the storerooms straight before resuming rounds with the travelling shop.

Wilberforce appeared in the doorway.

There's a coupla gents in the back yard asking for you, Mis' Mary-Ann. Probably salesmen, they don' look too dangerous.'

She smiled.

'Thanks, Wilberforce. I'll see them outside. I don't aim to buy any more. The shelves are packed, as it is.' She made her way along the corridor and stepped out into the yard.

Outside, the sun was high, and the bright light dazzling for a moment. She raised a hand to shield her eyes. The two men stood deep in conversation, but the younger one had turned in her direction when she appeared.

She paused, shocked. I must be imagining things, she thought dazedly. It was Alistair – young Alistair, as she had first known him – but it could not be!

'Mama! Don't you recognize me?' the young man said.

Mary-Ann gasped as realization dawned.

'Davey!' It seemed like a miracle, her boy grown into a man. She opened her arms with incredulous joy. She could have wept when she thought of the lost years, but she would not spoil this joyful moment with tears. Davey was safe, here in her arms. She hugged him and gave thanks.

Then she recognized the older man, and the shock of recognition was almost as great.

'Alistair!'

Davey disentangled himself from his mother's arms.

'Mama, won't you greet my father?' he said loudly.

Alistair glanced nervously over his shoulder.

'Davey, do be careful!'

'Why should I?' he declared defiantly. 'I am standing here with my own father and mother for the first time in my life. I want to tell everyone!'

Alistair touched his shoulder warningly.

'You cannot. We must be discreet – I explained why.'

The air of secrecy worried Mary-Ann.

'What is it, Alistair? What's wrong?'

'It's not important, Mary-Ann,' he lied.

She was more desirable than ever, he thought, but she did not look happy. He should not be pleased about that, but he was.

Davey, however, was not to be suppressed. Past events in his life had developed a healthy contempt for those in authority.

'The Governor-General says that if we do not keep our relationship dark, Mama, my father's career and your reputation will suffer. Not to mention my future prospects and the honour of Government House. It is a lot of rot, if you ask me!'

Mary-Ann drew back. She had lived in Sydney long enough to recognize the truth of the matter. This community thrived on sensational gossip.

Alistair was perturbed.

'Please, Mary-Ann, don't look like that! It will make no difference to us, my dear.'

He took her hand and raised it boldly to his lips.

She snatched her hand away.

'But it should! Have some sense, Alistair. The yard gates are open. What if some passer by had seen what you did? For myself, I do not care tuppence what people think, but there is your future to think of, and Davey's. He has been through enough to last him a lifetime, poor lad.'

Her son did not seem at all upset.

'Where are the others?' he demanded eagerly.

She explained that Danny would be home from school shortly, and Shona was at choir practice. Then she smiled.

'But Agnes is in the shop, dear. Why not give her the surprise of her life?'

Mary-Ann knew the suggestion would appeal to Davey, and she needed to have a word in private with Alistair Ross. There were important issues at stake. When her son had gone off into the back shop, she led Alistair across the yard to a bench screened by banksia bushes.

'We must talk.'

'Yes, Mary-Ann, we must.'

It was a delight to sit beside her, watching the play of light and shade on her skin. He turned his thoughts away with an effort to more immediate matters.

'They have pardoned Ewan and Davey. Did you know?'

She nodded.

'Yes. Ewan told me.'

That was a shock.

'You found him?'

She shook her head.

'He found us. But he would not stay. We have agreed to part, Alistair. He has found someone else, it seems, and is promised to her.'

To Mary-Ann the words sounded bare and final and infinitely sad, but Alistair could not conceal his joy.

'Oh, my dearest! I am sorry it has come to this, of course, but now you can forget Ewan Macgregor. We will spend the rest of our lives together. A fresh start for us all in a new land.'

He would have taken her in his arms, but she pushed him away.

'How can you, Alistair? I am still Ewan's wife. I made a promise when I married him, and I have never broken a promise in my life.'

Alistair looked at her in exasperation.

'For heaven's sake! He has gone off with another woman. That gives you licence to break a few promises, my darling!'

Laughingly, he caught her in his arms, but she struggled wildly.

'Are you mad?' she cried, 'If you are seen kissing me folk *will* talk with a vengeance. Government House will not stand for even a hint of scandal. You'll be sent packing, for sure.'

'Do you think I care?'

He laughed again, knowing she could not get away. This was a game he was determined to win.

Just then a shadow fell across the bench and Alistair's throat was caught in a hard, choking grip.

'Take your hands off her, mister!'

Mary-Ann stared at her rescuer, and gasped.

'Gideon!'

Alistair struggled free and leapt angrily to his feet, turning on his attacker. Mary-Ann watched in horror as the two men circled one another with raised fists.

And then quite suddenly she saw the funny side of this ridiculous scene. Two grown men brawling over an Irishwoman who was heading for middle age. Why, Danny had observed one or two silver hairs among the black already! She burst out laughing.

They paused with fists in mid-air and gaped in astonishment, which made her laugh all the more.

'What's so funny?' Gideon demanded.

'If you could see yoursel! Wee boys in the playground fighting over a toffee apple!'

She studied her two suitors with pity. Since Ewan had left, she had been forced to face hard truths about herself and her feelings. For weeks she had been drifting, uncertain what to do. Now she knew. The way ahead was plain.

Smiling gently, she smoothed Alistair's rumpled jacket, and set Gideon's hat straight with motherly hands.

'Come inside out o' the sun's glare, my dears, and I will tell you what I have decided,' she said . . .

Perhaps Ewan Macgregor's fine physique might have helped, but after what seemed to him only a few weeks after arriving at the diggings, he had unearthed a modest fortune. When the flecks and specks of gold he had panned were weighed and added to the whole, he reckoned he had enough and some to spare for Rose Bates to complete her bell tower.

Then he rolled his belongings in his old blanket and left the plundered earth behind. Trudging on foot, back the way he had come.

The voyage from the mainland across the strait to Van Diemen's Land was long and devious, and Ewan greeted sight of the familiar rugged green, mountainous scene with relief, as the cargo vessel approached the island. He was first down the gangplank in Hobart, finding himself once more among wharves and wool bales, wrinkling his nose against the stench of fish and rancid whale oil. He was lucky to hitch a ride on a farmer's cart to Launceston, and tramped the rest of the way to the lane skirting Miss Rose's land.

Ewan stopped abruptly when he came within sight of the kirk. The sun shone on pale stone, arched windows, leaded roof and buttressed bell tower, surmounted by a copper-clad spire pointing triumphantly to the heavens.

It was finished.

By mortgage and miracle, she had done it, with Enoch and the other lads to put the finishing touches.

He laid down his pack by the hedge and headed for the entrance porch. It was a grand affair adorned by Enoch's sure touch with the chisel. The double doors stood wide open, and he removed his cap and went inside, standing in the aisle.

It was peaceful here, after the restless pounding of seas and the frantic scrabble of ports and towns swamped by miners bound for the goldfields. Ewan had lost count of days, but he guessed from the silence all around it might be Saturday, half-holiday.

Enoch and his mates would be visiting the inn for a drink of warm, weak beer and a long blether. The kirk lay empty, sunlight slanting in upon wooden pews and carved pulpit, a perfume of cedar wood and flowers drifting in the still air.

He sank down in the nearest pew and let the peace and beauty of the place soothe his troubled mind.

'Ewan Macgregor! You kept your promise.'

Miss Rose had come in so quietly, he had not heard. She sat down beside him, smiling. He thought she looked pleased to see him. Well she might, Ewan thought bitterly, considering the promise he had made her, had cost him his wife.

'So. You have finished it!' He tilted his head and looked up at the roof. 'You have done well.'

She looked at him.

'No. It is not finished, Macgregor. There is no bell hanging in the bell tower. I would not let them break the mould, till you came.'

'Fancy you trusting a convict!'

'I knew you would keep your word,' she said quietly.

He drew from his inside pocket the small bag of gold he had been guarding all the way from Melbourne, and beyond. He handed it to her.

'I hope there is enough here to lift your mortgage.'

She held it in her hands. In deference to her surroundings she wore the ancient straw hat but her eyes shone bright beneath the brim.

'You did not need to do this, Macgregor – no!' She stopped his protests with a hand on his arm. 'Truly, you did not, because the community came to our aid. They are as eager as I am to have the church open. I don't know who told them about the mortgage – Enoch, I suspect – but these good folk started a trust fund. It raised enough, and more than enough. In the end, the Lord *did* provide.'

Her smile was impish; he would not have been surprised if she had added, 'So there!'

'I'm glad for you, Rose,' he said.

She pressed the bag of gold back into his hands.

'So – thank you – but you will need this for your future, and I have no need of it, for mine.'

She paused, lifting her pointed chin to survey pulpit, lectern and altar. 'The community abhors evil as much as I do, that is why they were so generous, I believe. No one wants the wicked men who burned my dead brother's church to triumph.'

At that, Ewan could not contain his outrage. He thought of his workmates, going on patiently month after month, silently bearing her bitter contempt, because they had loved their pastor and understood his weakness, only too well. All around him, Ewan could see the evidence of the love and devotion of these men.

He could not bear it a moment longer.

'Woman, they did not do it!'

She turned on him angrily.

'What are you saying? Of course they did!'

'Miss Rose, your brother set light to the church himself. It was an accident. He went there every night to drink whisky, and one night he must have stumbled and knocked over the lantern. Enoch was among the convicts who ran for the church and tried to save him. But it was too late.'

Her eyes were wide with shock and outrage.

'No! I don't believe you. You – you are a convict yourself, and my brother would not—'

He gripped her shoulders, forcing her to look at him

'He did! Think on it, Rose. Every night he went to the kirk alone, to pray. You told me so.'

'Yes – yes, he did, but—'

'Dear Rose, face the facts,' he said gently. 'He was chaplain at Port Arthur Prison, wasn't he? He had seen cruelty and suffering that would haunt him all his life, and whisky dulled the memories and eased the pain. Your brother was a brave, compassionate man, and I suppose he fought the secret craving as best he could, and hid it from his devoted sister. But it killed him, in the end.'

She sat quietly for some time in the peaceful church, so distressed and shamed he could have wept for her. At last she sighed and looked at him.

'I believe you. I was blind to the signs, but they were there.

I should have seen the truth, Ewan, but instead I blamed those
poor men. I made no secret of the fact that I hated and despised
them, and they shouldered the blame without a word. Why did
they do that?'

He took her cold hand and warmed it in his.

'As a tribute to your brother, my dear. A tribute to you.'

She despaired.

'How can I repay such a debt?'

He smiled at her.

'By not making a song and dance about it. By making sure
there's three good meals, a comfortable bunkhouse and steady
employment for old crawlers.' And then he laughed, a joyful sound
that echoed to the roof. 'I daresay they might attend your kirk
alongside the great and good, and even tolerate a wee prayer
meeting now and then at supper time, if the tucker's good.'

She smiled and pressed his hand

'Bless you, Ewan. I'll bear it in mind. So what now, Macgregor?'

'Now to hang a braw new bell in the belfry.'

'And after that?' She watched him with steady blue eyes.

'After that, we have decisions to make,' he said seriously . . .

The decision Mary-Ann had made, the memorable day her son
Davey returned to her, affected many more lives than her own.
Alistair and Gideon, of course, whose rivalry had appeared so
ridiculous it had finally made up her mind. She had been considering returning to Scotland, ever since Ewan had abandoned her,
and once the decision was made, the pace of life became fast.
Mary-Ann had welcomed the speed of events, which gave little
time for inevitable arguments and tears. The passage was booked,
and now, once more, she stood aboard ship, preparing to face the
longest journey in the world.

Louisa Polpatrick had wept copiously at the loss of her dear
friend and colleague, but Mary-Ann had no fears for Louisa's
future, although she too would miss her. Louisa would survive
and prosper in her adopted country.

Shona and Danny would accompany their mother on the
voyage, but Agnes's decision had been a shock to everyone. Agnes
had elected to stay, because she could not bear the thought of
leaving Mrs Louisa all alone.

'I love you dearly, Mama, but she needs me more, she really does!' Agnes had said, and there was no denying the truth of that.

Mary-Ann could see her daughter now, standing on the quay-side, hand in hand with Louisa Polpatrick, both in a companionable flood of tears. Behind them stood Gideon Jones, and she watched the young man put a comforting hand on Agnes's shoulder.

Gideon and Agnes? she wondered. Ah, what an asset to this new country that union would be! It was a thought that helped to ease the heartache of loss.

Then she looked down at Alistair, with Davey by his side, and even at this distance she could sense his desolation. Well, she was sad for him, but nothing would persuade her to stay. She had made a long journey to find where her real love and loyalty lay, and it was not here in New South Wales, not any more. She had lost Ewan, the only man she had truly loved. Ewan, her husband. And for a moment the scene on the quayside blurred.

Aye, all those years ago, she would certainly have married Alistair, if his father had not intervened, but would they have been happy? She could not see herself mingling with London society, always conscious of her humble background, unable to curb her outspoken tongue – what a liability to an ambitious politician!

Then Davey raised his hat in the air and gave a yell that rivalled the seagulls clamouring round fish boxes. She laughed. Aye well, this was the gift she had bequeathed to Alistair, her first love – a son to be proud of. Davey would make good out here. The lad had always been a free spirit.

Danny tugged at her sleeve.

'Ma, will I go to the Spoutie School when we get home to Forfar?'

Mary-Ann smiled and ruffled his hair. He was a clever laddie, his teachers said.

'We'll see – maybe the Academy. It depends whether your brother Matthew has made a success of the smiddy.'

'Will Pa be there?'

'No, darling. I think not,' she said sadly.

Shona was hanging on her other arm. Mary-Ann's tall, pretty daughter had sampled freedom, and discovered that she much preferred security.

'I wonder if they will want a soprano in the Parish kirk choir, Mama?'

'I wouldn't be surprised, my dear.'

The deep roar of farewell from the ship's siren drowned her words as hawsers were cast off. She put her arms round the precious remnants of her scattered family, and took a long, last look ashore at the people she loved.

Mary-Ann watched the far shore that was home now to her loved ones gradually fade out of sight into a misty haze of heat. Out of her sight forever, perhaps, but always close to her thoughts . . .

It was half-past five on a murky morning in Dundee as Janet Golightly trudged to the mill.

There was grey mist over the river, and chilly tendrils exploring Peep O' Day Lane and the tenements at Blackscroft. There wasn't a sprig of green or a blade of grass to be seen. There had been a tree standing once on this corner, a lime tree, fresh and delicate green against blackened stone. But it had been a casualty of the terrible storm that had struck Dundee in June last year.

She sighed. It was fully a year since Davey had left, and she was no nearer deciding what to do about him.

They were busy in the mill, making canvas tent ducks out of Egyptian flax for the gold diggers in Australia. Janet wondered if Davey had found gold and grown rich. It seemed a far-off prospect, nothing to do with her own concerns.

The gateman at the lodge hailed her when she reached the mill with the other workers.

'Letter for ye, Janet lass!'

A letter! She accepted it with trembling hands. It was a stained, far-travelled document, the corners dog-eared, but Davey's dashing script was clear enough. She hung her shawl on her hook, then scuttled into the lavatory and hastily scanned his letter.

Dearest Janet,

I am happily settled now in a braw house with Mr Ross, who is fostering my career in this wonderful country . . .

There followed a long passage detailing the wonders of Sydney and New South Wales, which were so far from the reality of life in Dundee, she skimmed lightly over them without much interest. But the letter ended with Davey's impassioned plea.

> *Janet, you must come out. If I work hard in this beautiful land, I am sure I can be very successful and rich one day. I could give you everything you ever dreamed of, dear one.*
>
> *Oh, Janet, write to me, say that you will come . . .*

But she was late. She stuffed the letter hastily into her pocket and ran to catch up with the others. She worked harder than ever that day. Her skilled hands at the loom flew fast as her thoughts, at times almost a blur, but unerring. By the end of a long working day, she had made up her mind.

It was a decision dictated by Dundee's horse-stained streets, the smells that drifted from East Whale Lane, endless days of unrelenting work and the broken ruins of a bonnie tree. But most of all, it was because of a love she had not realized was true and strong within her, till today.

That night at the weary ending of the shift, she approached the foreman and begged leave to hand in her notice. He was surprised and not well pleased, for she was one of his best workers.

'Your notice? What ails ye, Janet?'

'Homesickness, sir. I'm a country lass, Mr Fenton, and back home in Forfar there's a country lad whose heart is set on me. Truth to tell, I should never have left him.'

She left the foreman shaking his head, but he couldn't rightly blame her. She'd be a great loss to the mill of course, but a fine asset for some lucky country lad.

Janet smiled a secret smile as she donned her shawl and went out into the dark. If she had her way, she would prove the foolish tale – that the man who gave gloves to his lass, would never claim her hand – was just a lot o' blethers . . .

The hawthorn was in full flower when Mary-Ann, Shona and Danny arrived in Forfar. White drifts of mayflower lined the lanes and edged the lochside.

Mary-Ann shivered in the bracing air.

'Ne'er change a cloot till May be oot!' she quoted with a laugh. 'I'll maybe get out of my winter woollies one of these days.'

They were walking up through the town, carrying some of their hand baggage. Mary-Ann had considered that the surest way to announce their return, and it was working a treat. You could almost see the air vibrate with excitement as they passed. But it was a sad reminder that she had come home alone, without her husband.

Still, the smiddy looked splendid in the sunlight when they reached it. The doors were newly painted dark green and there was not a cartwheel out of place in the tidy yard. And there was Matthew, looking out curiously to see who the strangers were. Matthew, a young man now, well built and handsome, so like his father in the smith's leather apron it brought tears to her eyes.

Incredulous recognition dawned, and he pounded across the yard to hug her.

'Mama!'

Then Matthew lifted his sister off her feet, and finally whirled Danny round in an excess of joy. But Danny looked reproachful once he was back on his own two feet.

'Why did you miss the boat, Matt? I saw you chasing after us, but the boat went off without you.'

Matthew looked shamefaced.

'Och, I'd forgotten I had Davey's money sewn into my jacket, Danny. I kept it safe for him though, and he took it with him to New South Wales. It would give him a fine start.' He turned eagerly to his mother. 'Did you see him there, Mama?'

'Yes – yes dear, we did, and it was wonderful. It broke my heart to leave him there with Agnes, but it is what they both wanted, and at least they have one another in that far land. But –' she glanced at Danny with frown – 'Danny, dear, you never told me you had seen Matthew chase after us!'

'You never asked me, Mama,' he answered blithely. He looked around eagerly. 'Where's Wullie?'

Matthew laughed.

'Wullie will be here presently. He's away helping Mrs Wullie flit to a new house, next to Molly's bakery. Mrs Wullie has a steady job making steak pies and bridies for the shop, so we gave

her leave to go to a more convenient location. Besides, we needed
the room.'

'We?' Mary-Ann ventured.

'Aye, we.'

His eyes shone with mischief. Mary-Ann noticed the lad fairly
glowed with happiness. She smiled.

'Could this have to do with that lass you were keen on, Janet
Golightly?'

'Janet's back, and we're to be wed soon. Meantime, she's working
for the auld laird. He's as spry as you like, with a mind sharp as
a Lochaber axe. He often danders into the smiddy for a blether.'

'I'm glad,' she said softly.

And so she was. Matthew deserved to be happy. But as for
herself, life in the smiddy-seat would never be the same without
her husband. She was sadly resigned to that.

She glanced towards the open door.

'I'm sorry, Matthew, we interrupted your work. The forge is
roaring. You forgot the damper.'

'No' me, Ma!' he laughed. 'I'm never so careless. Go in and
see for yourself.'

Wondering, she left them and crossed the yard, prepared to
find some clever new device invented by this gifted lad. She went
through the double doors leading into a smoky gloom, brilliantly
lit at one end by the forge. She could just make out someone
standing by the anvil wielding tongs, ready to draw a bolt of
white hot metal from the blaze. He did not look round.

'Who is it, Matthew?' he called, in a voice so familiar and dear
Mary-Ann clutched the doorpost to steady herself.

'Dear love, it is your wife,' she said.

The tongs clattered unheeded to the floor and Ewan's cry
echoed through the smiddy.

'Mary-Ann! Oh, my Mary-Ann. How I hoped and prayed you
would come home!'

Even in his joy, this careful man paused, and Mary-Ann watched
with a patient smile while her husband damped the fire. Then
he crossed the workshop floor in two bounds and stood looking
down at her.

'I've travelled far and waited long for this, my only love,' he
said softly.

Mary-Ann smiled and stretched her arms out longingly towards her man.

'Ah, but Ewan, I promise you it will be worth the waiting...'

> *And fare thee weel, my only love,*
> *And fare thee weel a while,*
> *And I will come again, my love,*
> *Tho' it were ten thousand mile.*
>
> Robert Burns